VANISHING ANGELS

A Bailey Flynn FBI Mystery Thriller, Book One

Melinda Woodhall

Melinda Woodhall

Melinda Woodhall
Visit my website at www.melindawoodhall.com
Printed in the United States of America
First Printing: February 2024
Creative Magnolia

CHAPTER ONE

Cisco Silver moved swiftly through the fine, white sand, sticking close to the row of exclusive houses that lined the Florida coastline along Bellamy Beach. He was grateful for the thick clouds blanketing the night sky, shielding him from the unwelcome glow of the full moon. The darkness would protect him from prying eyes.

Coming to a stop, he pulled out the slim, military-grade flashlight he'd come to rely on during his recent road-trip, which had included stops at every upscale hotel and resort from Miami Beach to Key West and back.

After swiping cash, jewelry, and credit cards from dozens of hotel rooms, rental cars, and poolside cabanas along the way, Cisco had returned home to Belle Harbor with a respectable stash, which he'd quickly hidden away, like a squirrel hoarding nuts for the winter.

The thought of the stolen goods secreted under his bed stirred no feelings of guilt or remorse in Cisco as he surveyed the row of houses before him.

After all, it wasn't his fault tourists left room keys and valuables lying on their lounge chairs while they zoned out by the pool or sipped an overpriced pina-colada at the bar.

If he hadn't taken advantage of their carelessness, he was pretty sure someone else would have.

Besides, I need the loot more than they do.

And it still hadn't been enough. The stolen cash and valuables wouldn't pay off what he owed Lando Gutierrez.

It would barely be enough to replace the money he'd withdrawn from his grandmother's savings account before he'd left on his road trip.

Picturing the lined, careworn face of the woman who had taken him into her home when no one else would, he experienced a rare pang of regret.

Then he shrugged.

Nonna should have known better than to use my birthdate as her PIN. It's like she wanted me to have the money.

Dark hair blew into his eyes as Cisco scanned the wind-swept beach and zipped up his black nylon windbreaker, wishing he'd worn a heavier jacket.

The weather was always unpredictable in South Florida during hurricane season, and the ocean air carried a sharp chill as he approached a box-shaped house constructed of thick glass and shiny steel.

Ducking behind a lush sago palm, he studied the floor-to-ceiling windows with a frown, unsettled by the stark lines and sharp angles of the ultramodern architecture.

A sense of foreboding sent a shiver up his spine as he surveyed the dark, unwelcoming windows. He resisted the urge to turn and scurry back the way he'd come.

I should leave now. Before it's too late.

But a plan of action was already forming in his mind.

Sucking in a deep breath, he assured himself the target house was empty and that the sliding glass door leading into the kitchen would have been left unlocked.

The fat cat who lives here probably figures he's untouchable.

Resentment surged through Cisco as he wondered what it would be like to sit up on the terrace without a care in the world, sipping a glass of wine and watching the waves crash onto the shore.

The bastard must feel like he owns the whole damn ocean.

The bitter thought was interrupted by a flash of light behind him. Spinning around, he saw the beacon from the Belle Harbor Lighthouse flashing in the distance, illuminating the turbulent waves beyond the sand dunes.

The tide was coming in as quickly as Cisco's time was running out. He needed to get into the house, take whatever he could carry, and get out before he lost his chance.

Reaching into his pocket, he found his black ski mask and pulled it over his head. After adjusting the mask so that only his eyes were exposed to the stinging wind, he slipped on black leather gloves and positioned his backpack straps more firmly on his shoulders.

He started toward a flight of steep wooden steps that led up to the beach house deck, then stopped to listen.

Was that a voice behind him or was it just the wind?

Is someone coming along the beach?

The faint crunch of boots on sand and shells answered Cisco's question and sent him scrambling under the stairs.

Seconds later, a woman emerged from the darkness. She held a cell phone in one hand and a small flashlight in the other as she made her way along the shore.

Pulse pounding, he remained perfectly still as the woman strode forward, aiming the flashlight straight ahead, seemingly unaware that a masked stranger was hiding only a few yards away.

Cisco's eyes widened as he recognized Detective Emma Walsh's long, dark hair and heart-shaped face. A flutter of panic started up in his chest, making it hard to breathe.

Someone must have seen me skulking around and called it in. Or maybe the Belle Harbor PD knows about my recent road trip. Maybe this is some sort of trap they've set to catch me in action.

He thought of Lando Gutierrez, who'd given him the tip about the house being empty, then dismissed the idea. The drug dealer would never cooperate with the cops.

Not unless he has a death wish.

Leaning forward, he risked a glance at the detective.

It was obvious she hadn't seen him yet, but as soon as she did, she would know who he was and why he was there.

He had no doubt that Detective Walsh and every other cop in Belle Harbor would recognize him. Their database was filled with records of his petty crimes and arrests going back years.

Although his driver's license officially identified him as Francisco Ignacio Silveri, the local cops knew him by the street name he'd started using in high school.

Cisco Silver was one of the usual suspects they routinely hauled in for questioning after any break-in or burglary in the area. And they would have no doubt as to why he was creeping around outside the row of multi-million dollar beach houses.

Crouching in the darkness, he held his breath, hoping the detective would pass by. If he was lucky, he might be able to slip away unseen. He could head north up the coast, or even inland to Orlando, where he could hit the pricey family resorts around the attractions.

I can still get out of this if only...

But the detective had come to a sudden halt in the sand.

Peering out again from his hiding place, Cisco saw her staring up at the empty windows of the big beach house.

He jumped as she spoke.

"I'm here."

Her voice cut through the rush of wind and surf.

"Where are you?"

Heart stopping at the words, he was trying to decide if he should make a run for it when he noticed the soft glow of a phone screen next to the detective's ear.

"Let's get this over with," she said. "It's cold out here."

Just then, the faint tap of shoes sounded on the wooden planks above Cisco's head and a silent shadow passed over the gaps in the wooden stairs.

The dark figure of a man descended, moving swiftly down the staircase and onto the uneven sand, heading straight toward Emma Walsh.

The detective gasped as the man stepped into the bright circle of light cast by her flashlight.

"I didn't see you coming," she said. "Where'd you-"

"You said you wanted to talk," the man cut in. "So, here I am. Although, I'm not sure what more there is to say."

The man's back was to the stairs, preventing Cisco from getting a good look at his face. Taking a menacing step toward Emma, the man lowered his voice to a deep growl that Cisco had to strain to hear.

"You think I had something to do with that dead girl?"

The man slid a hand under the back of his jacket as he took another step forward.

"I know you've been watching my house," he said, not waiting for the detective's response. "I saw you parked across the street last night. Did you think I wouldn't see you? Do you think I'm a fool?"

"I think you're a killer," she said. "And I can't let you-"

Her words ended in a gasp as the man pulled a knife from under his jacket and thrust the long blade toward her.

Emma ducked out of reach and made a grab for her gun but the man was too fast. He managed to deliver a vicious blow to the side of her head before she could pull her weapon from its holster.

With a cry of pain, she staggered backward, fighting to keep her balance in the uneven sand, her arms pinwheeling in the dark air around her as the man began to slash the blade toward her again and again.

Spinning away, Emma sidestepped the sharp edge of the knife, regained her footing, and ran north toward the lighthouse, her long hair whipping in the wind behind her.

As her pursuer gave chase, Cisco scrambled out of his hiding place, running forward just in time to see Emma disappear into the dark shadows of the sand dunes that lay between the house and the ocean.

He reached for his phone to call 911, then hesitated.

If I call for help, how will I explain why I'm even out here?

There was no good reason to be on the beach by himself at midnight. And when the cops found he'd used an untraceable burner phone to make the call, they'd know he'd been up to no good.

Besides, did a cop with a gun really need his help?

She's likely already called for backup anyway. And why was she out here on her own in the first place?

As Cisco turned toward the water, the clouds parted and a soft glow of moonlight illuminated the empty shore. To his relief, Detective Emma Walsh and the man who'd been chasing her were gone.

Standing alone on the beach, he jumped as a terrified scream rose over the howl of the wind only to be swallowed again by the crash and roar of the waves.

His feet, heavy with dread and sand, started moving toward the sand dunes of their own accord, carrying his reluctant body with them into the black shadows ahead.

He didn't realize how far he'd wandered into the scrubland beyond the dunes until his foot caught on a vine and he fell to one knee, dropping his backpack, and spilling out its contents, which included several wallets he'd stolen on the boardwalk earlier that evening.

Pulling out his phone with a shaky hand, Cisco thumbed the flashlight icon and aimed the resulting beam toward the ground as he gathered the wallets.

As he moved forward, he expected the man with the knife to leap out at him at any minute, but the circle of light revealed only a small, sandy hill covered with a profusion of dune grass, sea oats, and vines.

No, that's not all. There are footprints, too.

He shone the light on the deep set of prints that led forward, further into the dunes.

If the police show up, there's no denying I've been here now.

Swinging the light back toward the lighthouse, he froze as the beam fell on a body lying face down in the sand.

"Detective Walsh?"

His voice was a dry croak.

"Are you okay?"

Something moved in the sand to his left and he stumbled back, aiming the light at a little ghost crab who quickly disappeared back into its burrow.

Cisco swallowed hard, then crept forward and knelt next to Emma's prone body, his eyes watering from the wind and sand as he lowered two fingers to her limp, outstretched hand, intending to check the pulse in her wrist as he'd seen people do in the movies and on TV.

Her skin was damp and cold, and he felt no movement as he called her name again.

"Detective Walsh?"

Moving the light over her body, he winced as he saw the rip in the back of her jacket and the red, sodden patch of sand beneath her chest.

He reached over and pushed a heavy strand of damp hair off her face, then jumped back with a hoarse cry as he saw her open, unblinking eyes staring out toward the ocean.

Emma Walsh was dead.

CHAPTER TWO

Acold gust of autumn air greeted Special Agent Bailey Flynn as she exited the FBI field office in Washington, D.C., and followed Ludwig onto 9th Street. The German shepherd was eager to stretch his legs after spending the last two hours cooped up in the team meeting SAC Roger Calloway inexplicably scheduled each Monday at eight a.m., and Bailey was in dire need of a double espresso to get her through the rest of the morning.

Six months earlier, the field office's Special-Agent-in-Charge had invited Bailey to join his new special crimes task force, assuring her she would be working side by side with the best agents in the Bureau, handling federal investigations and partnering with local police on challenging cases across the country.

He'd never mentioned the Monday morning meetings.

Hurrying into the coffee shop on the corner, she and Ludwig joined the long queue waiting at the register.

She'd just given her order to the barista and was browsing through the available selection of boxed sandwiches when her phone buzzed in her pocket.

Her mother had sent a text.

With a sigh, Bailey tapped on the message, expecting to see one of Jackie Flynn's usual warnings about recalled lettuce or the rising rates of cancer in women under thirty.

Instead, the simple sentence her mother had typed out made Bailey's stomach drop.

Emma Walsh is missing and I thought you'd want to know.

Reading the words again, Bailey frowned. Surely her mother was just being dramatic, as usual.

And why does she think I'd want to know anyway?

After all, it was no longer Bailey's business if her former best friend and police academy roommate Detective Emma Walsh had gone missing.

Bailey hadn't been back to her hometown in six months. And she hadn't spoken to Emma in years.

When she'd moved up to D.C., Bailey had tried to tell her mother she wanted to put her past and everyone in her hometown behind her so she could make a fresh start.

But Jackie Flynn had never been easily dissuaded and over the last few months, she'd sent her daughter a constant stream of updates from Belle Harbor in an effort to *keep her in the loop* with the persistent hope that she could lure her youngest daughter back home.

"Why does she always think she knows best?" Bailey muttered under her breath as she inched forward in line.

She looked down at Ludwig, hoping the dog would commiserate with her but he was busy staring at the selection of food in the display window with hungry eyes.

After reading the text for the third time, Bailey reluctantly tapped in a reply.

What do you mean by missing?

It took only seconds to receive a response.

I mean the police are looking for Emma. She's gone.

She stared at the words for a long beat, then lifted the phone and scrolled through her contacts, stopping on a name she should have deleted long ago.

She hadn't called Zach Walsh since he'd ended their engagement five years ago.

Her finger hovered over the phone.

"Bailey?"

She jumped as the barista called her name.

Grabbing her double espresso off the bar, she carried it to a table by the window and sank into a chair.

As she peeled back the plastic wrap on her sandwich and fed Ludwig a slice of cheese off the top, she once again looked down at Zach's number.

Biting her lip, she tapped on the screen and then held her breath. Her ex-fiancé answered on the second ring.

"Emma?"

Bailey heard both hope and dread in his voice, and her throat tightened. For a minute, she wasn't sure she was going to be able to speak.

"No, it's Bailey," she finally managed. "My mother just texted me. Is Emma really missing?"

She held her breath, half-expecting him to hang up on her. Or maybe to ask why she was calling now, after years of stony silence, but he only sighed.

"Yes, it looks like she's been gone since Friday night," he said dully. "I went camping over the weekend. Me and some buddies from law school. We were out of range in the Ocala National Forest on Sunday night. When I got home..."

His voice wavered and he coughed and cleared his throat.

Bailey could picture Zach's square-jawed, handsome face creasing into a frown as he ran a hand through his light brown hair, the way he'd always done when he was upset.

"When I got home she wasn't there," he finally managed to say. "I could see from the security system that she'd never come home Friday night."

He grew more animated as he continued.

"I called the station...called everyone I could think of. No one had seen her since she left work Friday afternoon. When she still hadn't gotten home this morning, and she didn't show up for work, I reported her missing."

Wondering why he'd waited all night to file a report, Bailey took a long sip of her espresso and slipped Ludwig the last slice of her cheese.

"Jimmy Fraser, he's Emma's partner now, he took the report this morning. He was really worried and-"

"Has he located her phone yet?" Bailey interrupted, looking at her watch to see how much time she had.

Calloway's meeting would resume shortly.

"No," Zach said. "I've tried calling a dozen times. It goes straight to voicemail so I'm guessing she's turned it off."

"Has he looked through her calls and texts?" Bailey asked with a frown. "That could tell him her last location."

A muffled voice sounded somewhere behind Zach, and Bailey realized he probably wasn't alone.

"Look, I don't have a clue what Fraser's doing to find

her," Zach said, suddenly frustrated. "You'd think since she works for the police department someone would-"

The voice in the background spoke again.

"Here, let me talk to her."

A crisp, authoritative voice that she recognized as Judge Gavin Walsh spoke in Bailey's ear.

Zach's father sounded considerably calmer than his son.

"As far as we can tell, Emma's phone has been turned off," he said. "The police were able to determine that it last pinged off a tower near Bellamy Beach."

Lowering his voice, he adopted a confidential tone.

"In my opinion, Zach should have waited to get the authorities involved. Emma may have simply gone off somewhere to *find herself* as women are known to do."

He gave a long-suffering sigh.

"In any case, we'll all just have to wait and see what happens," he added. "Now, I think Zach needs to get some rest. I'm sure he appreciates your call after all this time. Perhaps the two of you can talk later. Bye-bye now."

The connection dropped as Bailey stared at the phone.

Draining the last drops of the rich coffee from her cup, she threw it in the trash and looked down at Ludwig.

"Let's go, boy," she said. "Calloway will be waiting."

But as she walked out onto the street, she saw a taxi pulling up to the curb to let out a fare.

Impulsively, she crossed the sidewalk and looked in at the driver, who had just activated the *Taxi for Hire* sign on the top of the car.

"Where are you headed?" he asked.

13

Looking down at Ludwig, she made a decision.

"We need to make a quick stop in Georgetown," she said. "And then we're going to the airport."

* * *

The flight to Miami was only half-full, which had allowed Bailey to secure a front-row seat. As Ludwig settled in at her feet, she pulled out her phone and typed out an email to Calloway, requesting a few days off for personal reasons.

Looking out the window at the cloudy sky, she hoped she'd managed to pack everything she would need. The quick stop at the small studio apartment she was subletting in Georgetown hadn't given her much time to plan.

But then, she didn't expect to be gone long.

With any luck, she and Ludwig would join the search for her one-time best friend and make it back to D.C. within a matter of days.

Hopefully, before Calloway becomes too irate.

The thought of her SAC's possible reaction was unsettling, but she assured herself that her boss would understand once he read the email and understood the situation.

Resting her head against her seat, Bailey closed her eyes, hoping the soothing hum and gentle vibration of the plane would ease her anxiety about returning to Belle Harbor.

She'd secretly been relieved after her new assignment to the special crimes task force had necessitated a move to

Washington, D.C. six months earlier.

Confident the change of location would allow her to move on from her painful past, Bailey had jumped at the chance to move to a city where no one knew she'd been dumped by her fiancé two weeks before their scheduled wedding, only to discover he had married her best friend instead.

A city where she didn't have to take the long way to work every day in order to avoid driving past the park where she'd killed a man while trying to save a little girl's life.

No longer would she have to be reminded on a daily basis that twelve-year-old Dolores Santos had died because she'd arrived too late, or that a fellow agent had gotten shot in the line of duty because her bullet had hit its mark too late.

It was easier to forget in a new city. Easier to just pretend none of it had ever happened at all.

Closing her eyes, she laid her head back against her seat and tried to block out all memories of the past. Memories from which she'd moved a thousand miles away to escape.

But as she hovered on the edge of sleep, the mental lockbox where she kept the memories swung slowly open.

Summerset Park simmered in the Florida sunshine as Bailey parked the black Interceptor in the lot and climbed out.

A knot of uniformed police had gathered under an oak tree, trying to find relief in the shade. They turned to her as she approached, their eyes looking to her for answers.

"The K-9s and their handler went that way," one of the officers said, pointing to the west. "Looked as if the dogs picked up a scent over by the playground. They ran off toward the trail and

Agent Morley ran after them."

A female officer gestured to a woman who was being interviewed by two men in plain clothes next to a Belle Harbor PD cruiser.

"That's the girl's mother," she said. "She claims her twelve-year-old daughter Dolores was riding her skateboard outside the house one minute, and the next, she was gone."

The officer's expression was grim.

"A neighbor was gardening at the time and saw a van stop beside the girl. He had the sense to write down the license plate number. That's how we knew it was Ronin Godfrey. The guy's a registered sex offender with a record as long as my arm."

Bailey nodded solemnly, her mind on Sid Morley.

She knew the agent was one of the Bureau's most seasoned handlers, and that his search and rescue dogs had a top-notch reputation. If Godfrey and the girl were still in the park, Morley and his dogs would find them.

Checking the holster under her lightweight jacket, she began to jog west, moving quickly past the basketball court and soccer fields toward the five-mile nature trail that circled the park.

She had just passed the entrance to the trail when she heard the dogs barking. As a shout came from her right, she turned toward a forested area surrounding a murky pond.

"Put the gun down, Godfrey," a deep voice called out. "And let the girl go. No one has to get hurt."

Slowing to a walk, Bailey pulled her Glock from the holster as she took up a position behind the scratchy trunk of a pine tree.

She peered out to see a skinny man in jeans and a dirty white t-shirt standing on the opposite shore of the pond. The man was *pointing a gun at Sid Morley as two German shepherds in K-9 vests barked and pulled on their leashes.*

"I'll shoot them dogs if you don't shut 'em up," the man yelled. "I'll shoot you, too. Got nothin' to live for anyway."

Bailey saw the pink tennis shoe sticking out from the undergrowth behind Godfrey just as she heard the metallic click of his gun as he cocked it.

Her finger instantly squeezed the Glock's trigger, planting a bullet between the man's eyes, and sending him staggering backward.

"No!" she cried as she ran forward.

But she already knew she'd been too late.

A soft cry escaped Bailey's lips as the dream played behind her eyes, causing Ludwig to shift on the floor at her feet and nuzzle her hand.

Sitting up straight with a start, she managed to stifle the shout of panic that hovered in her throat, pushing back images of the dead girl she'd arrived too late to save and the man she'd killed too late to stop.

Sucking in a deep breath, she looked down at Ludwig and scratched the fur behind his ears, grateful he'd woken her before she could scream out as she usually did after her dreams about Ronin Godfrey.

"Let's check the news from Belle Harbor," she murmured to the dog as her pulse returned to normal. "We'll see if we can find out what's going on back home."

She opened her browser, logged into the plane's Wi-Fi, and searched for the latest news from Belle Harbor, Florida, something she hadn't allowed herself to do for months.

Clicking on a video report from Channel 3 News, she watched as a female reporter with short blonde hair stood outside the Belle Harbor Police Station.

"I'm Sabrina West reporting live from Belle Harbor, where a search is underway for Detective Emma Walsh, who hasn't been seen since last Friday," the reporter said in a solemn tone. "An official investigation was opened this morning after the detective's husband reported her missing. Anyone who has seen Emma is asked to contact the Belle Harbor PD Tipline."

A photo appeared on the screen.

Bailey stared at Emma's familiar heart-shaped face and dark hair with a growing sense of unease.

Oh Emma, what have you done now?

CHAPTER THREE

Full night had fallen as Cate Flynn fought rush hour traffic toward Miami International Airport. Bailey's flight in from D.C. was due in on time for once, and Cate was definitely going to be late to meet it. Of course, in her defense, she had been in court delivering closing arguments in a felony assault case when she'd received her mother's frantic text.

Gripping the steering wheel in both hands, Cate imagined for just a moment that it was her mother's neck.

Why'd Mom have to call Bailey and tell her Emma is missing?

If only her mother didn't always feel the need to stick her nose into Bailey's business, always worrying and giving unwarranted advice to her youngest daughter.

Jackie Flynn's anxiety had all started when Bailey had announced during her senior year at Miami University that she wasn't going on to law school but instead had enrolled in the Belle Harbor Police Academy.

Her sister's acceptance at the FBI Academy in Quantico, Virginia a few years later, and her subsequent assignment as a special agent in the Bureau's Miami field office, had only served to exacerbate her mother's neurotic tendencies.

And the traumatic circumstances around the death of little Dolores Santos and Ronin Godfrey had confirmed Jackie's fears about the dangers of Bailey's chosen career.

Cate had hoped that Bailey's recent move to D.C. would improve the situation, allowing her mother to relax.

Out of sight is out of mind, right?

But the distance had only made matters worse.

And now her mother had managed to involve Bailey in whatever mess Emma Walsh had concocted this time even though, as far as Cate was concerned, the Flynn family had no obligation to Zach Walsh or his blushing bride.

After all, Bailey's former fiancé, along with her one-time best friend, had betrayed them all in the worst possible way.

Why come running back now just because Emma decided to up and disappear?

She's probably shacked up somewhere with her new guy, unaware of all the fuss she's causing.

Or maybe Emma was aware and enjoying the attention she was receiving. It certainly wasn't out of the question. Not after what she'd done in the past.

Catching a glimpse of the bitter expression on her face in the rearview mirror, Cate felt a sudden pang of doubt. Perhaps she should be more forgiving. Like her sister.

Bailey can put a positive spin on just about anything.

But then, it wasn't in Cate's nature to turn a blind eye.

Her uncompromising principles had kept her working in the Summerset County prosecutor's office rather than moving into private practice in nearby Miami and raking in the big bucks as a defense attorney.

She just couldn't see herself working for people who had committed the kind of appalling crimes she prosecuted on a daily basis.

Rubbing elbows at the defense table with thieves, abusers, and killers? No, thank you. That's not for me.

She wasn't about to sell her soul, no matter what the financial incentive might be.

Pulling up to *Arrivals* twenty minutes later than she'd planned, Cate was taken aback to see Ludwig standing at the curb beside Bailey.

She'd almost forgotten about the search and rescue dog her sister had taken in after the terrible incident with Ronin Godfrey. The black and tan German shepherd appeared too big to fit in a plane seat. How had Bailey managed it?

Cate's eyes flicked to the pristine leather seat of her shiny new Lexus as she slowed to a stop beside Bailey, watching as the dog clambered into the backseat, his sharp canines on display as his tongue lolled out.

Hopefully, his claws aren't as sharp as his teeth.

Deciding to keep the thought to herself, she waited as Bailey sank into the passenger seat with a weary groan.

"Sounds as if someone's glad to be home," Cate said dryly. "Do you want me to take you straight to Mom and Dad's, or do you want to grab a bite to eat first? We could stop by-"

"I want to go to Bellamy Beach," her sister said, trying to stifle a yawn. "As soon as possible, if you don't mind."

Cate nodded and pulled back into traffic, then frowned.

There were only a few people who knew where Emma's

phone had last pinged. How did Bailey know the Belle Harbor PD was focusing their search on the beach?

"Have you spoken to Zach?" she asked.

"Yes, I called him before I decided to come down here."

Raising an eyebrow, Cate glanced at her sister.

"I'm surprised you agreed to come down here at all after everything he and Emma did to you, and after-"

Bailey cut her off before she went any further.

"That's all in the past now," she said firmly. "It's taken me a while, but I've moved on. You should, too."

Cate opened her mouth to protest, then decided not to waste her breath. Bailey prided herself on being a glass-half-full optimist. She'd never admit that there were betrayals you could never forgive.

Driving the rest of the way in tense silence, they passed over the Summerset County line and then the Belle Harbor city limit, each mired in their own thoughts of the past.

* * *

As Cate's Lexus pulled into the visitor's parking lot adjacent to the Bellamy Beach boardwalk, Bailey woke up Ludwig, who had dozed off in the backseat.

"Let's go find Emma," Bailey murmured to the sleepy dog as she hooked on his leash. "It's time to go to work."

The German shepherd wagged his tail happily as he jumped out of the car and took in the dark, windy beach and crashing waves beyond the sand.

"At least one of us is glad to be home," Bailey said,

ruffling the soft fur between the dog's ears.

She turned to Cate.

"We need to find Jimmy Fraser," she said with a sigh. "I hear he's Emma's partner now."

Cate followed Bailey to the edge of the lot where a solidly built man in a navy blue Belle Harbor PD windbreaker was talking to a uniformed officer.

As he pushed back his hood and called out a greeting, Cate recognized his friendly face and pleasant Jamaican lilt.

"Detective Fraser," she called out, zipping up her jacket as a gust of wind picked up her auburn hair and whipped it around her face. "Any progress in the search?"

"Not yet, Prosecutor Flynn," he replied solemnly. "But thank you for bringing your sister. We'll need all the help we can get to find Emma."

He turned anxious eyes to Bailey.

"Officer Rourke and I made a first pass down the beach earlier without success. And now that it's full dark, we have little hope of finding anything out there on our own."

Cate glanced at Killian Rourke, noting the uniformed officer's clenched jaw and furrowed brow as he stood behind Fraser. Catching her eye, he quickly turned on his heel and stalked back to his cruiser.

"What's his problem?" Cate asked Fraser. "Is he upset about Emma going missing?"

Fraser looked after the man and shrugged.

"Rourke's upset, but not in the way you might expect," he admitted. "The guy's had a bad attitude ever since Emma made detective. Now, he's mad he's out here at night looking for her. Thinks she's just seeking attention."

"That seems to be the common theme I'm hearing from a lot of people," Bailey said, giving Cate a reproving look. "They all seem to think Emma must have gone off on her own accord. But, I don't see it that way."

She looked over at Fraser.

"We think she's been missing for almost seventy-two hours now, right? And as far as we know her phone's been off that whole time?"

Fraser nodded.

"And she never showed up for a job she loves, and never bothered to call and inform her partner she'd be out?"

"That's right," Fraser said. "I didn't even know she was missing until this morning."

He ran a nervous hand over his close-cropped hair.

"As soon as Zach called and asked if she'd shown up for work, I had a feeling something was wrong. He said her phone had been turned off."

"When he told me what was going on this morning, I asked Zach to check her cards and bank accounts. He said there's been no activity all weekend, but I didn't start to panic until I checked the current location for the Interceptor she's been driving."

He pointed to a black SUV at the edge of the lot.

"It's a department vehicle so it's got a GPS tracker which can't be turned off," he explained. "The SUV's parked over there, but Emma's gone."

"How far did you search up the beach?" Bailey asked.

She was staring toward the expanse of white sand.

24

"It was close to dark by the time we got started," Fraser admitted. "We did what we could..."

Cate cleared her throat, not sure it was her place to question what they were doing, but unable to resist.

"How can you know for sure Emma even went onto the beach?" she asked. "She could have met up with someone in the lot and left with them voluntarily."

She ignored the glare Bailey threw her way.

"Or she could have stopped at the beach after work for a run and someone could have taken her against her will."

Cate gestured around at the near-empty lot.

"If it was nighttime then it would have been easy for someone with bad intentions to..."

Her voice faded as a black BMW pulled into the lot and parked beside the Interceptor Emma had been driving the night she disappeared.

She frowned as two men climbed out.

Zach Walsh wore a hooded jacket that covered his light brown hair, but she recognized him at once, along with his father, whose gray hair was still as thick as his son's.

As Bailey started across the lot toward the two men, Cate called after her, but her sister didn't look back.

"You don't like him very much, do you?" Fraser asked, noting the angry expression on Cate's face.

"Which *him* are you talking about?" she shot back. "Although, just between me and you, you'd be right in either case."

Fraser smiled and shook his head.

"Your secret is safe with me," he said. "Now, I'm going

25

to get a few more flashlights before we get started."

Cate watched Fraser hurry off toward one of the cruisers, then made her way over to the BMW, curious as to what Bailey and her ex-fiancé had to talk about.

She stood silently with her hands in her pockets, trying to warm them as she studied the man who would have been her brother-in-law if things had worked out differently.

Now he was a stranger. Someone she didn't know at all.

As Bailey spoke to Zach in a quiet voice that Cate couldn't quite hear, she wondered what they could be talking about.

As far as she knew, Bailey hadn't seen her ex in person since the night he'd told her he was in love with her best friend and that the wedding they'd spent months planning would have to be canceled.

"How have you been, Cate?"

Gavin Walsh was suddenly standing beside her.

"It's been a while since I've seen you at the courthouse."

"Oh, I've been there," Cate replied stiffly. "But lately all my cases have been assigned to Judge Inglebert. I'm starting to think you said something to Inez."

Ignoring her comment, along with the implication he'd asked his clerk to keep her off his courtroom docket, the judge leaned forward and lowered his voice.

"I suspect Emma hasn't always been honest with Zach."

"You've just figured that out?" Cate asked, lifting an eyebrow in mock surprise. "Because I've suspected she couldn't be trusted since the day she announced her engagement to my sister's fiancé."

"I think Emma's been hiding something," the judge

continued as if Cate hadn't spoken. "If that's the case, she may have left on her own. She doesn't want to be found."

Cate wasn't surprised by the older man's comment. She'd heard the rumors about Emma's marriage.

There had been talk of another man, although for Bailey's sake, she'd kept the information and her opinion to herself. Her sister wouldn't appreciate her spreading gossip.

As Judge Walsh continued to expound on his theories about what might have happened to his daughter-in-law, Cate's eyes landed on a dusty Dodge pickup parked nearby.

A fair-haired man leaned against the truck, dressed for the weather in a sturdy jacket and waterproof boots.

He appeared to be watching Bailey and Ludwig with great interest. His eyes followed her sister as she called to the dog, and they stayed on her as she jogged over to Jimmy Fraser, who had returned with flashlights.

Who the hell is he, and what does he want with Bailey?

Hurrying to catch up with Fraser as he followed Bailey and Ludwig to the beach, Cate put a hand out to stop him.

"You know that guy by the pickup?" she asked.

Glancing back, Fraser nodded.

"That's Dalton West," he said. "His search team found that girl over by the Summerset Mall last month. Or, I guess I should say, they found her body."

Cate raised an eyebrow as they started walking again.

"He used to be a bounty hunter, but now he runs a private investigation and security company," Fraser explained. "The company does a lot of pro bono work. I met Dalton when Tori Cabot went missing a few months back.

Her parents brought him in to help with the search."

Fraser exhaled, suddenly sounding tired.

"When his team found Tori, it was too late."

He stared after Bailey, who was nearing the water.

"Luckily, Dalton West's services won't be needed tonight now that Bailey and Ludwig are back in Belle Harbor."

Turning to Cate, he gestured toward the edge of the lot.

"Best to stay off the beach for now," he said. "It's about time for the search to begin."

CHAPTER FOUR

Jimmy Fraser followed Bailey to the edge of the water and looked over at the lighthouse, squinting his eyes against the wind. A mix of sand and salty spray stung his face as a fog horn sounded in the dark. He sighed and wondered for the thousandth time where Emma could be.

Could she be out there in the ocean? Did everything just get to be too much for her? It would be so easy to get lost in the waves.

Emma had been Fraser's partner for over a year now but he still felt as if he didn't really know her.

At least, not well enough for her to confide in him.

All he knew for sure was the woman had demons that she had tried to keep hidden. But on occasion, Fraser had witnessed the signs.

And of course, he'd heard about the drama between Emma and Bailey. At least the part that made some people in the department call Emma a homewrecker and worse.

But he didn't like to pry or ask questions.

Despite all the gossip, he had decided not to discuss the rumors about Emma's past with anyone, even Linette.

Things at home were already tense enough.

His wife of ten years spent most evenings at home taking

care of their two young daughters on her own while he worked late into the night.

She hadn't been pleased when he'd been partnered up with the attractive, newly promoted Detective Emma Walsh, and his wife's frosty attitude whenever he spoke about his partner prompted him to heed the advice his father had often dispensed when he was growing up.

He could hear his father's deep voice even now, after all these years, as if it was carried to him on the waves crashing around his boots.

Talk and taste your tongue, Jimmy.

Fraser's father, a cautious, soft-spoken man who'd been a police constable in Jamaica before he'd moved to Miami, had used the phrase to remind his impulsive son to think before he spoke. It was advice that still served him well.

Turning to Bailey, Fraser saw a rare frown of concern. He wondered what she was thinking.

She gave the impression she'd moved on and made peace with Emma. But could anyone really be that forgiving?

I doubt I'd be so gracious if I'd been betrayed by two of the people I loved the most.

He could certainly understand why she'd quit the Belle Harbor PD as soon as she'd gotten accepted into the FBI Academy up in Quantico.

And why she had jumped at the opportunity to move up to D.C. for good when given the chance. Belle Harbor was a small town, and it was impossible for her to live there and not run into the ghosts of her past on a daily basis.

"Did you bring something of Emma's to use as a scent?"

Bailey asked as she turned to Fraser. "Ludwig may not be able to find her without it."

Fraser grimaced and motioned to Rourke, who was standing at the edge of the parking lot next to Cate.

The officer jogged down toward them, his pale, freckled face hardening into a mask of irritation as his booted feet sank into the sand.

"Go to my Interceptor and get the jacket I left in the front passenger seat," he instructed. "And hurry."

Throwing the keys to Rourke, Fraser watched in amusement as the officer turned and jogged back toward the parking lot, kicking up damp sand as he went.

"I bet you don't get this kind of excitement up in D.C.," he teased as they watched Ludwig run in excited circles while they waited for Rourke to return. "How is the new assignment going, anyway?"

Bailey cocked her head and squinted her eyes as if trying to recall something that had taken place a long time ago.

"D.C. seems a million miles from here," she said, looking north as if she might see the lights of the Washington Monument glowing in the distance. "But the new task force is pretty much the same as any other."

She shrugged her shoulders as if it was no big deal.

"Although we just closed out a serial arson case that was really interesting. I learned so much. As did Ludwig. He's trained to search in any conditions, you know."

"Sounds like a great opportunity," Fraser said, feeling a pang of envy. "And they're lucky to have you. Both of you."

He smiled as Ludwig chased a wave that had thundered

onto shore, then watched it slip quietly back into the ocean.

"How often do you speak to Sid Morley?" he asked, suddenly thinking of the gruff FBI agent who had originally trained Ludwig and most of the other search and rescue dogs used by law enforcement in the area.

"You know, the only time I ever saw Morley crack a smile was when he was with those dogs," he added before she could reply. "He always loved it when they caught a scent and took off running."

Fraser hesitated, suddenly remembering the shoot-out at Summerset Park. He doubted old Morley was doing much running these days. Ronin Godfrey had seen to that.

Glancing at Bailey, he saw that she was looking back toward the parking lot as if impatient for Rourke to return.

"You know he has a prosthetic leg now," Fraser said, trying to sound upbeat. "He still gets out and about with that old dog of his. I saw them a few months ago."

When she didn't respond, he decided to drop the subject.

He knew Bailey had a habit of ignoring unwelcome or unpleasant questions or comments.

He'd noticed it when they'd worked together at the Belle Harbor PD before she'd moved on and up to the FBI.

She liked to focus only on the positive even when there was nothing positive in sight.

Nowadays some people might call the habit *toxic positivity*, but Jimmy Fraser knew it was just the way Bailey coped with the stress of the job.

And with a job that could end with the blast of a bullet at any time, who could blame her?

Suddenly, Rourke was back holding out the jacket Emma had left in Fraser's Interceptor the week before.

Bailey took the jacket from Rourke and studied it.

"Yes, this is Emma's," she said quietly. "I can smell her perfume. She always liked Chanel. She said it smelled expensive."

A wistful expression flashed across her face.

Then it was gone and she was turning to Ludwig. Holding out the jacket, she allowed him to sniff the dark material as she gave a firm command.

"Find her, Ludwig," Bailey said. "Go find her!"

The dog lifted his nose high into the air and issued a high-pitched bark.

Fraser's pulse jumped as the German shepherd scrambled into action, deftly making his way along the sandy shore.

CHAPTER FIVE

Bailey followed Ludwig through the sand dunes, praying the dog would be able to pick up Emma's scent despite the windy conditions on the beach. As she jogged behind the German shepherd, she silently reminded herself what Sid Morley and his fellow SAR trainers had taught her when she'd been learning to handle Ludwig in a search and rescue situation.

A dog's sense of smell can be a thousand times stronger than a human's, and they can pick up on a scent a mile away or even further if conditions are right.

But were the conditions right?

Lifting her own nose into the air, she detected the faint odor of sulfur and rotting seaweed.

And is that a hint of Chanel...or just my imagination?

The sweet, floral scent of the perfume always conjured memories of Emma. The first time they'd met, Bailey had asked her what scent she was wearing and was impressed a trainee police officer could afford the expensive brand.

Later, after they'd become fast friends, Emma had confided in Bailey that she often stopped by the department store to spritz her wrists with a tester bottle of the pricey fragrance since she couldn't afford her own.

Emma had also confessed that her unwed mother had only been sixteen when she'd given birth and that they'd always struggled to make ends meet.

The possibility of going to college had seemed unattainable, but Emma had managed to work her way through Belle Harbor Community College before applying to the Belle Harbor Police Academy.

That's where she'd met Bailey, who had recently graduated from Miami University with a four-year degree in criminal justice.

Emma had been shocked to learn Bailey applied to the academy after tearing up her acceptance letter to law school in response to the sudden realization that she didn't want to become a lawyer like her parents and her sister.

Bailey had wanted to be out in the field, stopping crime and catching criminals. Not stuck in a courtroom or boardroom dealing with endless meetings and paperwork.

Her family had tried to change her mind, but she'd refused to give in, saying only that she had her reasons, and in the end, they had to let her go.

When she'd met Emma in the academy, the two young women had quickly bonded, and after working together day in and day out for several years, they'd become best friends.

At least, that's what Bailey had believed until...

No, I can't go there. Not here. Not now.

Running along the shore, she pulled her thoughts back into the cool night air. She couldn't afford to lose focus, not when Ludwig was pulling impatiently on the leash.

The dog was heading toward the maze of sand dunes and scrubland that bordered the beach, his tail wagging eagerly as he stopped briefly to sniff at a clump of railroad vines, before racing on, pulling Bailey behind him.

She aimed the flashlight toward the ground, moving the bright circle of light back and forth as they moved further into the shadowy dunes.

Ludwig's sudden, loud bark started her heart pounding.

The dog ran forward, pawing and scratching at the sandy ground, giving a clear signal that he'd found what they'd been searching for.

Stepping forward, Bailey focused the beam of her flashlight on a black boot lying in the sand.

As the German shepherd barked again, she moved the beam along a slim leg, clad in black pants.

She continued tracing the body with the beam until she came to the mass of dark hair tangled in dune grass.

With a soft moan, she knelt beside the body.

"Oh, Emma...why?"

Her words were followed by more barking.

Looking over, Bailey saw that Ludwig was confused by her reaction. He'd tracked the scent and found the target.

Why wasn't she happy?

Forcing herself back to her feet, she leaned down and patted the dog on the back, ruffling his soft fur.

"Good job, Ludwig!" she said in a positive, upbeat tone, despite her grief. "You found it! What a good boy!"

As she patted the dog's back and gave him the treat he expected, she blinked hard against the wind and sand that stung her eyes, staring up at the row of expensive houses that lined the beach, thinking that the dark windows looked like silent, mournful eyes.

"I heard Ludwig barking. Did you find something?"

It was Fraser, breathing hard as if he'd been running.

When Bailey just nodded, the detective moved closer.

He stopped with a gasp as his beam fell on Emma's body. "Is she..."

The words stuck in his throat as he saw the bloody jacket and the gaping wound in her back.

"Someone must have come up behind her," he said, clenching his fists as he looked up at Bailey. "She still has her service weapon in her holster. She didn't even get a chance to defend herself."

Bailey patted Ludwig again and inhaled deeply, urging herself to stay calm and focused.

Now that she'd found Emma, she would need to do everything in her power to find the person who'd killed her.

In a voice that sounded much steadier than she felt, Bailey told Fraser to call for the medical examiner.

"And get Rourke and the other officers to cordon off the area," she said. "We need to keep everyone out while we wait for the CSI team to get here."

As Fraser started to make the calls, she heard a voice she recognized coming closer.

"Where is she? Where's Emma?"

Spinning around, Bailey saw Zach coming toward her, his face wet with tears and twisted with grief.

Fraser tried to block his path, but Zach pushed past him.

He stared down at his wife's body in shock.

"I'm sorry, Zach," Bailey said, coming up behind him. "It's just so terrible. But we will find whoever did this."

Taking Zach's arm, Fraser led him back the way he came, with Bailey bringing up the rear.

She watched as Zach stumbled through the sand, supported by Fraser, his broad shoulders deflated in grief.

When they finally reached the parking lot, Gavin Walsh was waiting for his son.

"Did you find her?" the judge asked. "Was it Emma?"

"She's dead," Zach said, starting to cry again. "She's dead and she's not coming back."

As Zach allowed himself to be led toward his father's black BMW, Bailey felt someone step up behind her.

"Karma really is a bitch, isn't it?"

She turned to see Officer Rourke.

"Don't get me wrong, it's sad and all, but you of all people have to admit it's ironic," he said. "I mean, Emma Walsh was an expert at stabbing people in the back, and now...this."

He met Bailey's eyes and held them, his expression unreadable. Before she could respond, Fraser was there.

"How did Zach Walsh get past you?" he snapped at Rourke. "Make sure no one else gets past the tape while we're waiting for the M.E. and the CSI team."

He looked over at Bailey.

"I'll make sure Zach gets back to his car," he said, then added under his breath. "I want to speak to him before he leaves the scene. I'll ask him to come down to the station for an official interview later tonight or tomorrow."

He hesitated as he looked back down the beach.

"I'm used to having a partner to tag team with," he said with a sigh. "Would you mind going back and waiting with the body until I get there? It won't be long."

Before she could respond, he walked away, leaving Bailey to trudge back through the sand to where the body of the woman she'd once called her best friend lay.

Emma had been the one person she'd entrusted with all her secrets. The last person she'd expected to betray her.

In many ways, Bailey had grieved the loss of Emma's friendship more than the loss of her relationship with Zach.

As she stared out at the churning Atlantic, she realized the anger and hurt she'd kept locked up inside for so long was gone as if it had been caught up in the relentless tide or carried away by the icy wind.

CHAPTER SIX

Mason Knox stifled a yawn as he steered the big white van past the yellow crime scene tape and into the Bellamy Beach parking lot. The medical examiner for Summerset County had been on his way home after a busy day in the autopsy suite when he'd gotten the call that a woman's body had been found on the beach.

County budgets being what they were, he had only one assistant examiner on staff, and Finola Lawson was already out in the field, collecting a body from the Summerset County Medical Center. That left only him to attend the scene, which meant it was going to be another late night.

It was only his first year working in South Florida, and the bite of the wind that greeted him as he stepped out of the van was an unpleasant surprise.

Isn't Florida supposed to be warm and balmy year-round?

Of course, Mason knew the weather up north would be miserable come winter, and that he would undoubtedly be grateful for the mild Florida climate, but it had been a long day and he wasn't in the mood to be reasonable.

Pulling out a fresh set of protective coveralls, cap, and boot covers, he waved to Detective Jimmy Fraser, who was standing in the parking lot next to a black BMW.

As the car rolled onto the highway, Fraser returned the wave and motioned toward the beach.

"The body's over there in the sand dunes," he said. "Agent Flynn is waiting with the body while our officers are setting up a perimeter. I'll be there shortly."

As Fraser turned away, Mason pulled the protective gear over his street clothes and slung his bag over his shoulder, deciding he'd come back for the gurney once he'd had a chance to examine the body.

Starting off toward the beach, he studied the dark sky, then hesitated and walked back to the van, hefting out a portable light with an audible groan.

When he finally stepped onto the sand, he headed north, following the deep trail cut through the sand by a series of heavy boots that left no question as to the scene's location.

So much for preserving the crime scene.

He saw the beam of light just as he was starting to think he might have made a wrong turn through the sand dunes after all.

A woman was holding a flashlight. As he approached, she turned and held up her badge.

"Are you with the CSI team?" she asked, pushing back the tangle of dark blonde hair that flew around her face.

"No, I'm Dr. Mason Knox, the medical examiner for Summerset County," he said, pushing back his cap and pulling down his mask so she could see his face.

"I'm Special Agent Bailey Flynn with the FBI."

He looked down at the body, which was half-hidden by

sand and shadows, and sighed.

"It's good to meet you, Agent Flynn."

"Please, call me Bailey."

She nodded toward the German shepherd.

"And that's Ludwig. He's search and rescue."

"You work in the Miami field office?" he asked, setting down the portable light and dropping his bag on the sand.

"I used to, but I relocated to D.C. about six months ago."

Mason lifted an eyebrow as he unfolded the legs to the portable light and switched it on, illuminating the area.

"Emma? Is that the victim's name?"

Bailey nodded slowly and cleared her throat.

"Yes, her name is...*was*...Emma Walsh."

"*Detective* Emma Walsh?"

Mason's heart sank as Bailey nodded.

"She worked with the Belle Harbor PD."

Pulling out his camera, he began to snap photos of the scene and the victim in situ.

"Did you know her?" Bailey asked, watching as he knelt to examine the body.

"Not well," Mason admitted. "I've only been with the medical examiner's office about a year. However, I consulted with the Belle Harbor PD on a homicide victim a few months back. Detective Walsh appeared to be very passionate about her job. Very persistent."

"Yes, she was," Bailey said.

He looked up to see the agent wiping at her eyes.

"There's so much sand blowing around," she said, blinking hard. "That's probably why it took so long to find

Emma. She was covered with sand...hard to see."

Mason dropped his gaze to the German shepherd, who stared back at him with dark, assessing eyes.

"Why'd they send a handler from D.C. down to South Florida for a missing person case?" he asked, suddenly curious about the duo. "Surely they have search and rescue dogs in Miami. Is Detective Walsh's death somehow linked to a federal investigation?"

Bailey hesitated as if she wasn't quite sure why she was there. Or maybe wasn't allowed to say.

"No, I actually came here on my own when I heard Emma was missing," she admitted. "I used to be her partner at the Belle Harbor PD. Back when we were both in uniform."

She'd dropped her hand, giving up on trying to control her wind-swept hair, allowing the dark blonde strands to billow out behind her.

"Detective Fraser invited me to join in on the search," she said. "He thought with a search and rescue K-9, we might be able to find Emma."

Her green eyes softened as she looked down at the dog.

"And he was right. Ludwig ran straight to her."

Mason nodded his head in approval.

"Nice work," he said to the dog.

Bailey crouched beside the German shepherd and rubbed his black and tan coat with obvious affection.

"Yes, nice work, Ludwig," she echoed. "You found Emma. Now we've got to find out what happened to her."

She stared down at the body in the sand.

Melinda Woodhall

"Can you tell how she died?"

"This likely has something to do with it."

Using gloved hands, Mason pulled back the torn, blood-stained material that clung to the dead woman's skin.

"Looks like a single stab wound to the back."

The sight was disturbingly familiar, and he frowned as he realized what he was seeing.

Pulse quickening, he checked higher up on Emma Walsh's back, pulling the stiff material of the jacket away from her left shoulder. The skin was discolored but intact.

Finally, he checked both her arms, but there were no signs of track marks.

"What are you looking for?" Bailey asked.

"She certainly doesn't match the profile," he murmured, confused. "But the injury..."

"What profile? What injury?"

The agent was staring at him in confusion.

He couldn't really blame her. He was confused, too.

"I've seen something just like this three times before," he admitted. "Three different women have been on my dissection table over the last year with this exact wound."

"An eighteen-year-old named Wren Dempsey was the first," he explained. "She was found behind a rest stop in Bonneville. Her body had been dumped in the woods.

"The stab wound was unique, as was the mutilation to her back. A four-by-four inch patch of skin had been removed. Carved off her back with a knife. It was strange. Of course, that kind of thing stuck with me."

"So when I responded to another call a few months later

44

and saw Tori Cabot discarded in a field just north of the Summerset Mall, the similarity between the injuries was impossible to miss."

Glancing up, he saw she was listening with rapt attention, her wide green eyes wide with interest.

"I told the Bonneville and the Belle Harbor Police that they were possibly looking at the same killer."

"You told the police here in Belle Harbor?"

Mason nodded.

"I spoke to Detective Walsh myself," he said. "She assured me she would look into it."

"Then, when Hallie Kwan was discovered over in Sun Creek last month, I submitted a written report to all three departments, requesting confirmation on my findings."

He clenched his jaw as he thought of the latest email he'd been working on. It was still sitting in his *Drafts* folder.

"I never heard anything back," he said. "I was planning to send Detective Walsh another email this week."

"And you think whoever killed those girls could have also killed Emma?" Bailey asked.

"I can't say for sure," he admitted. "However, based on her injuries, I'd say it's very likely the same perp."

The agent looked doubtful.

"But I haven't heard anything about a serial killer in Summerset County," she said. "And I didn't see anything on the news about three connected homicides."

"I'm not surprised," Mason said. "As you probably know, Summerset County encompasses fourteen different cities and towns, including Belle Harbor. The local police don't do a great job of talking to each other."

Bailey cocked her head as if she'd had a sudden idea.

"Did any of the local police departments enter the homicides in CODIS?" she asked. "That would tell us if the homicides appear to be connected."

Mason shrugged as he knelt and prepared to take the dead woman's temperature.

"If they have, they never told me about it," he said. "I've escalated my concerns, but as far as I know, nothing's been done to pursue the connection between the homicides."

"I wonder why?" Bailey asked. "Why would the local departments ignore the connection?"

A frown accompanied her soft words, and Mason hesitated, figuring the FBI agent was likely just thinking aloud, not asking for his opinion of the local police departments' motives and actions, or lack thereof.

Although, some things just need to be said.

Clearing his throat, he looked up at Bailey.

"I have a theory."

He got to his feet, brushing the sand from his knees.

"The police said the deaths were almost certainly drug-related. As if that explained everything," he said. "I got the impression they didn't want to cause a public outcry and bring more attention to the drug activity in their communities. I'm guessing it isn't good for tourism."

"So, you're saying they just want tourists to feel safe?"

Mason nodded.

"Otherwise they'll just stick to Miami and Orlando," he explained. "None of the police I've spoken with wanted to acknowledge the deaths could be related to other homicides. They want to believe it's just a coincidence that the victims were all mutilated and killed with the same sort of knife."

He knew he sounded bitter, but he was tired of dissecting people who should have had decades left to live.

"Even after this, I doubt any of the police departments involved will admit there might be a serial killer stalking Summerset County."

"Although, the press are starting to put the pieces together. It's only a matter of time before we'll hear a special news bulletin about the murders. Maybe then the murders will get some attention."

Bailey nodded slowly as if she was still trying to process the information.

"I think you're exactly right, Dr. Knox," a voice said from behind him. "And you've certainly got *my* attention."

Mason turned to see the slim figure of a young woman in a royal blue pantsuit standing just past the sand dune.

A camera bag was slung over one shoulder and a press badge hung from a lanyard around her neck. As Mason gaped at her, the wind ruffled her short, fair hair.

"I'm Sabrina West with Channel 3 News. I heard the call on the police scanner and came straight over."

Her eyes flicked to the body in the sand.

"Is that the latest victim you two were talking about?"

As she slipped the camera out of its bag, Bailey stepped forward and held out a hand.

"This is a restricted crime scene," she said, blocking the reporter's view of the body. "You need to leave the area and stay behind the tape."

Sabrina West ignored the agent as she stepped closer, aiming the camera at Mason.

"Do you really think there's a serial killer stalking Summerset County?" the reporter asked.

She sounded hopeful.

"Agent Flynn told you to leave," he shot back. "I suggest you do so before you contaminate the scene."

The reporter started to protest, then thought better of it as she saw several figures approaching.

Mason was relieved to see Jimmy Fraser's solid frame leading a group of uniformed officers.

The detective was walking next to Madeline Mercer, the lead crime scene technician for the Belle Harbor PD.

"Hey, what's she doing here?" Fraser called out.

Scowling at Sabrina West, he quickened his step.

"Ms. West was just leaving," Bailey assured Fraser, lifting a placating hand as if to stop any further discussion. "Perhaps an officer can escort her back to the parking lot."

Once the reporter was out of earshot, Mason turned to Fraser, feeling as if he should express his condolences.

Emma Walsh had been Fraser's partner, after all. The man was bound to be upset. Maybe even emotional.

He was still human, even if he was a cop.

"I'm sorry for your loss, Detective Fraser," he said softly. "I know Emma was your partner, and I can speak to someone else about my findings so far if you think-"

"No, I'm okay," Fraser assured him. "This is my case. And there's no way I'm gonna let the dirtbag who did this to Emma get away with it."

Mason nodded, accepting the response without further comment, figuring he'd probably feel the same way if he were in the detective's position.

"Okay, then," he said briskly, reverting to his all-business tone. "As I was telling Agent Flynn, Emma suffered a single stab wound in the back. The cause of death will likely be massive hemorrhaging and exsanguination. The manner of death is definitely homicide."

"Based on her temperature and the conditions out here, I'd guess she's been dead for at least forty-eight hours. I'll know more after the autopsy."

"I need to take some more photos before I move the body. And I'll need some help with that if my forensic technician doesn't get here soon."

He checked his watch.

"Finola's responding to another scene as we speak, and I'm not sure how long that will take."

Fraser nodded, then turned to Bailey.

"You really don't have to be here," he said softly. "You did what you came to do. You found Emma. You can head back up to DC now. You can try to forget Belle Harbor all over again."

Mason looked up to see Bailey shaking her head.

"Whoever killed her is still out there," she said, lifting her chin in defiance as she gestured toward the dark beach beyond. "And I'm not going back to D.C. until I find him."

CHAPTER SEVEN

T he widescreen TV was turned to Channel 3 News, broadcasting live from Bellamy Beach. On the screen, yellow strips of crime scene tape fluttered against a background of gray skies and darkly crashing waves as a solemn-looking young woman in a royal blue pantsuit spoke into an oversized microphone.

"For those of you just joining us, I'm Sabrina West, reporting live from Bellamy Beach in Belle Harbor, Florida, where a woman's body was discovered last night following a search by local police and the FBI."

The fair-haired reporter raised her voice against the gusty whoosh of the wind and the low roar of the waves.

"Sources within the Summerset County Medical Examiner's Office have confirmed the woman's identity as Emma Walsh, a detective with the Belle Harbor PD who had been reported missing early yesterday morning."

"Channel 3 News has learned that this has been the fourth fatal stabbing in Summerset County this year, with one source suggesting that last night's homicide could be the latest in a string of attacks by a serial killer some people are calling the Summerset Stalker."

The words earned a worried frown from the man on the sofa, who was watching the report with growing concern.

"The Summerset Stalker?" he muttered as he shifted in his seat. "Is that what they're calling me?"

The idea was unsettling.

If the press had given him a nickname, the public would soon take notice. People would start to panic.

Sensationalized reports on the Summerset Stalker would fill the news cycle and spread fear throughout the county, maybe even the state.

There would be pressure on the local cops and the FBI to find the Stalker and send him to death row.

An image of the electric chair flashed through his mind.

Do they still use Old Sparky up in Starke?

He knew the state's only execution chamber was located in the little North Florida town, but he couldn't remember if death sentences were carried out by lethal injection or the electric chair.

Maybe both? Maybe you get a choice as to how you die.

The thought wasn't comforting.

The Stalker, as he was already starting to think of himself, knew he'd have to be more careful going forward if he didn't want to find himself making that choice.

Turning back to the television, he watched as footage taken the previous evening began to play.

A young woman with dark blonde hair held the leash of a black and tan German shepherd. She stood next to a woman he recognized. A tall, thin woman with auburn hair.

"Prosecutor Cate Flynn was at the scene last night as was the

Summerset County medical examiner, Mason Knox."

Sabrina West's earnest face was replaced by video footage of the medical examiner wheeling a sheet-covered gurney to a white van.

"Stay tuned to Channel 3 News and we'll bring you the latest news on the Summerset Stalker as soon as it becomes available."

As the station cut to a commercial break, the Stalker shut off the television and began to pace the room, wondering how much the FBI knew about him so far.

Has a task force been assigned to investigate the murders?

If so, there could be a knock on his door at any minute.

He'd known that eliminating Emma Walsh and the threat she'd presented would be dangerous. But he'd never thought her death would be connected to the others so quickly, if at all.

Anxiety bloomed in his chest as he dug in his pocket for the bottle he'd gotten that morning from a girl not much older than Tori Cabot had been.

Her sullen face and glazed eyes hovered in his mind as he unscrewed the lid, shook out two benzos, swallowed them dry, and then shook out two more.

He'd need to stay calm. He couldn't afford to have another one of his panic attacks.

Reaching for the leather sheath on his belt, he slid out the big combat knife he kept nestled against his back.

The heavy weight of the handle felt good in his hand, instantly granting him a heady sense of power and control.

His thumb lightly traced a path along the serrated edge of the knife as he pictured his father, who had often used a handkerchief to polish the knife's stainless steel teeth.

The combat knife was the only thing he had left from his childhood, other than a handful of faded photos and a few best-forgotten memories.

Would his father have wanted him to make good use of the knife? Would he be proud? It was impossible to know.

His father had been a hard man with an unbending sense of duty. And once he'd joined the army, his duty was to kill.

The transition back to civilian life hadn't been easy.

His mother had whispered to him about his father, saying he'd come back from overseas a changed man. She'd sounded sad, maybe even scared, whenever she'd spoken of him, although he'd been too young to understand why.

Of course, that had been before she'd gone up to heaven.

A familiar ache took its usual place in his chest at the thought, and his father's deep voice echoed in his head.

"Your mother's not coming back, boy. She's dead."

At first, he hadn't believed it. His father had to be mistaken or even lying. After all, he wasn't a godly man.

His mother had admitted as much to the reverend when she thought her six-year-old son wasn't listening.

For once, he had dared to talk back to his father.

"You're wrong, Daddy! Reverend Cheever said that people worthy of the resurrection can't die anymore...they're like the angels. It says so in the Book of Luke."

He'd stiffened, bracing for a blow, but instead of the slap he'd expected, his father had delivered an indifferent shrug.

"Then maybe she's an angel now, son. Maybe she's got her wings and she's flown away. We'll have to make do without her."

That terrible day, and his father's callous words, had marked a turning point in his life.

Though he remembered little of the funeral, he could still picture the stony expression on his dead mother's face as Reverend Cheever spoke over her coffin in a stern, forbidding voice.

One verse had stayed with him all these years.

"...God spared not the angels that sinned, but cast them down to hell, and delivered them into chains of darkness..."

Sometimes the verse would still come to him at night, whispered in his ears by unseen demons as he slept, conjuring images that had haunted him since childhood.

All light and joy had ended the day his mother had been buried, replaced by a gloomy loneliness that had grown darker and darker as his father descended into the depression and madness that eventually took him away.

In the end, the only thing he'd been left with was the memory of his mother and the sure knowledge that she watched over him from some mysterious place in the sky, far from the empty hopelessness of the world below.

Her memory was sacred and nothing and no one could be allowed to tarnish it. Not his father, and not the girls who'd tried to wear her wings.

Anger began to simmer at the thought of Wren Dempsey. She'd been the one who'd started the trouble.

All this is her fault.

As he ran his thumb along the knife's sharp blade, a thin line of blood appeared in the thickly scarred skin.

Closing his eyes, he remembered.

She was waiting on the corner for him just as he'd instructed, the street light reflecting off her long blonde hair as she climbed into the passenger seat and handed him a brown paper bag.

"It's in there," she said stiffly. "This is the last time. I'm done."

Pulling away from the curb, he looked in his rearview mirror, worried that someone might be following him.

That he might be seen.

He knew too well that the local police regularly patrolled the area but had been compelled to take the risk anyway.

The last of the Devil's Breath was gone and he needed a new supply. He also wanted more of the benzos, which kept him calm.

The other pills he'd taken made him tense and jumpy.

Merging onto the highway, he drove west, then exited at the Bonneville rest stop. He parked behind the long single-story structure and turned off the engine, eager to dip into the goodies in the bag.

Once he'd swallowed a few pills and snorted a whiff of the fine white powder, he turned to Wren, studying her delicate profile.

She was young. Only eighteen.

But that was old enough to know better.

Old enough to know right from wrong.

She'd been in and out of rehab more than once, but as she turned to look at him, her big, blue eyes still had that hungry look that told him she hadn't fully kicked the habit.

That maybe she never would.

Telling himself she'd be back on the pills before too long, with or without his influence, he spilled a few of the pills onto his palm and held them out to her like an offering.

"I don't want them," she said, shaking her head. "I told you, I'm done with that. I'm clean now."

"Clean?" he mocked. "Is that what you think you are?"

As he reached for her, she jerked back, grabbing for the door handle, sensing the sudden change in him, desperate to get away.

His head began to spin from the pills and the powder as he lunged across the front seat, managing to grab hold of Wren's blouse before she tumbled out onto the grass, leaving him holding only a ragged strip of silk.

Wrenching open the door, he scrambled out after her, racing around to intercept her as she made a run toward the highway.

He seized hold of one thin arm, pulling her back as she continued to struggle. A flash of pain tore through him as she kicked out, the hard toe of her boot making contact with his knee.

With a cry of pain, he grabbed his knee as she bolted toward the side of the building, then tripped over a root, falling with full force on the hard ground.

Instantly he was on her, grabbing her by the hair, his face a red mask of rage as he snarled in her ear.

"You'll regret this, I promise you I'll..."

His words ended abruptly as he saw what was on her shoulder, clearly visible under her torn blouse.

Gaping in disbelief as he realized what he was looking at, he blinked and tried to focus his eyes. Was he having a delusion?

After all, the Devil's Breath could have strange effects.

Or maybe it was a vision sent by God.

He stared in horror at the intricate pattern of red, raised scars.

"What's that on your back?"

Wren gasped out the words.

"Wings," she said. "They're...angel wings."

Shaking his head, he squinted down at the scarred flesh as his father's words echoed in his head.

"Maybe she's an angel now, son. Maybe she's got her wings..."

The words burned through him, summoning the darkness that came with the memories of his childhood.

As Wren tried to twist away, he grabbed her by the throat and then pulled his father's combat knife from its sheath.

Another voice began to whisper to him as he held the knife above her. Reverend Cheever's words echoed in his ear.

"...God spared not the angels that sinned, but cast them down to hell...and delivered them into...darkness..."

Clenching the knife in his hand, he gave a sudden, vicious thrust forward, lodging the knife in the girl's back.

"You're...no...angel," he panted in her ear.

Hot blood ran over his hand as he yanked the knife free of bone and tissue, leaving her lifeless on the ground.

He looked down at her with disdain, then knelt beside her, knowing what needed to be done.

Working deftly with the knife, he cut around the scarred flesh, scraping off clinging nerves and tissue before dropping the patch of skin into an empty paper bag from Summerset Subs.

His rage started to fade and the darkness began to recede as he dumped her body into a clump of trees behind the rest area, already feeling lighter.

The girl had been asking for it. Had gotten what she deserved.

As he walked back toward his car, he looked up at the night sky with expectant eyes, but the stars were hidden by clouds, as was the waning moon. The heavens were dark above him.

Opening his eyes, the Stalker stared down at an angry red splotch of blood on the floor, then looked around the room, surprised to find himself at home and not in the woods behind the Bonneville rest area.

Perhaps the psychoactive effects of the Devil's Breath hadn't worn off. Or maybe regular use of the drug was causing permanent damage.

Maybe I should lay off for a while. Maybe I should get clean.

The thought circled through his aching head as he stared into the black eyes of the raven mounted on the top of his china cabinet.

Turning on his heel, he walked into his bedroom, his eyes scanning the frames of mounted butterfly and moth specimens that covered the far wall.

He crossed to a white wooden frame, admiring the skins he'd carefully stretched, dried, and pinned to the mounting board behind the glass.

The raised pink lines that formed the angel wings were basic and unrefined when compared to the intricate designs on the butterfly wings in the other frames.

But they added a certain originality to his collection.

Wren had been his first fallen angel.

Now there were three sets of angel wings on display. And there was room for more.

CHAPTER EIGHT

Bailey sat up with a start, woken from a fitful sleep by a loud bark coming from the floor below. A beam of sunlight streamed through a crack in the bright white curtains, dimly illuminating a room she barely recognized now that nothing of the familiar décor or memorabilia from her childhood remained.

Sitting up in bed, she looked around with tired eyes, trying to picture the way the room had looked when she'd lived at home, back before she'd learned that some monsters were real and that the world beyond the four walls could be deadly.

Her plush pink carpet, collection of stuffed animals, and bookshelf full of young adult vampire romances were all gone, replaced by beige walls and sensible furnishings that still came as a shock sometimes, stirring up emotions Bailey didn't like to analyze.

While she'd always known her mother would repurpose her childhood bedroom someday, Bailey hadn't expected Jackie Flynn to convert it into a guest room and donate all her possessions to Goodwill without warning or discussion.

She suspected her own last-minute decision not to go to

law school may have inspired the drastic remodeling project, and in some ways, she could understand her mother's disappointment.

The whole family had expected her to be a lawyer, and she'd shocked them all by signing up for the Belle Harbor Police Academy before moving on to the FBI.

It wasn't the path any of them would have chosen for her, and Jackie Flynn took every opportunity to make sure Bailey knew it.

Another bark from below had Bailey climbing out of bed, wondering how Ludwig had gotten downstairs.

Ignoring the missed call notifications on her phone for the time being, Bailey opened her suitcase and dug through the clothes she'd hastily thrown in the day before.

After pulling on a slightly wrinkled pair of navy blue pants and a white woolen sweater, she went downstairs, following the scent of coffee into the kitchen, where her father sat at the breakfast table reading the newspaper.

Duchess, her mother's white Siamese cat, was lounging by the back door. She'd taken over Ludwig's usual spot but was keeping her big, blue eyes on the German shepherd, who was sitting beside her father.

The dog looked up at Bailey with a guilty smile, licking his jowls with satisfaction.

"I've already taken him for a walk and he's had his breakfast," Chris said with an equally guilty grin.

"What have you been feeding him?' she asked, knowing her father could rarely deny the dog's dark, imploring eyes.

An animated voice drew her attention to the television on

the counter before her father could answer.

Bailey looked over to see Sabrina West on the little screen. The reporter was standing in the Bellamy Beach parking lot still wearing the same royal blue pantsuit she'd had on the night before as if she'd never left the scene.

"...a woman's body was discovered last night following a search by local police and the FBI. Sources within the Summerset County Medical Examiner's Office have confirmed the woman's identity as Emma Walsh..."

Crossing the room, Bailey turned up the volume.

"Channel 3 News has learned that this has been the fourth fatal stabbing in Summerset County this year, with one source suggesting that last night's homicide could be the latest in a string of attacks by a serial killer some people are calling the Summerset Stalker."

She shook her head in dismay.

The reporter's claim that there was a serial killer on the loose was bound to start a panic, and her decision to dub the killer the Summerset Stalker would make sure it spread across the entire county, maybe even the state.

"You really think Emma was murdered by a serial killer?" her father asked, frowning at the television. "Do you have any leads, yet?"

"I'm not officially working the case," Bailey reminded him as she switched off the television.

She'd had enough of Sabrina West for the time being

"Besides, her body was found less than twelve hours ago, so I don't imagine the BHPD has any leads yet either, other than the usual suspects the police investigate whenever a woman is killed."

She crossed to the refrigerator and took out a carton of orange juice.

"They'll look at her husband first," she said. "And then anyone else she might have been involved with."

"You think Zach could have done this?"

Pretending not to hear the question, Bailey focused on pouring juice into a glass while trying to block the image of Zach's tear-streaked face from her mind.

"Well, whoever did this, once they catch the guy, your sister will send him to jail for a good long time," Chris said with confidence. "They showed Cate on television earlier, you know. They said her name, too."

"Yes, Cate was at the beach last night when Emma was found," Bailey said. "But Ludwig is the true hero. He's the one who should be on TV since he found Emma's body."

Chris glanced down at Ludwig and shook his head.

"And you were right behind him, I'm sure," her father said with a shiver. "The maniac who did this could have still been there. Remember what happened to Sid Morley."

Bailey's back stiffened at the unnecessary reminder.

"I'll never understand why you didn't follow me into corporate law," Chris said, not noticing the grimace that flashed across his daughter's face at his words. "There's no danger in the boardroom."

"That's not true," Bailey shot back. "If I spent all my time writing up contracts like you do, I'd die of boredom."

Jackie Flynn tutted as she came into the room, dressed in wide-legged black trousers and a silk blouse of the palest blue. Her short, silver bob was slicked back from a face that seemed perpetually creased into a concerned frown.

"Bailey, that's a terrible thing to say to your father," she scolded as she crossed to the espresso machine. "He's just worried about you, as am I."

She raised a stern eyebrow in her daughter's direction.

"And don't forget that without your father's connections, you might never have gotten a place in the Bureau."

"How could I forget when you remind me every time I see you?" Bailey replied with a forced smile. "I'm sure Dad knows I'm eternally grateful for everything he's ever–"

"I just can't believe Zach killed her," Jackie cut in as if no one else had been speaking. "Of course, I heard rumors at the club that Emma was seeing someone else. And I can't say I was surprised after what she did to you and–"

Bailey jumped up and grabbed Ludwig's leash.

"I've got to go downtown. I need to give a statement to the Belle Harbor PD and–"

"But how are you going to get there?" Jackie protested. "If you wait I can drop you off on my way into the office. We can have a nice chat about–"

"I can take the Camaro," Bailey said, turning bright eyes to her father. "You don't mind, do you, Dad?"

Her father's eyes widened with dismay at the thought of his youngest daughter driving his restored '67 Camaro.

"Ludwig and I will be very careful," she promised as she plucked the keys from the hook on the wall. "And we'll be back by midnight."

* * *

Bailey smiled as she pulled onto the highway and sped past Grand Harbor Boulevard. The police station would have to wait. She had an important stop to make first.

Driving west to the outskirts of town, she slowed as the cherry-red Camaro neared the Mariner's Rest subdivision, and looked into the tiny backseat at Ludwig, who was wagging his tail in happy anticipation.

By the time she'd parked the classic car in front of Sid Morley's modest bungalow, the front door had opened and a large, furry figure was bounding toward them.

"Amadeus!" a gravelly voice called. "Come back here!"

The big black German shepherd paid no attention as he raced around the car and barked, prompting a happy bark from Ludwig in response.

Bailey watched as the smaller tan and black dog jumped from the car and greeted his ex-partner with excited sniffing and more tail wagging.

The two dogs hadn't seen each other for months, and they were obviously glad to be reunited.

Turning to the modest house, Bailey saw former special agent Sid Morley emerge.

He descended the porch steps slowly, taking them one at a time. Once he'd reached the smooth concrete of the driveway, he moved more confidently as if he was getting used to his new prosthetic limb.

"Ludwig, my boy!" he cried out. "I've missed you!"

Morley ruffled the smaller dog's fur with obvious

pleasure, his eyes bright as he looked up at Bailey.

"You should have told me you were coming," he said. "I could have had food ready. I've been learning to cook you know. Retirement isn't all bad."

A pang of guilt shot through Bailey as she watched the older man walk stiffly toward a length of rope, bend slowly to pick it up, and then throw it into the yard for the dogs to retrieve and return.

No matter how many times Morley had reassured her he didn't blame her for the loss of his leg, she couldn't stop replaying the events at Summerset Park in her mind, wishing she'd acted more quickly.

"I hear that you and Ludwig had a successful search last night at Bellamy Beach," Morley said with an approving smile. "You even made the news. I'm proud of you."

"Thanks," Bailey said. "I was proud of Ludwig. He's amazing. There was so much wind and sand, but he found Emma almost right away."

Morley cocked his head.

"You don't seem happy about it," he said. "Why not?"

"The woman who was missing...she was my friend," Bailey admitted. "Or she used to be. We went through the police academy together."

Wincing at the news, Morley sighed.

"I'm sorry, I didn't realize you knew her. It makes the search much harder if you know the one you're looking for," he said. "That's a lesson they can't teach you in handler's training. You have to learn that one for yourself."

Bailey swallowed hard, knowing he was right.

But she was eager to change the subject. She wouldn't have much time to spend with Morley and she wanted to make sure he'd been doing okay.

"So, enough about me and Ludwig," she said. "What have you and Amadeus been up to since I've been gone?"

"Oh, not much," Morley said. "Although we have been picking up the odd search and rescue job here and there."

The extra gruffness in his voice told her he was pleased, but she was instantly concerned.

"Search jobs? Who with? Is it safe?"

Morley waved a dismissive hand at her.

"Stop fussing," he said, sounding amused. "I've been running search and rescue ops since you were toddling around in diapers. Not gonna stop now, not if I'm needed."

He led her toward a shady tree, where several chairs had been arranged, and sank down into a rocker with a sigh.

"I've worked a few jobs with a P.I. named Dalton West," he said. "The guy owns his own investigation company. He specializes in search and rescue. Takes on pro bono cases whenever he can."

Leaning back in the chair, he watched the dogs, who were still wrestling with the rope.

"Dalton brought me and Amadeus in to help with searches for several different missing girls."

The older man grimaced.

"Although me with one leg and Amadeus with his hips..."

"Dalton West?" she said. "The name sounds familiar but I don't think I know him."

"He's not been in South Florida long," Morley said as he

began to absently rock back and forth. "He was in the military before moving into private security overseas. Did a few years as a bounty hunter before he moved to South Florida and started up his latest enterprise. I get the feeling he wanted to be close to his sister."

He rolled his eyes.

"You'll have heard of *her* for sure," he said. "Sabrina West...the reporter for Channel 3 News?"

Thinking of the aggressive reporter's sudden appearance the night before, and her unsubstantiated report that morning about a serial killer in the area, Bailey nodded.

"You'll have seen her on the news today," Morley said. "She's figured out what's going on, although her brother's tried to keep her out of it. He's the protective sort."

"What do you mean?" Bailey asked. "What is going on?"

Morley scratched at the stubble on his chin.

"Girls are going missing and turning up dead," he said. "There's been three so far that I know about."

His words sounded eerily familiar.

"Wren Dempsey was the first girl we looked for," Morley said. "Dalton offered to conduct the search pro bono. We found her in the woods out in Bonneville. After that, there was Tori Cabot and Hallie Kwan. Both found dead."

"Let me guess, they'd been stabbed in the back and mutilated before being dumped."

The older man frowned.

"How'd you know?"

"Because you're talking about the same homicides the M.E. was telling me about last night. It seems as if everybody knew about these women except the police."

Morley scoffed.

"The police didn't *want* to know," he said. "Just like they didn't want to search for those girls. I think they'd rather we hadn't found them either."

"So, Dalton told his sister about these women," Bailey said, speaking more to herself than to Morley. "He gave her the lead on the story."

That's why Sabrina jumped on the serial killer angle so quickly when she heard Mason discussing the murders. And why she had the Summerset Stalker nickname already picked out.

But the reporter had needed someone working in an official capacity to confirm it. Someone like Mason Knox.

As Bailey mulled over the information she'd learned, the opening notes of Beethoven's Symphony No. 5 began to play somewhere nearby.

"Sorry, that's my ringtone for Dalton," he said, digging in his pocket and glancing down at the screen. "He's almost here."

Shifting in his seat, he prepared to stand.

"He's been taking me to my appointments," he explained as he pushed himself up and onto his feet. "It's still a little hard for me to drive, you see."

A flush of color rose into his cheeks as he escorted her back to the car, and Bailey realized he was embarrassed.

"I'm sorry," she said, blinking hard. "If I'd gotten to the scene sooner. If I hadn't stopped to-"

"You saved my life," he cut in softly. "That's enough."

She nodded miserably as a big black Dodge pickup pulled

onto the driveway.

"There's Dalton now," Morley said as a man climbed out.

Dalton West had the same fair hair as his sister, but that's where the similarity ended.

He was lean and fit, with a strong, clean-shaven jaw and a golden tan that revealed he spent plenty of time outdoors.

Lifting a hand in greeting, he was waylaid by Amadeus, who ran up to greet him, tail wagging.

Bailey watched as Dalton took the length of rope from the German shepherd's mouth and pretended to wrestle with him, laughing as Ludwig jumped into the fray.

Once Dalton slipped past the dogs, Morley made gruff introductions, leaving Bailey and Dalton standing beside each other to make awkward small talk as he went inside to get his wallet and lock up the house.

"I've heard a lot about you from Morley," Dalton said. "And I've seen a little, too."

Bailey cocked an eyebrow.

"On the news," he explained. "And last night at Bellamy Beach. I have to say, you and Ludwig make a good team."

"I'm lucky to have him."

Her cheeks grew warm under his approving gaze.

"I'm grateful Morley trusted me to take him on."

She opened her mouth, tempted to add that she was also grateful Dalton was there to help Morley, and to take him to his appointments, then closed it again.

No need to state the obvious, especially when it might embarrass Morley, or make Dalton uncomfortable.

Instead, she silently watched Ludwig and Amadeus chase

a lizard around the yard while surreptitiously studying the man whom Morley obviously held in high regard.

If Sid Morley had spent time with the ex-bounty hunter and found him worthy, who was she to say otherwise?

"I actually have a question for you," Dalton said, lifting a hand to block the sun from his eyes. "I was wondering what it would take to get the FBI to officially open a homicide investigation into the three women who were killed in Summerset County over the last year?"

He cleared his throat.

"It's just...I helped search for those women and have met their families," he said. "It seems as if nothing's being done and now another woman has been killed."

His words stung for some reason, and Bailey felt her back stiffen, although she wasn't sure why.

"I don't know what the local police or the FBI plan to do about the homicides," Bailey said. "But Emma Walsh used to be my partner, and I can assure you, I intend to find her killer. With or without their help."

CHAPTER NINE

Dalton opened his mouth to respond to Bailey's impassioned statement, then closed it again as Morley appeared behind them, coming back down the driveway, moving at his usual slow but steady pace, calling to Amadeus and Ludwig as he approached.

"I'm glad you stopped by," Morley said, taking Bailey's hand and squeezing it. "Come by again before you head back to D.C., I'll make you something special for dinner."

"I'll see what I can do," she said, stopping to scratch Amadeus behind the ears. "I better get going, too. I told Detective Fraser I'd stop by the station and give him an official statement about last night."

As she started back toward the Camaro, Dalton called out to her, feeling as if he'd left something important unsaid.

"If you need help finding the man who killed Emma Walsh, I'm willing to do whatever I can," he said, digging in his pocket for a business card. "Don't hesitate to call if-"

"Thanks," she called back. "I'll keep that in mind."

Rewarding him with a faint smile, she opened the car door and let Ludwig climb into the back seat.

She had already backed out onto Mariner Trail when he

realized he'd never handed her his business card. Although, if he thought about it, that shouldn't really matter.

She's an FBI agent. If she wants to find me, she will.

He watched the little red car pull away, then helped Morley into the Dodge, wondering if he'd said the wrong thing or come on too strong.

He had to admit he was intrigued by the woman who had saved old Sid Morley's life, and who handled Ludwig like a seasoned pro.

Of course, Bailey Flynn was a beautiful woman, that went without saying, but his attraction went way beyond that.

Perhaps it had started with the footage Sabrina had shown him after the shoot-out with Ronin Godfrey.

Bailey had been hounded by the press as she'd left the Summerset County Medical Center where Morley had been transported.

In the footage Sabrina had captured that day, Bailey had still been wearing a bloodstained jacket, and the expression on her drawn, pale face was one he'd seen plenty of times before in his line of work.

The young FBI agent had been in shock and grieving.

For whom he couldn't be sure.

For her fellow agent who'd been shot?

For the little girl who'd been killed before she arrived?

For the monster Bailey had taken out with a single bullet between the eyes?

What had put that look in her eyes?

Even then, it was a question that had intrigued Dalton.

And now that he'd gotten to know Morley and had seen

Bailey in action the night before at Bellamy Beach, he was even more curious to know what was going on behind those guarded green eyes.

A frown fell over his face as he realized she'd be going back to D.C. soon and he may never get a chance to find out.

As he backed the truck out of Morley's driveway and headed for the doctor's office, he wondered if he'd see her again.

If I leave it up to her, I sincerely doubt it.

He grimaced at the thought, releasing an unhappy sigh.

Looking over at him, Morley chuckled

"Bailey Flynn is a complicated woman," he said as if reading Dalton's mind. "So, if you're looking for easy..."

"I'm not looking for anything," Dalton said defensively. "I was just trying to be friendly."

"Okay, my bad."

Morley lifted his round shoulders in an indifferent shrug.

"I just thought that moronic lovestruck look on your face might mean you were interested."

He turned his eyes back to the road ahead.

"But it's probably best you aren't."

"And why is that?

Feeling suddenly indignant, Dalton glanced at Morley, who showed no emotion as he answered.

"She's out of your league. She's one of the good ones."

Now Dalton was truly offended.

"And what am I? One of the bad ones?"

Morley chuckled again.

"No, you're alright," he conceded. "But you have a way

of getting around. You like variety. And that's not going to work with a woman like Bailey Flynn."

His voice had grown serious.

"Especially after everything she's been through."

Before Dalton could ask what Morley meant, they had arrived at the doctor's office.

Jumping out of the truck, Dalton circled around to help Morley climb down, but the older man waved him away.

"I'll do it myself," he said. "Not everyone needs you to save them, you know."

Dalton sighed and stepped back, allowing Morley to get down on his own. Before the older man could walk past him, he lifted a hand and put it on Dalton's arm.

"Thanks," he said. "I know I can be a pain in the ass."

He didn't give Dalton a chance to reply as he began walking in an unsteady gait toward the entrance.

"Wait up," Dalton called. "That offer I made to Bailey...to help find the man who killed Emma Walsh. I was serious about that. And you could help, too."

"Oh no," Morley said. "My days of searching for killers are over. How do you think I lost my leg?"

A pained look crossed his face and then was gone.

"From now on, I'll stick to looking for people who are missing, not people who are murderers."

* * *

Dalton drove east toward the coast, feeling restless. He'd left Morley in the doctor's waiting room after the older man had insisted he would get an Uber home, and he wasn't quite sure what to do with the rest of his day.

After hearing that Emma Walsh had gone missing the day before, he'd cleared his schedule for the week in anticipation that his search services might be needed.

However, Bailey had arrived to save the day, and the missing woman was already lying in the morgue.

The only thing left to do was to catch her killer.

And I think I know the best place to get started.

Steering the Dodge further north up the coast, he caught sight of the Belle Harbor Lighthouse in the distance and was soon pulling into the Bellamy Beach parking lot.

I guess I'm not the only one who thought coming here was a good place to search for a killer.

The Belle Harbor CSI van was parked at the edge of the lot, along with several news vans, including the white unmarked minivan his sister drove when she was working.

Parking his pickup beside the van, Dalton climbed out and strode onto the sand, where Sabrina appeared to be shooting her own footage for her next special report, using a video camera propped on a tripod.

She ignored him until she'd finished recording, then walked over to where he was standing, her eyes searching his face with a curious frown.

"What brings you out here, big brother?" she asked. "And what's got you looking so down?"

"A woman died out there," Dalton said, not liking the amused gleam he saw in his sister's eyes. "A man is killing women and no one is doing anything about it."

Putting her hands on her hips, Sabrina sighed.

"Don't be so morbid and depressing," she said. "If there's a stalker in town abducting women, it'll be good for business. For both of us."

Dalton stared at her with narrowed eyes.

"Don't joke about this," he said, looking around to see if anyone was listening. "Nothing about this is funny."

He shook his head in disgust. His younger sister seemed to have a one-track mind. All she wanted was to be the next big name in crime reporting and she wasn't about to let anything or anyone get in her way.

"I've been on three different searches for missing women this year where I've found a dead body dumped out like trash," Dalton said. "These women were younger than you, Sabrina. They had their whole lives ahead of them before someone murdered them in cold blood."

Sucking in a lungful of ocean air, he continued.

"It gets to you, after a while, you know? And all these dead bodies are giving my company a bad reputation. Bringing in West Investigations is like putting a curse on the person who's missing."

Sabrina waved away his concern.

"People don't call in a private investigator unless they've tried everything else. If the police can't find them, it means they don't want to be found or that they're a victim of foul play. Either way, it's not your fault."

Dalton knew that in her own practical way, Sabrina was trying to make him feel better. But her analysis of the situation only made him feel more depressed.

Leaving her to finish up her special report, Dalton walked further along the shore, deciding to head north up the coast toward the lighthouse and see what he might find.

If the Stalker had attacked Emma on the beach after she'd parked in the lot, he might have chased her into the sand dunes where her body had been found.

Would the Stalker then risk going back toward the lot where someone might see him? No, most likely he would head out in the opposite direction.

Avoiding the yellow crime scene tape that fluttered in the breeze, Dalton walked past the first few dunes, then made his way up toward the row of luxury houses along the shore, keeping his eyes on the sandy ground as he went.

He hadn't expected to really find anything, so when he saw the corner of the black leather wallet sticking out of the sand, he assumed it was trash someone had left behind.

As he got closer, he saw that the wallet looked fairly new and that it appeared to be full of cash and credit cards.

"Hey, what are you doing there?"

A man's voice called out and Dalton spun around to see Jimmy Fraser striding toward him.

"I was just looking around and I saw *that*."

His eyes moved back to the wallet at his feet.

"Not sure if it could have anything to do with the scene here," he said lightly. "Although, I guess the killer could have dropped it while he was running away."

The words were meant to be a joke but Fraser didn't crack a smile as he stared down at the wallet.

"Why were you looking over here?"

The detective raised both eyebrows.

"Well, it's kind of obvious," Dalton said. "If the Stalker followed Emma onto the beach from the parking lot, he probably would have run off in the other direction."

Fraser continued to study him with suspicion.

"Has someone retained your services regarding this case?" he asked. "Are you investigating Emma Walsh's murder? Because, if you think you can interfere-"

"I don't think finding three homicide victims can be called interference," Dalton said, his temper starting to rise. "Especially when the police sat on their hands and did nothing for those poor families."

He matched the detective's stony glare with his own.

"So, you coincidentally found three dead bodies on your own, and then stumbled across a wallet associated with a fourth victim?" Fraser said. "How do you think that looks?"

"It looks as if I'm doing the job you and the other local cops couldn't," he said, indignant at the accusation. "The families of three young women asked me to help. I did what I could but it wasn't enough."

Suddenly his anger melted away.

"Those parents had to *bury* their daughters."

His shoulders sagged as he pictured Tori Cabot's parents, weeping over their daughter's grave.

"So, my question to you, Detective Fraser, is what are *you* going to do about it? How are you going to stop this man from killing again?"

CHAPTER TEN

Jimmy Fraser watched Dalton West storm off down the beach, wondering if the man's show of concern was genuine. He wasn't an expert at detecting liars, but Fraser thought the P.I. had sounded sincere. Of course, the man had been involved in the discovery of three different women, so there was no question he would have to be considered a person of interest until proven otherwise.

Jogging back toward the parking lot, Fraser waved down Madeline Mercer, the CSI team leader for the BHPD.

"I've found a wallet that could be linked to the scene," he said. "We need to bag it. But first, let's look inside."

Madeline's sleek dark bob fluttered in the wind as she snapped on a second pair of gloves and pulled an evidence collection bag from her pocket.

She took out a small camera and snapped several photos of the wallet as it had been found, then bent over and used a single gloved finger to flip open the flap.

The plastic window inside the cover held a Georgia driver's license in the name of Sean Ellerman, a fifty-year-old resident of Atlanta

Madeline snapped several more photos, then slid the

wallet into the paper bag and sealed it.

"I'll take this to the lab and get the wallet and its contents tested for prints and trace evidence," she said.

"And I'll look up Mr. Sean Ellerman as soon as I get back to the office," Fraser said, checking his watch. "In fact, I'm heading back there now. Zach Walsh is scheduled to come in for an interview at noon."

Hurrying back to the station, Fraser found that Zach had not yet arrived. Sitting down at his computer, the detective ran the ID from the wallet through the system.

His eyes widened as he saw the results on his screen.

Sean Ellerman had filed a report Friday night claiming that someone had stolen his wallet on the boardwalk.

Fraser was on the phone to Madeline within minutes.

"You know that wallet we found? Someone stole it off the boardwalk Friday night," he said. "That's the night Emma Walsh was killed. We've got to test it for prints right away."

He sucked in an excited breath of air.

"Whoever stole the wallet could be a witness," he said. "Or better yet, the pickpocket could be a suspect."

"Okay, I'll get on it right away," Madeline assured him. "Oh, and I meant to tell you we found a second phone in Emma's pocket when we were going through her clothes."

Fraser felt his pulse quicken.

"A second phone?"

"Yeah," Madeline said. "Looks like a burner phone. I sent it over to the digital forensic examiner. I'll let you know when we hear back."

As he ended the call, his phone buzzed in his hand.

It was Linette.

"Hey there, beautiful," he said, wondering what he'd forgotten this time. "How's your day going?"

"It'll be going just fine if you tell me you'll be home on time to take Tiana to ballet while I pick Sasha up from school," she said. "You do remember your daughter has a rehearsal this afternoon, don't you? The play's on Friday."

Automatically checking his watch, he tried to calculate how much time he had left.

"Of course, I'll be there," Fraser assured his wife with more confidence than he felt. "Now, I have to go."

He exhaled loudly as he ended the call.

Both Sasha and Tiana were in school now with full schedules of extracurricular activities. With both him and Linette working, it was a challenge every day to juggle all the drop-offs, pick-ups, and playdates.

But as much as it stressed him out, he wanted to be involved. His daughters were growing up fast, and he didn't want them growing up without him.

Being a good father and a good cop wasn't easy, but he was doing his best. He would just have to think and act more efficiently. Especially now that his partner was gone.

Emma's not just gone. She's been murdered. And if I'm going to find the bastard who killed her, I'm going to need help.

He tucked the thought away as a knock sounded at the door and Officer Rourke stuck his head in.

"Zach Walsh and his lawyer are here," he said. "They're waiting for you in Interview Room A."

Fraser stood and followed Rourke out the door,

wondering if the uniformed officer was about to get his wish.

He's wanted that promotion to detective for years and now Emma's no longer here to stand in his way.

Brushing past the uniformed officer into the interview room, he saw Zach Walsh slumped at the wooden table, looking tired and deflated, wearing a rumpled sweater.

His law partner on the other hand appeared to be alert and freshly shaven, wearing an expensive-looking suit and tie, his dark, curly hair slicked back from his craggy brow.

"Detective Fraser, good to see you," Anthony Brunner said. "I'll be representing Zach in this matter."

The criminal defensive attorney rose and held a well-manicured hand out to Fraser, but the detective ignored it.

Instead, he turned back to Rourke who stood at the door.

"Coffee would be good if you don't mind."

He saw a flash of resentment cross the officer's freckled face, then Rourke nodded curtly and was gone.

Closing the door, Fraser turned back to the table.

"Thanks for coming in, Mr. Walsh," he said. "I know this is a difficult time for you and your family, and I'll try to make this as brief as I can."

Zach nodded numbly.

"I've reviewed your initial statement and just wanted to clarify a few things," he said as he sank into the chair across from the two men and opened a folder in front of him. "I understand you were out of town camping over the weekend with your college friends."

He frowned.

"When did you decide to go on this trip?" he asked.

Shrugging his shoulders, Zach looked over at Brunner.

"I don't really remember..."

"I'm sure you can appreciate that my client is grieving," Brunner cut in. "He's in a state of shock. And I'm not sure what his travel plans have to do with anything."

Fraser sat back in his chair. When he spoke, he addressed his words to Zach, ignoring Brunner altogether.

"It's just that we've spoken to the men you were with in Ocala," he said. "And while they all corroborate your alibi, they also say the trip was planned at the last minute, and that you arrived late on Friday, after everyone else."

"That's right," Zach said, nodding slowly. "Emma said she was going to have to work most of the weekend. There was a new development in the homicide she was working. So, I asked the guys if they wanted to go camping."

He dropped his head into his hands.

"Things had been stressful at home and I just...wanted some time away," he said, his words muffled.

Studying Zach's bent head, Fraser wondered what development Emma could have been talking about.

The only homicide they'd been working on was the Tori Cabot case. The girl who'd gone missing, and whose body was eventually found behind the Summerset Mall.

As far as Fraser knew, there had been no new leads.

"Based on the timeline we've calculated, I'd say it's possible you would have had time to follow Emma to Bellamy Beach, confront her, and still have time to get to Ocala in time to solidify your camping alibi."

Brunner's fist struck the table at Fraser's words.

"That's ludicrous. My client is here voluntarily and is cooperating fully. He has answered your questions, and-"

Ignoring the lawyer, Fraser stared straight at Zach.

"You're a lawyer, right?" he prodded. "So, you know all about establishing an alibi, don't you? What do you think? You think your alibi will hold up in court?"

Zach lifted red-rimmed eyes to Fraser.

"I specialize in family law," he said dully. "Not alibis. That's why I brought Tony. He's the criminal attorney."

"Okay, so can Brunner tell me why you didn't report your wife's disappearance until yesterday morning?"

He leaned forward and spoke softly.

"Were you hoping her body would never be found?"

"No!" Zach protested.

"Then why?" Fraser demanded. "Why not report her missing as soon as you got back Sunday night?"

Dropping his head in his hands, Zach shuddered.

Fraser opened his mouth to press his point, then closed it again when he realized the man was crying.

Finally, Zach looked up, his eyes wet and swollen.

He sucked in a deep breath and swallowed hard.

"I thought maybe...maybe she was with someone else."

"That's enough, Zack," Brunner said sharply.

He grabbed his partner's arm.

"You don't have to say anything else. Not until we talk."

"That's right, Zach," Fraser said. "You don't have to say anything. Because if your wife was sleeping with someone else, it'd give you a hell of a motive for killing her."

CHAPTER ELEVEN

Bailey stood behind the one-way glass, listening to Zach Walsh's sobs, and watching his broad shoulders shake as Fraser sat across from him. The detective surreptitiously checked the clock on the wall and then tried again to get the grieving man's attention.

"Listen, Zach," Fraser said quietly. "Just tell me what really happened and we'll figure out what to do together."

"Oh, please," Brunner snapped. "Don't think I'm going to let you manipulate some sort of half-assed confession out of my client. He's obviously in shock and grieving."

Turning her eyes to the lawyer, Bailey assessed Tony Brunner with distaste. She had to admit she'd never liked Zach's law partner.

The darkly good-looking man was arrogant and condescending, and his smarmy, smooth-talking attitude had always given her the creeps.

"Let's go, Zach," Brunner said. "You need some rest."

The lawyer rose and helped his sniffling client to his feet.

"If you have any other questions for Mr. Walsh, you can work through me," Brunner said. "And if you're thinking of stopping by his house, make sure you bring a warrant."

Waiting until Brunner had slammed out of the interview room, dragging a stumbling Zach behind him, Bailey stepped into the hall, leading Ludwig behind her.

Fraser turned in surprise.

"I didn't know you were watching," he said. "I would have put on a better show."

He offered a weak smile and rubbed at his eyes.

"Let's go down to my office," he said. "I need coffee."

"You really think Zach did it?" she asked as she and Ludwig followed him down the hall and into a small room with two metal desks and a dented filing cabinet.

A well-used coffee pot sat on a table under the window.

Closing the door behind him, Fraser poured steaming coffee into two mugs as Ludwig curled up in the corner.

"Zach's got an alibi for Friday," Fraser said after taking a long sip. "Although, it's hardly airtight. And if Emma's murder is connected to Tori Cabot and the other women, as the M.E. is suggesting, what would Zach's motive be?"

When Bailey didn't answer right away, he narrowed his eyes and studied her as if he were trying to read her mind.

"You know him a whole lot better than I do," he said as he sank into his chair. "What do you think? Is Zach Walsh capable of murder?"

"I don't know that I've got the best track record when it comes to analyzing Zach," Bailey admitted, sitting down across from him. "I didn't think he was capable of cheating on me with my best friend and dumping me two weeks before our wedding. You can see where that got us."

Fraser sighed and sipped at his mug.

"I guess Zach would be the easy answer, wouldn't he?" he murmured. "Our suspect list is depressingly short."

"And you have no other leads?" Bailey asked.

She tried not to show her surprise.

"Well, we did find a wallet," Fraser said. "Actually, Dalton West found it on Bellamy Beach not far from where Emma was attacked. The wallet had been reported stolen from the boardwalk on Friday."

Upon hearing Dalton West's name, Bailey leaned forward with interest.

"I gave the wallet to Madeline Mercer to check for prints," he said. "So, maybe that'll lead us to a witness or even another suspect."

"Dalton West sure gets around, doesn't he?" she said, thinking of the man she'd met that morning at Morley's house. "Didn't he find the three other women who are thought to be victims of the Stalker?"

Fraser nodded.

"Yes, I had a chat with Mr. West," he said. "Seems a little odd that he has discovered the body of each victim, other than Emma Walsh. And we aren't sure yet that her homicide is related to the others."

His words prompted a sudden thought.

"What is it?" Fraser asked, seeing Bailey's frown.

"What if the three women Dalton West found weren't the only other victims? What if there are more out there?" she asked. "The families of these three women hired Dalton, and he used Amadeus, a very talented search and rescue dog to find them, along with the help of a retired FBI agent."

"What if there are other victims out there? Women who didn't have families desperate to find them, or private investigators and search and rescue dogs looking for them? What if we don't find them in time either?"

An image of a pink tennis shoe flashed into her mind before she could push it away. The shoe that Dolores Santos had been wearing the day Ronin Godfrey had kidnapped her.

The shoe that-

"Bailey? You okay?"

She blinked at him, then nodded numbly.

"Yes, sorry," she said. "I guess I was just...thinking of something else."

Fraser lifted his hands.

"Let's not get tangled up in all those *what-ifs*," he said, sounding frustrated. "We have enough confirmed homicides right now to keep us busy for a long while."

He pointed to some files on his desk.

"I only have details on the Tori Cabot case," he said, opening a folder. "Emma and I investigated her death, but I'd never heard of Wren Dempsey or Hallie Kwan before Mason Knox mentioned them at the scene yesterday."

Flipping through the contents of the folder, Fraser shook his head and sighed.

"It's a sad story," he said. "Tori grew up in Belle Harbor with a good family. A solid home. But she got caught up in drugs as a teen. Ended up spending a few months in the Summerset County Women's Detention Center."

He tapped on a report in the file.

"She got out and went to rehab. Her parents were happy.

They thought her life was back on track."

His voice was grim.

"But less than a year later her body was found behind the Summerset Mall, and she had drugs in her system," he said. "Her parents suspected her old dealer might be responsible. A man they knew only as Lando, but Tori had always refused to talk about that part of her life, and we had no evidence and no witnesses."

He took another long drink from his mug.

"Emma entered the details into CODIS, but there was no hit. No link to other cases," he said. "But she wouldn't give up. She was determined to find the man who killed Tori."

"Now that you know there *are* other cases, do you think it's time to ask the FBI to join in the investigation?" Bailey asked hesitantly, not sure how Fraser would react. "That would allow you to get information on the crimes that had occurred outside your jurisdiction."

She was relieved when he slowly nodded his head.

"I've been thinking the same thing," he said. "But I'd want you working the case with me, not some stranger. Do think that's possible? Would your SAC allow it?"

Bailey felt a flush warm her cheeks, thinking of the message she'd sent her special agent in charge earlier.

"We'll know soon enough. I've already sent Calloway a message asking for permission to stay and investigate Emma's death, and that of the other women," she admitted. "I told him if he doesn't approve, I'll need to take time off to handle the matter on my own."

She checked her phone. Still no response from Calloway.

Sucking in a calming breath, she impulsively tapped on Calloway's number.

The phone rang four times, and Bailey was already mentally preparing the voicemail she would leave when her boss answered the call.

"I'm in a meeting with Argus Murphy," Calloway said, skipping the usual greeting. "We're going over the results of one of his damn algorithms. It's giving me a headache."

Bailey smiled despite her nerves.

She had first met Special Agent Argus Murphy, an analyst and profiler with the Behavioral Analysis Unit in Quantico, six months earlier while working on a serial case in Tempest Grove, West Virginia.

Since then, he'd helped Calloway's new task force compile lists of possible suspects in several other high-profile cases.

She wasn't sure how he did it. All she knew was he collected as much data as possible on victims and crime scenes and built complex algorithms to analyze the data to identify patterns and connections and create a profile.

The agents working the case could then use the results to identify possible suspects who fit the profile, saving lots of time and investigative effort.

"I read your message," Calloway said. "You really think you could have a serial killer on your hands down there?"

"I'm almost sure of it," Bailey said. "And the last victim was a police detective. My old partner."

Calloway cleared his throat, quickening Bailey's pulse.

Would she really have the nerve to defy him if he denied

her request? Was she willing to give up everything she'd worked so hard to achieve?

"I've already sent a message to Ford Ramsey at the Miami field office telling him to expect you," he said. "If he approves you working the case out of his office, I'll approve it on my end."

Bailey met Fraser's eyes and gave him a thumbs up.

"And tread lightly, Agent Flynn," Calloway warned. "I don't want you stepping on any toes down there."

Someone spoke up in the background before Calloway could end the call. Bailey recognized Argus Murphy's voice.

"Let me know if you need any help while you're down there," the analyst called out. "In fact, if you send me the data you have, I can start working on an algorithm for you."

At that, Calloway ended the connection.

* * *

Bailey led Fraser into the ultra-modern, eight-story building that houses the FBI's Miami field office, feeling as if she'd been away for six years instead of six months.

She'd made it off the elevator and halfway down the hall to SAC Ramsey's office when someone called her name.

"Bailey?"

She turned to see Aisha Sharma walking toward her.

The special agent offered a wide smile that lit up her eyes, which were the color of warm honey.

Her dark silky hair was cut into a stylish, chin-length bob, and the slim-fitting suit she was wearing fit her lean, athletic body as if it had been custom-tailored.

Feeling a little underdressed in her simple blue pants and sweater, Bailey lifted a hand to self-consciously smooth back her dark blonde hair, which fell onto her shoulders in messy waves.

"SAC Ramsey asked me to be on the lookout for you," Sharma said, her eyes flicking to Fraser.

"Oh, sorry," Bailey said, stepping to the side. "This is Detective Jimmy Fraser with the Belle Harbor PD. He's running the investigation I'm here to discuss."

Fraser exchanged pleasantries with Sharma as she led them into a conference room off the hall.

As soon as she closed the door, she turned to Bailey.

"I should warn you Ramsey wasn't happy to get the message from D.C.," she said. "Resources are tight, and you know he doesn't like to feel pressured into anything."

The agent lowered her voice.

"But he says you've identified a possible serial murder case here in South Florida?"

Bailey nodded.

"I came down here to look for my ex-partner at the Belle Harbor PD," she said. "She'd been missing since Friday, and we found her body over on Bellamy Beach yesterday."

Shock and sympathy played over Sharma's face as she reached out and squeezed Bailey's hand.

"The responding M.E. recognized the stab wounds on Emma's back as similar to three other homicides he'd responded to in Summerset County over the last year," she continued. "But the connection was never made until now."

"I'm so sorry," Sharma said. "You must be devastated."

Bailey shook her head, wanting to clarify the situation.

"I hadn't been close to Emma in a long time," she admitted. "We'd had a falling out and hadn't spoken in years. But she was a good cop, and she was trying to do her job. She deserves justice. As do the others."

A knock sounded on the door, making both women jump.

Turning around, Bailey saw Ford Ramsey enter the room.

The special agent-in-charge was leanly muscled and fit for a man of fifty. Below his pale, thinning hair, the tanned skin of his forehead was perpetually creased.

His narrow eyes were impassive as they fixed on Bailey, as was his voice when he addressed her.

"Back so soon, Agent Flynn?" he said. "What happened? Calloway seems to be in quite a hurry to get rid of you."

"Maybe so," Bailey said, not allowing the SAC's usual sarcasm to bother her. "But I believe a serial killer has been active in Summerset County over the last year."

"Detective Fraser at the BHPD has asked me and the Bureau to join the investigation as multiple jurisdictions are involved, and one victim was a detective in Belle Harbor."

Ramsey continued to stare at her as if waiting for more.

"We'll need to start looking for a connection between the crimes and the victims, as well as for possible other victims outside Summerset County," she added. "There could be others in Miami-Dade or Palm Beach..."

Her voice trailed off as Ramsey crossed his arms over his chest and cocked his head.

"But there's been nothing flagged in CODIS?"

The question caught her off guard.

She couldn't confirm why the FBI's Combined DNA Index System hadn't alerted any of the local departments to a possible connection between the homicides.

"I don't think the Bonneville PD or the Sun Creek PD entered the homicides into CODIS," Fraser said.

As Ramsey's eyes turned to him, he cleared his throat.

"They determined the deaths were drug-related, despite the Summerset County M.E.'s report alerting them to similarities with other suspicious deaths in the county."

"Once we enter all the data into CODIS, we'll likely get an alert right away," Sharma said. "And I have the bandwidth to help Agent Flynn if needed."

Throwing a grateful look at the agent, Bailey wondered what else she could say to sway Ramsey's decision.

"Calloway's arranged for one of the BAU analysts in Quantico to assist as well," she said. "If needed, that is."

"Which analyst?" Ramsey asked.

"Argus Murphy."

The SAC looked impressed, as did Sharma, who seemed unflustered by Ramsey's perpetual frown.

"The local police consider the deaths to be drug-related," she said. "Which may mean the unsub is active in one of the trafficking gangs working that area. We could look into it."

The possibility seemed to rouse Ramsey's interest. The bored look in his eye turned into a gleam.

"Okay, fine," he said with a curt nod. "Agent Flynn can work out of the office on this one. I'll let Calloway know."

He moved toward the door.

"Agent Sharma, you can help as needed as long as you keep up with your other investigations."

Pinning Bailey with a final glare, he opened the door.

"I want an update on my desk by the end of the week."

Once the door had closed behind him, Sharma flashed Bailey a smile.

"Well, you got what you came for," she said. "Now it's time to get to work. I want to make sure all the victims are entered into CODIS. You mentioned that the Summerset County M.E. has the data?"

Bailey nodded, thinking of Mason Knox.

The medical examiner had been the one to catch the connection first, and at this point, he potentially knew more about the murders than anyone else.

"Fraser and I will call the M.E. and see if we can stop by his office on the way back to Belle Harbor," she said. "Hopefully, you'll have what you need later this afternoon."

CHAPTER TWELVE

Mason Knox ended the call and dropped the receiver back onto its cradle. Turning on his heel, he walked down the hall, looking for Finola Lawson. He found the assistant medical examiner in the break room eating a banana and a pot of strawberry yogurt, her long, coppery hair pulled back into a neat bun.

"Sorry to ruin your lunch, but we've got guests on the way," he called out as he crossed the room to pour himself a cup of coffee. "I just invited Special Agent Bailey Flynn with the FBI and Detective Jimmy Fraser with the Belle Harbor PD to observe the Emma Walsh autopsy."

Finola kept her eyes on the television in the corner as she took another bite of yogurt. It was tuned to Channel 3 News.

"I'll prep the body in a minute," she said, pointing to the screen. "Did you know there's a serial killer in Summerset County? They're calling him the Summerset Stalker."

"Actually, I did."

Mason took another drink of the weak coffee, before setting the half-full mug in the sink.

He considered telling his assistant that the woman they were about to dissect was likely a Stalker victim, then decided against it. Best not to get ahead of himself.

Ten minutes later, when he stopped outside the cooler room, he saw Finola dressed in protective gear, positioning a gurney in front of a stainless-steel drawer.

As she opened the drawer to reveal a sheet-covered body on a stainless-steel tray, he hurried in and helped her slide the tray onto the gurney, then watched as she pushed the gurney into the autopsy suite.

Checking his watch, he went out to the reception area and found Bailey Flynn and Jimmy Fraser already waiting.

"Come on back," he called. "We're about to get started."

Leading them down the hall, he waved them into a small prep room next to the autopsy suite.

"There are protective coveralls and masks on the shelves," he said, noticing the pale pallor of Bailey's skin. "And shoe covers over by the door."

As he pulled on his own protective gear, layering on two sets of gloves, and positioning his face shield, he attempted to make small talk, but both of his guests seemed nervous and remained silent as he led them into the autopsy suite where Emma Walsh was already waiting, covered with a stiff white sheet.

Catching the bright, panicked shine in Fraser's eyes as they gathered around the dissecting table, Mason hesitated.

"Are you going to be okay with this?" he asked. "It's just that you both look a little nauseous."

"I'm good," Fraser said, nodding stiffly.

"Yeah, me too," Bailey added, although Mason could see a drop of sweat starting to slide down her forehead.

Still not convinced his guests were ready, he pointed to an industrial sink mounted on the wall.

"If you feel sick, use the sink. Not the floor."

Moving to the head of the metal table, Mason motioned for Finola to pull down the sheet.

Bailey gasped at the sight of Emma Walsh, her wide blue eyes glued to the stiff, discolored face, her hand rising to block the sickly-sweet smell of decay that wafted up.

Mason understood her reaction. He always felt an initial jolt of surprise whenever he looked at death and witnessed its power to destroy what had once been alive and beautiful.

As he studied the dead woman, he couldn't recognize the persistent police detective he'd consulted with only weeks before. All the passion, energy, and life force inside Emma Walsh was gone, leaving behind only the sad, decomposing figure on the table.

Clearing his throat, he nodded to Finola, who clicked on a small recorder as he began to speak.

"The body before me is that of a white female measuring sixty-eight inches and weighing one hundred thirty-six pounds. Her appearance is consistent with her recorded age of thirty years. Her eyes are closed."

Mason continued speaking in a modulated tone as he worked his way down the front of Emma's body, conducting a quick external examination, noting any abrasions or contusions on the front of her body.

He and Finola then turned her over, exposing discolored skin and an ugly red wound in her back.

As Mason described the sharp force injury to the back,

Finola took a series of photos and measurements and collected a specimen of the blowfly larva that had infested the open wound for testing.

Mason expected that tests on the larva would confirm a time of death that corroborated his own estimate that Emma had been dead at least forty-eight hours by the time her body had been discovered.

As he studied the ugly red wound, he grew more convinced that the knife used to kill Emma matched the knife used to kill the other three women he'd dissected.

The depth of the cut, the size, and shape of the wound. It seemed to all match up to one weapon, and one killer.

But they couldn't know for sure until they opened her up.

"We need to examine the internal organs now," Mason said. "That's where we'll see the true damage done."

Both Bailey and Fraser nodded stoically as Finola and Mason turned Emma over again.

With practiced ease, Mason sliced a y-shaped incision into Emma's chest before lifting the skin to reveal the ribs.

Using a small electric saw, he cut away the cartilage holding the ribs in place before getting Finola's help in lifting out the rib cage.

As she took photos, Mason removed and weighed each internal organ, until all that was left was the heart.

"The decedent suffered a penetrating heart injury that caused a massive, fatal hemorrhage."

He swallowed hard as he surveyed the damage.

"The blade appears to have entered the right ventricular cavity, penetrating the ventricular septum and the aortic tissue below the right cusp of the aortic valve."

Looking up, he saw Bailey staring at the damaged heart in his hands, her eyes wide with shock and pain.

Mason stepped back and pushed up his plastic face shield, before removing his bloody, outer layer of gloves.

"That's pretty much it," he said. "Finola will collect samples for a complete toxicology screening. I'll request a full blood panel, but I don't imagine we'll find anything to impact our findings."

His words prompted Bailey to look away from the body.

"What's the official cause and manner of death?"

"It's a homicide by knife wound to the back, resulting in a fatal hemorrhage," he said. "Just like the others."

* * *

Leaving Finola to collect the blood and tissue samples needed for testing, Mason led his guests down the hall.

Both Bailey and Fraser were pale and dazed.

"I've seen my fair share of dead bodies," Bailey said, shaking her head. "But I'd never observed an autopsy."

"Me either," Fraser admitted. "And now death seems much more *real*. Like *too* real."

Mason waved them into his office with a sympathetic smile, surprised that they'd both made it through the autopsy without running to the sink.

"Well, for first-time observers, I'd say you both did very well. It's never easy to watch the autopsy of a friend, no matter how seasoned and jaded you might be."

"Before we leave, I actually have a favor to ask," Bailey said. "It's about the three homicides you mentioned last night. The ones you said are linked to Emma's."

"I called my boss at the FBI and told him what you said, and he's agreed to open an official investigation. He also said I can stick around Summerset County and work the case with Detective Fraser."

Mason stared at her in surprise.

"You work fast," he said. "I've been trying to get someone to take me seriously for months and it's only taken you a few hours."

He exhaled with relief.

"So, you're going to treat the cases as connected, right? It'll be a serial murder investigation?"

"Yes, based on your information about the knife and the mutilation of the skin, we plan to treat the murders of Wren Dempsey, Tori Cabot, and Hallie Kwan as serial killings," Bailey said. "I'm not sure about Emma."

A frown creased her forehead.

"I know you said the same type of knife was used with Emma and the others, but she wasn't mutilated," Bailey said. "Not like the others were. You said they all had skin carved from their backs. What do you think it means?"

"I thought maybe the killer was trying to cut off an identifying mark," Mason said. "Like a birthmark or a tattoo, to hide the victim's identity. And I've had some people ask me about removing and preserving tattoos from their dead relatives. So, I thought maybe the killer could be collecting trophies."

A shiver ran down his back at the thought.

"But I asked the families and none had heard that the women had tattoos, although they couldn't guarantee it," he said. "Tori's mother told me she hadn't seen her daughter's bare shoulder since she'd gotten home from rehab. She claimed Tori had been traumatized from her experience and didn't like to be touched."

"It's definitely unusual," Bailey said. "Which is why we want to enter all the details of each homicide into CODIS. That way we might find other victims, scenes, or even suspects that are connected to these murders."

She took out her phone and began to tap on the screen.

"I'm sending you the contact information for Special Agent Aisha Sharma at the Miami field office. If you send her all the data you have on these women, she can get it entered into CODIS and we can identify any matches."

"I'll send everything I have as soon as possible," he agreed. "I've taken DNA samples and fingerprints of each victim I autopsied. So far, we haven't managed to find any DNA or prints at the scenes that didn't match the victim."

The mention of prints brought back another memory.

"You know, I did think it was kind of strange, though. When we submitted the fingerprints for each victim, we got back results saying they each already had a record in the database," Mason said.

"The database?" Fraser asked. "You mean AFIS?"

"Yes, whenever we autopsy a homicide victim we submit their prints to the Automated Fingerprint Identification System," Mason confirmed. "That lets the investigators compare their prints to prints collected at the crime scene."

"In this case, we were told the victims already had records in AFIS. I tried to find out why and was told all three of the victims had prior arrest records."

The information didn't seem to surprise Fraser.

"I knew Tori Cabot spent time at the Summerset Women's Detention Center," he said. "Emma told me Tori had been convicted on drug charges."

Mason nodded. He had discovered the same.

"Tori's parents told us everything they knew," Fraser continued "But she had refused to talk to them about the circumstance leading up to her arrest. The only thing they remembered was her mentioning a man named Lando. She'd told a friend she was scared of what he might do."

The name sounded familiar to Mason, but he couldn't be sure where he'd heard it.

"I figured Tori might have been talking about Lando Gutierrez," Fraser said. "He's a local dealer. Real bad news."

"Did you talk to Lando?" Bailey asked.

Fraser shook his head.

"We couldn't find anything to connect him to the scene and he lawyered up. He refused to talk to us."

A gleam entered his eye at the memory.

"Emma was so mad. She couldn't believe that her husband's partner had taken on the case."

"Tony Brunner was this dealer's lawyer?" Bailey asked.

Producing an angry smile, Fraser nodded.

"Still is as far as I know," he said. "I overheard Emma

arguing with someone on the phone about it just last week. I assumed it was Zach. She sounded really mad."

'What about Wren Dempsey and Hallie Kwan?" Bailey asked. "Were their records drug-related as well?"

Mason shrugged.

"I tried to find out...I even requested their arrest records, but I was told the records had been sealed by the judge."

Fraser and Bailey turned to stare at each other with the same look of surprise, before turning back to Mason.

"That's really strange," Bailey said. "I'll look into it."

She looked at her watch.

"In fact, I may even be able to get my sister to help with this one," she said. "Cate's a prosecutor for Summerset County. If she can't get a copy of their records, no one can."

CHAPTER THIRTEEN

Cate stared down at her computer and yawned, barely able to keep her eyes open after the late night out at Bellamy Beach. She'd had a meeting scheduled at the Summerset County Courthouse first thing that morning and had gotten less than six hours of sleep.

Looking forward to going home and curling up in bed with a good book, she had just glanced up at the clock, wondering if she could find an excuse to head out early when she heard a soft knock on her office door.

Bailey stood in the open doorway, dark circles under her blue eyes and her blonde hair mussed and spilling over the shoulder of her white sweater.

"Looks like you had quite a day," Cate said as her sister crossed the room and sank into a chair.

"I need a favor," Bailey said.

Propping her elbows on the desk, she produced the same pleading smile she'd always used to get her way when they were little girls wanting to play with the same toys.

"Of course you do," Cate replied dryly. "Why else would you be here? You certainly wouldn't just stop by to see your big sister now, would you?"

"I need you to look up some records for me," Bailey said, ignoring the sarcastic comment as she reached into her bag and pulled out a slip of paper. "We think these three young women were victims of the same man who killed Emma."

She slipped the paper to Cate.

"But we can't seem to access their records to find out the circumstances around their arrests," she said. "I thought you might be able to help."

Cate reached out and picked up the paper, reading the three names with interest. If there really was a serial killer stalking Summerset County, she may be called upon to prosecute the case if it ever came to trial.

Prosecuting a serial killer and getting a conviction would be the pinnacle of her career.

Of course, she couldn't let Bailey know she was interested in helping her catch the Summerset Stalker.

Oh no, that wouldn't do at all.

Best to let her little sister think she was doing her a favor out of the goodness of her heart.

"I guess I can look this up," she said as she looked at the paper and typed the name *Wren Dempsey* on her keyboard. "Although, the clerk of the court could have just as easily..."

The words died away as she saw the red *Records Sealed* alert pop up on her screen.

She cleared the screen and typed in the next name.

Again, the bright red alert appeared across her screen.

"Is something wrong?" Bailey asked, her blue eyes wide and innocent as she stared at her sister.

Fingers moving quickly, she typed in the last name.

"You knew those records were sealed," she said, staring at her screen in disgust. "Why didn't you just say so?"

Bailey shrugged.

"I thought maybe you had special access," she admitted. "I guess your access is just normal, like everyone else."

Exhaling loudly, she sat back in the chair.

"So, what do we do now? How do we get the records?"

"We'll need a judge to issue a court order to unseal the records," Cate said. "It's the only way."

The idea didn't seem to bother Bailey.

"Okay, so get the judge to issue a court order," she said.

"It's not that simple. At least, not in this instance."

She bit her lip, trying to think.

"What do you mean?" Bailey asked.

"I mean, is that in most cases I would submit a request to the clerk of the court, who would most likely pass it on to Judge Walsh. That's one of the things about living in a small city. Everyone is somehow connected to everyone else."

Bailey blinked.

She'd almost forgotten that Zach's father was one of the few judges in the county, having worked first as a prosecutor and then as a defense attorney for decades before being elected to the bench.

"You don't need to mention a connection to Emma's death, do you?" she asked. "I mean, three deaths of young women in the same county with similar wounds should be sufficient to get a look at the sealed records."

Cate wasn't so sure.

"I can give it a try," she agreed, having a feeling she

Melinda Woodhall

would regret it. "But it's too late to submit the request now. I'll take care of it first thing in the morning.

* * *

The next morning Cate made sure to arrive at the courthouse early, parking the white Lexus in her reserved space in the courthouse parking garage on Central Avenue, and hurrying inside.

Seeing that her law clerk hadn't arrived yet, she typed up the request to unseal the records herself and printed out two copies. One for the judge and one for her records.

As she walked the request over to Judge Walsh's office, she saw that his clerk was just arriving.

Inez Flores offered her a concerned smile.

"You aren't on the judge's schedule today, are you?" she said. "He's been trying to clear his calendar as much as possible to take bereavement leave. You know about his daughter-in-law, don't you?"

"Yes, I had heard," Cate said.

She held out the request with the same pleading smile Bailey had used on her the day before.

"But I have an urgent request. It's related to a homicide case and really can't wait."

Looking down at the document, Inez sighed.

"Judge Walsh has a meeting first thing," she said. "But I'll make sure he gets this as soon as he gets out."

"Thank you, Inez, you're the best," Cate said as she spun around and bumped straight into Nigella Ashworth.

The long-serving Summerset County commissioner shot her a dirty look as she pushed past her into the judge's chamber.

"Still thinks she owns the place I see," Cate said in a low voice to Inez, who flashed a conspiratorial smile.

"Well, she owns almost everything else in town, and she is getting on in years, so maybe she's a little confused," the clerk shot back with a wink.

An hour later Inez called.

"Judge Walsh reviewed your request," she said. "He doesn't seem very happy about it. He wants to see you in his chambers right away."

* * *

When Cate stepped into the judge's office, she was relieved to see that Nigella Ashworth was gone.

"He'll see you know," Inez said. "You can go in."

Pushing through the door to the judge's chambers, Cate saw Gavin Walsh sitting behind his desk, staring down at the same request she was holding in her hand.

"How is Zach doing?" she asked as she crossed the room.

The judge shook his head sadly.

"He's still in shock. And he can't even make funeral arrangements until the medical examiner releases the body, so he's in limbo for now. It's torture for us all."

He cleared his throat and looked down at her request.

"But that's not why you're here, is it?"

He tapped a long finger on the printout.

"Your request is highly unusual," he said. "Asking to unseal three different records?"

Cate cleared her throat, preparing to explain, but he held up a weary hand to stop her.

"I'm well aware of the circumstances of the cases that were sealed," he explained. "Although I wasn't aware that any of these young women had gotten into further trouble. What have they done to warrant your personal attention?"

Cate raised an eyebrow.

"They haven't done anything," she said dryly. "Other than getting themselves killed."

The judge just stared at her with his mouth open and eyebrows raised as if waiting for a punchline that would never come.

"The three women in question are all deceased," she continued bluntly. "They were all found over the last year, victims of homicide."

"That's...impossible," he protested. "I would have heard about that. It would have been in the news if nothing else, and I-"

His protest faded away as he met her hard gaze.

"The news is breaking now," she said. "Channel 3 News is already airing reports that there's a serial killer in Summerset County. If the identities of the victims aren't in the news yet, they soon will be."

She held up her hand before he could reply.

"And I agree with you. We all should have heard about these three young women being stabbed to death," she added in an icy tone, allowing her anger to surface. "But three different police departments were involved. And the Belle Harbor PD was the only department to enter the information into CODIS, so an alert was never triggered."

"I guess the police figured that since these women's deaths were thought to be drug-related, they didn't really matter."

Noting the pained grimace that had settled onto the judge's face, Cate resisted the urge to tell him that the connection between the victims might never have surfaced if Emma's body hadn't been found with similar wounds.

It was best not to go there.

If Judge Walsh determined he had a personal connection to the case, he might decide to recuse himself from making a decision on her request.

If that happened, Cate would have to wait for Judge Ingelbert to return from vacation before the petition could be considered since the only two other judges in the county had recently vacated their seats, one by retiring and the other by dying.

Both seats were now awaiting either an appointment from the governor or the next election.

Leaning forward over the desk, Cate cocked her head.

"Can you enlighten me as to why these three records were sealed, Judge Walsh?"

The judge hesitated, then shrugged as if it didn't matter.

"The three young women in question were each picked up on various drug charges," he said. "As you know, for drug offenders in Florida, the Offender Review Commission considers each case prior to release. The Commission investigates the circumstances of the crime and in some cases requires mandatory addiction recovery supervision for the offender in a private rehab program."

"And that's what happened with these cases?"

Judge Walsh nodded.

"The Committee determined rehab was required in all three cases and recommended that the records be sealed."

"But why?"

Judge Walsh shrugged his shoulders.

"The details of each case have been documented in the investigator's report," he said. "But from what I remember, concern for the offenders' safety was a factor."

He looked suddenly nervous.

"I believe there were indications the women had been coerced into committing their offenses. But they refused to lodge a complaint or point the finger at anyone."

Cate could see the judge's mind working.

If he and the State had known these women were at risk, and failed to protect them, there could be repercussions.

Lawsuits and press coverage were real possibilities.

"So, how do I get a copy of the investigator's findings?" Cate asked. "We need to find out everything we can about these women if we hope to find out who killed them."

"I guess you'll have to petition the Commission," he said, shifting impatiently in his chair. "If they approve your petition, I'll be happy to unseal the records. Now, I need to get back to work. I'm hoping to leave early so I can stop by and check on Zach."

He stood, looking relieved to have quickly passed a

potential problem on to someone else.

Cate got to her feet, then hesitated.

"Please pass on my condolences to Zach," she said, feeling awkward. "You can assure him we're all determined to find the person who killed Emma."

"Has there been progress on the case?" he asked, his eyes suddenly alert. "Do they have any suspects?"

"I'm not sure," she admitted. "But I believe a task force has been formed between the local police, the FBI, and the medical examiner's office. I'm sure together they'll be able to find the person responsible."

She opened her mouth to say that Bailey would be helping with the search, then closed it again.

As Emma's husband, Zach was bound to be a suspect.

There was no need to share details with his father about the investigation while it was ongoing.

Thinking of her sister, Cate realized she'd have to call Bailey and give her an update.

She would have to let her know she hadn't been able to get the reports unsealed. At least, not yet.

CHAPTER FOURTEEN

Bailey ran down Claremont Street and turned left onto Rampart Road, determined to keep up with Ludwig's swift pace. Lifting her face to the early morning sun, she reveled in the cool breeze and the much-needed reprieve from her mother's constant stream of questions and advice.

Jackie had greeted her that morning with her latest idea, which, like all her other ideas, involved Bailey going to law school. Only this time, she had couched it as an exciting opportunity to move up within the FBI.

"The Bureau is always looking for talented attorneys," Jackie had informed her in a hushed voice as if giving Bailey an inside scoop. "You could do so much good working behind the scenes, where you'd be safe. I hear the pay is..."

Bailey had blocked out the rest of her mother's words as she grabbed Ludwig's leash and headed for the door.

Now, as she and Ludwig circled the block, she began to mentally sift through the known details of the Stalker case.

Strange how it's less stressful to think about a serial murder case than my mother's alternative plans for my future.

The thought was interrupted by the buzzing of her

phone, and she immediately dug in her pocket, glad for the excuse to slow down to a comfortable walk.

Checking the display, she saw that Cate was calling.

"Mom's driving me crazy," she said before her sister had a chance to speak. "Can I sleep on your sofa until I go back to D.C.? I'm not sure how long it'll take, but I promise, you won't even know I'm there."

As Bailey waited for Cate's response, she earned an impatient look from Ludwig who had been enjoying the opportunity to burn off some energy.

"Um...okay, I guess so," Cate agreed in a put-upon tone. "Although, I seem to remember the last time you slept on my sofa you ended up staying for almost six months."

"That was an exceptional circumstance," Bailey objected.

"And the murder of your ex-police partner by a potential serial killer isn't?" Cate shot back.

Heading back toward Claremont Street, Bailey ignored the question, not wanting to think about the six months she'd spent bunking on Cate's sofa after Zach had called off their wedding.

"I'll bring my stuff by tonight," she said. "And thanks."

"It's no problem," Cate said. "Although Mom may not agree. Have you told her yet?"

Once again Bailey ignored the question, preferring not to think about Jackie's reaction until she absolutely had to.

"I'm sure you weren't calling about that," Bailey said, hoping to change the subject. "Did you get the records?"

"I went to see Judge Walsh this morning and submitted a request for a court order to unseal the records," she said.

"Unfortunately, since the offenses are drug-related, it's not that simple."

Bailey didn't like the sound of that.

"Florida law stipulates that an Offender Review Commission investigate the circumstances of each offender before they're released after serving a sentence," Cate explained. "It can result in mandated rehab, which is what happened in these cases."

"Okay, we know they went to rehab," Bailey said. "But why were the records sealed?"

She pulled on the leash, not ready to go home just yet.

"According to Judge Walsh, the records were sealed to protect the offenders. He implied they had been coerced."

The words stopped Bailey in her tracks.

"You mean, someone forced them to transport or distribute drugs?" she asked. "Who was it?"

"That's what we need to find out by reviewing the records," Cate said. "Judge Walsh said we'll need to petition the Commission to unseal the records, along with their findings. I expect all relevant details will have been included in the Commission's investigative report."

Bailey grimaced at the thought of all that paperwork.

She hated paperwork.

"Otherwise, you could go to the Commission and try to talk to an investigator in person," Cate said. "I'd go with you but I'm in back-to-back meetings all morning."

"Send me the address and I'll see if I can talk to someone over there," Bailey instantly agreed. "Then I'll pick you up after your meetings and we can have lunch."

Walking back into the house, she stopped in the kitchen where her parents were having breakfast with Duchess lounging at their feet.

"I really appreciate you guys letting me sleep here the last couple of nights," she said, biting her lip. "But Cate and I will be working on this investigation together so I ask Cate if I could sleep on her sofa for the duration."

Jackie's back had stiffened, but she simply nodded as if she knew the decision had been made.

Scooping Duchess up in her arms, she carried the cat toward the living room, calling over her shoulder.

"You can't take your father's car!"

"I just need it for another day or two," Bailey said as her father poured himself another cup of coffee. "I'll get a car from the Bureau's pool as soon as possible."

Chris Flynn just shrugged as if he wasn't concerned, but he lowered his voice so his wife wouldn't overhear.

"Fine," he said. "Bring it back by the end of the week."

Bailey went outside and started loading her suitcase into the trunk of the Camaro, making a mental note to herself to ask Ford Ramsey if she could use a car from the FBI's pool.

She saw Duchess in the front window, watching her with an air of satisfaction as if she'd arranged the whole thing.

Sticking her tongue out at the cat, she turned around to see Sabrina West pull up in a white minivan.

"Agent Flynn, you're still here," the reporter said as she stepped onto the sidewalk. "How long are you planning to stay in Belle Harbor?"

"As long as it takes for me to finish my business here,"

Bailey replied airily.

Sabrina smiled.

"Just what is your business?" she asked. "Are you working on the Emma Walsh homicide? I mean, you were on Bellamy Beach with Dr. Knox Monday night, right?"

The reporter lifted her perfectly arched eyebrows.

"I've got to say, he's the only hot medical examiner I've ever met. Although, he's not very talkative."

Picturing Summerset County's tall, dark, and handsome M.E., Bailey couldn't disagree, but she wasn't about to share the thought with Sabrina West, who wasn't exactly a model of discretion.

"You were the agent who killed Ronin Godfrey last year, weren't you?" Sabrina continued as if she hadn't noticed Bailey's lack of a response. "Didn't you also save that K-9 handler and his dog?"

The questions and comments kept coming as Bailey closed the trunk and walked to the driver's side door.

"But you moved on to D.C., right? Did you just come back to look for Emma Walsh?"

Sabrina followed after her, still talking as Bailey opened the door and slid into the driver's seat.

"You and Emma used to be partners when you were on the Belle Harbor PD. Now that she's been found, does that mean you'll be leaving?" the reporter asked. "Or will you be working on the Stalker case? Will the Bureau be starting up a task force with local authorities?"

Bailey wondered where Sabrina West was getting her information. The reporter worked fast.

"If there's a serial killer in Summerset County, maybe I can help you find him," she called out as Bailey started the engine.

Deciding she couldn't afford to alienate the press, Bailey summoned a smile and rolled down her window.

"I admire your persistence," she said to the reporter. "If there's anything you can do to help, I'll let you know."

* * *

Bailey steered the little red Camaro onto the downtown exit, merged onto Grand Harbor Boulevard, and made a right turn into the Summerset County Administration Complex parking lot.

She carefully parked the classic car in an empty space at the far end of the lot, hoping no one would park beside her and accidentally ding her father's car.

Leading Ludwig inside the main building, she checked the directory before taking the elevator up to the office of the Offender Review Commission on the third floor.

Approaching the young woman seated behind the reception desk, Bailey flashed her credentials.

"I'm Special Agent Bailey Flynn with the FBI," she said. "I need to speak to someone about several investigations the Commission conducted over the last year."

She held up the printouts Cate had given her with the offender names and court record numbers.

"I'm hoping to review the findings in these files."

"Is anyone expecting you?" the clerk asked, her eyes

wide behind rimless glasses as she glanced down at Ludwig.

"No, unfortunately not," Bailey admitted with an apologetic smile. "But Judge Walsh referred me to your office. Could you see if someone's available?"

Ten minutes later she was sitting in a conference room tapping out an update to Roger Calloway on her phone when the door opened and a man with a shock of thick, dark hair stepped into the room.

"Agent Flynn?"

Tucking the laptop he was holding under his arm, he crossed to Bailey and held out a business card.

"I'm Chad Hearst, the commission's lead investigator for Summerset County," he said as she jumped up and took his card. "I understand you have some questions?"

"Yes, I believe three cases your office investigated over the last year are relevant to a case I'm working on," Bailey said. "Do you have a few minutes?"

The investigator hesitated.

"I actually just stepped out of a staff meeting," he said, frowning down at his watch. "And I'm due on a conference call in about ten minutes."

"Well, thank you for talking to me on such short notice," Bailey said, taking his hesitation as a yes. "I'll try to make this quick."

She held out the printouts she'd brought with her.

"I'm looking for information on several women the Commission investigated prior to their release from the Summerset Women's Detention Center," she said. "As the lead investigator for Summerset County, I assume you sign off on all investigations? Are you familiar with these?"

Hearst pulled reading glasses from his shirt pocket and studied the three sheets of paper, then shook his head.

"Sorry, but these names don't ring a bell," he admitted. "Our office investigates hundreds of offenders each year, so it's impossible to remember them all."

"Would it be possible for you to access the records?" Bailey asked, hoping his obvious time crunch would work to her advantage. "If you can send me copies, I can let you get on with your conference call."

Glancing at his watch again, Hearst sighed, then set his laptop on the conference table.

"I'll check online," he agreed as he started to tap on the little keyboard. "All reports are stored in the system but..."

His words faded as he studied the screen.

After another bout of frantic typing, a frown formed between his eyes and he reached for the phone on the table.

Picking up the receiver, he held it to his ear and punched in an extension number.

"Hey, this is Chad. Can you please let the Committee know I'm going to be late for the ten o'clock conference call?" he said. "Something's come up with one of the investigations. Oh, and I need a favor."

He glanced uneasily at Bailey and then back at the phone.

"I need you to bring me the official hard-copy files for three offender investigations. I'm sending you the file numbers now."

After tapping out a message on the laptop, he turned back to Bailey and cleared his throat.

Her heart dropped at his next words.

"You realize these records have all been sealed, right?"

"Yes, I do," she said. "Which is why I'm here. Judge Walsh told me that after the investigations were completed, the records were sealed to protect the offenders. He said the only way to review the findings was to work through you."

Hearst nodded.

"Judge Walsh is correct," he said. "Each of the women listed here were suspected victims of criminal coercion by an unidentified perpetrator."

He cleared his throat.

"However, these women refused to identify or testify against the person they claimed victimized them," he continued. "They chose not to contest the charges or provide evidence of coercion. Instead, they had accepted short custodial sentences."

"So, they agreed to go to prison instead of testifying against their abuser?" Bailey asked.

Closing his laptop, he nodded.

"I'm afraid so," he said. "And after serving their sentence, they were assigned to post-release addiction recovery supervision in a private rehab program."

It took Bailey a minute to interpret what he was saying.

"They were required to go to rehab? Where?"

"Ashworth Recovery Center."

Bailey raised an eyebrow.

"They all were sent to the same facility?"

Hearst nodded.

"But why were their records sealed?"

"It was the determination of the Commission that these young women were victims of coercion by an offender they would not name. Likely a drug dealer or even a member of a cartel. None of the women had agreed to testify against the person responsible for their predicament, and-"

"And I can understand why," Bailey interjected. "They were all so young. And if they'd already been victimized, they must have been terrified."

"I'm sure they were," Hearst agreed. "But based on their refusal to give evidence to support their claims, the judge refused to expunge their convictions. The best we could do to protect them was to seal their records."

"Unfortunately, that wasn't enough," Bailey said.

Hearst raised an eyebrow.

"What do you mean?"

"I mean these three women are dead," Bailey said. "And it appears they were all killed by the same perpetrator."

The investigator stared at her with a startled expression.

"I'm guessing you hadn't heard of their deaths?" she asked after a long beat of silence.

"We have so many cases," Hearst said weakly. "I can't keep track of what happens after we..."

His voice trailed off and he swallowed hard.

"I understand," Bailey said. "But I'm here as part of a task force investigating these homicides. I'm trying to figure out who these women were being protected from. That might help us figure out who harmed them."

"As I said, the women refused to name any names."

Bailey wondered if that had been part of the problem.

"And the fact that they refused to name the person or gang who had coerced them wasn't made public? Their records were sealed and their silence was kept a secret? Which means their coercer couldn't be sure if they'd given evidence against him or not?"

Hearst shifted in his seat, clearly unsettled.

"Are you suggesting the outcome is somehow the Commission's fault?" he asked. "You think those women were killed because we sealed those records and their abusers thought they'd given evidence against them?"

Bailey quickly shook her head.

"No, that's not what I'm saying," she assured him. "But I do think whoever coerced them into transporting drugs could be involved with their deaths."

"It's possible," Hearst agreed. "Coercion isn't unusual."

Their conversation was interrupted as the woman from reception entered the room and handed Hearst three files, which he set on the table.

"Feel free to review the files and take notes," he said. "But the files can't leave the office."

Picking up the top file, Bailey scanned through Tori Cabot's report as Hearst stood and tucked his laptop back under his arm.

"Tell me, why were Tori and the others assigned to Ashworth Recovery?" she asked him. "Why that facility?"

"It's in the offender's county and it offers a competitive rate," the investigator said. "I guess it just makes sense."

He hesitated as his eyes fell on Tori Cabot's open file.

"I noticed the name Lando Gutierrez is mentioned in all

three reports," he said. "Lando's a dealer who's rumored to work for the Tumba Cartel. He's a dangerous man."

* * *

Bailey was on her way to the Summerset County Courthouse to pick up Cate for lunch when her phone buzzed on the dashboard.

Madeline Mercer's name flashed on the screen.

"I'm trying to get in touch with Fraser," she said as soon as Bailey answered. "He's not picking up and I've got results on the wallet he found on Bellamy Beach."

The CSI team leader sounded excited.

"What did you find?"

"Prints," Madeline said. "And there's a match in AFIS. A perfect match for a man with a very long criminal record."

She paused as if for dramatic effect.

"Okay, I'll take the bait," Bailey said. "Who is he?"

"His legal name is Francisco Ignacio Silveri," Madeline replied. "But he's unofficially known as Cisco Silver. I'm sending you his last known address and phone number."

The message came in just as Bailey was pulling up to a red light. Picking up the phone, she tapped on the message to open it.

According to Madeline, Cisco's last known address was over on Neptune Way, a street she recognized. It was in a decent neighborhood, and the house was owned by a senior citizen named Teresa Silveri.

Probably Cisco's grandmother.

Impulsively, Bailey tapped out the phone number Madeline had provided and held the phone to her ear.

The call was picked up on the third ring, but there was only quiet breathing on the other end.

"This is Special Agent Flynn with the FBI," Bailey said briskly. "I need to speak to Cisco Silver."

There was a long pause before the woman spoke.

"Cisco isn't here," she said. "He hasn't been home in a while. But I'll let him know you called."

"Yes, please do," Bailey said. "And thank you."

She hung up, satisfied she now knew where Cisco Silver lived. And while he wouldn't be calling her back, she would be stopping by his house later to find out what he'd seen on Bellamy Beach, and what he knew about the Stalker.

CHAPTER FIFTEEN

The Stalker was waiting for Cate Flynn when she emerged from the Summerset County courthouse. His eyes followed the prosecutor as she looked up and down Central Avenue, lifted an impatient hand to push back a silky strand of auburn hair, then pulled out her phone. As she began to pace anxiously along the curb, he studied her tall, slim figure, wondering what she was planning to do next.

Instinctively, his hand reached for the combat knife hidden in the sheath under his jacket, craving the heavy feel of the warm metal in his hand.

He'd been thinking about the prosecutor and her sister ever since they'd shown up at Bellamy Beach after Emma Walsh's body had been found.

The sisters worried him. Especially now that a connection had been made between his fallen angels.

The two women were a definite problem, although he wasn't sure how much they knew.

They can't know about me, can they? They can't know about my special collection.

Catching sight of the cherry red Camaro as it turned onto

Central, he watched it stop at the curb in front of Cate.

The Stalker's eyes narrowed as he caught sight of Bailey Flynn behind the wheel, his hands clenching into fists at his side as Cate climbed into the passenger seat and the classic car pulled back into traffic.

Turning on his heel, he walked quickly to the corner, not sure where he was going, knowing only that he had to calm down. He couldn't afford to bring attention to himself.

He'd be fine as long as he didn't lose control as he'd done with his first fallen angel.

He hadn't planned to take Wren Dempsey's life. But then he'd seen the wings and the Devil's Breath had taken over.

The white powder makes me do bad things.

Wren had been the first. And once he'd mounted her wings on his wall, he'd suspected she wouldn't be the last.

But he hadn't been sure until he'd seen Tori Cabot again.

She'd met him at the mall just as he'd instructed, and when he asked her for the drugs, she'd reached into her shirt to pull out the baggie she'd hidden in her bra.

Seeing the angel wings, half-hidden under the thick, chestnut hair that fell past her shoulders, he had known what he had to do. He had done what needed to be done.

He'd gone home with the next set of angel wings in his pocket. They had been added to his collection.

But they hadn't been the last.

No, Hallie Kwan had lured him to Sun Creek with the hope of another set of wings to mount.

Standing on the corner, waiting for the light to change, he pictured the young woman as she'd run from him through the forest, her terror making the angel wings tremble as the Devil's Breath urged him on.

Suddenly a car horn honked loudly beside him as a delivery van jerked to a stop inches away.

Realizing he'd stepped into traffic, the Stalker stepped back onto the curb, ignoring the wildly gesturing driver as he calmly headed north to the parking garage, anxious to return to the privacy of his vehicle.

Once he was safely back in the driver's seat, he reached into his pocket and took out his pill bottle, shaking six benzos into his hand.

The four he'd taken that morning hadn't been enough.

He closed his eyes and gripped the steering wheel, willing himself to stay calm.

Sucking in a deep breath he felt the benzos start to do their work. They'd make all his worries go away.

And the Devil's Breath will do the rest.

The fine white powder had given him the courage to take what he wanted. It had allowed him to build his collection.

He'd used it when he'd been forced to take care of Emma Walsh after she'd started asking questions and making threats. He'd had no choice but to silence her.

And now that Cate and Bailey Flynn were out there looking for him, he needed to get more of the white powder. He would need more Devil's Breath soon.

CHAPTER SIXTEEN

C isco Silver stood just inside the little house on Neptune Street and peered out through a crack in the curtains. His panicked, bloodshot eyes watched as Lando Gutierrez walked slowly up the driveway, stopping to look into his Grandmother's old Buick, before continuing up the flower-lined pathway.

"Who's out there, Cisco? What's going on?"

Gesturing wildly for his grandmother to be quiet, he kept his eyes on the drug dealer, who was now walking up the steps to the front porch, his big black boots leaving muddy prints on the smooth concrete.

Lando was tall and rangy, with shoulder-length, inky black hair that framed close-set eyes, a long, thin nose, and a narrow, pointed chin.

As the dealer lifted a big hand to knock on the door, Cisco turned back to his grandmother and put a finger to his mouth, motioning for her to be quiet.

They both jumped at the sudden pounding on the door.

"Open up, Cisco! I know you're in there."

Another round of pounding was followed by the rattle of the doorknob, prompting an outraged gasp from Teresa

Silveri, who opened her mouth and let out a loud protest before Cisco could stop her.

"Get away from my door!"

Wincing at the shrill words, Cisco clutched at his grandmother's thin arm.

"Nonna, you have to tell him I moved to New York," he whispered. "Tell him I've been gone for weeks, just like you did with that FBI agent on the phone."

His grandmother shook her head stubbornly, sending a white curl falling onto her lined cheek.

"This man doesn't scare me," she said.

"Well, he should," Cisco hissed. "He's a dangerous–"

His frantic words were drowned out by a deep voice from the porch. Lando sounded angry.

"I want my money, Cisco. Now, open this door before I kick it down. Or maybe I should just burn down this–"

Slipping from his grasp, his grandmother yanked open the door and glared up into the drug dealer's sneering face as he towered over her.

"I'll call the police if you don't leave right now!" she yelled, her voice cracking with outrage. "My grandson doesn't want to talk to you. He's a good boy."

"Well, he's going to be a dead boy if he doesn't come talk to me and pay off what he owes," Lando said.

His voice morphed from angry to amused as he stared down at the little woman.

"You tell Cisco to come by Lando's house and pay up before midnight," he said, sticking a big finger in her face.

She called after him as he backed down the path, despite

Cisco's desperate whispers for her to close the door.

"Don't you come back here, or I'll call the police."

"The last person who called the cops on me is buried over in the Summerset Cemetery," Lando called back with a nasty laugh. "Now, if you know what's good for you, old woman, you'll pass on the message."

Recoiling as his grandmother slammed the door, Cisco followed her into the kitchen where she grabbed up the receiver from the phone hanging on the wall.

"Nonna, you can't call the cops," Cisco said, plucking the phone from her hand. "You don't want Lando Gutierrez as an enemy. Besides, I can't afford to have the cops poking around asking questions."

His grandmother stared at him with suspicion.

"What have you done this time?" she demanded as he replaced the receiver.

"I didn't do anything," he said. "Well, I might have stolen a few things here and there..."

He winced as she began to shout at him in Italian.

"Calm down, Nonna, it's no big deal," he assured, following her into the living room. "At least, the stealing part is no big deal. But, I...saw something."

The color drained from his face as he pictured Emma Walsh's dead, staring eyes.

"What did you see?" his grandmother asked, suddenly suspicious. "What's happened to make you look like this?"

Looking into his grandmother's worried eyes, he sighed.

"You know the police detective they've been showing on TV? The one who was murdered on Bellamy Beach? Well, I saw what happened. I saw the man who killed her."

His grandmother stared at him in shock.

"You saw someone kill that poor woman, and you didn't tell anybody?" she asked. "You didn't call the police?"

Cisco shook his head.

"I'm in real trouble this time, Nonna," he said. "And I don't know what to do."

* * *

Checking to make sure his grandmother was still in her bedroom, Cisco quietly snuck out of the house.

He needed to go see Lando. He'd have to give him what money he had and hope the dealer would wait for the rest.

Slipping into his grandmother's old Buick, he drove slowly out of the neighborhood, taking the backroads in an effort to avoid any possibility of being seen by the cops.

The little house Lando was living in on Kennard Street had an overgrown lawn and a *Guard Dog on Duty* sign in the front window.

As he parked the car along the curb, he looked around, scared the police might be watching the house, but the neighborhood sat silent in the mild afternoon sunshine.

Stepping out of the car, Cisco walked up the cracked path and knocked softly on the front door, mentally rehearsing the excuses he would give Lando as to why he didn't have the money he owed.

But his excuses fell away when a young woman opened the door and frowned out at him.

From what Cisco could tell, underneath the heavy makeup, she was little more than a teenager.

The tips of her dark hair had been dyed blue, and her eyes were heavily lined with royal blue liner. She squinted out at him as a deep voice called out from behind her.

"Who is it, Jazz?"

The girl cocked her head and frowned.

"Who are you?"

Her words were slightly slurred and her eyes were glassy.

"I'm Cisco Silver," he said, pulling the cash from his pocket. "Lando asked me to come by. I've got some-"

Before he could finish his sentence Lando was looming up behind the woman, pushing her out of the way.

The dealer grabbed the wad of cash from Cisco's hand and began counting it as he watched with distaste.

What had his life come to? How had he ended up doing business with a low-life like Lando?

I may be a criminal and a thief, but I'm a gentleman thief.

It was the story he'd always told himself. A way to justify his actions. He'd come up with the idea after watching *To Catch a Thief*, an Alfred Hitchcock movie he'd seen with his grandmother as a boy, not long after he'd moved into the little house on Neptune Way.

I'm no Carey Grant, but I'm not an animal. Not like Lando.

Looking past the dealer, he saw the girl Lando had called Jazz sink onto her bare, bony knees. She tipped forward, falling face down onto the floor.

"Hey, what's wrong with her?" he asked.

Lando shrugged and kicked at the girl with a big boot.

"She does that sometimes," he said, turning and walking back into the house. "She'll be okay."

Stepping inside, Cisco crouched beside the girl, pushing her hair back to see if she was still breathing, hoping he wasn't about to witness another pair of staring eyes.

But her eyes were closed, and he decided that she had passed out but was still breathing.

Cisco started to get back to his feet, then recoiled as he saw the angry red scars on her back below her left shoulder. Red, raw lines had been burned into the tender flesh.

"They look like *wings*," Cisco muttered stupidly, not sure what he was seeing. "What the hell have you done to her?"

He stared down in horror, then turned to Lando.

"I gave her my mark," Lando said. "That way nobody'll mess with her. And they'll know whatever she's carrying belongs to me."

The dealer sounded proud.

"Most dealers use ink to mark their mules, but that takes too long," he added. "This dude in prison was into scarification. He told me all about it. You just carve or burn designs straight into the flesh. It's a lot quicker."

The image of burning flesh caused Cisco's stomach to clench and for a minute he thought he was going to be sick. Jumping to his feet, he started for the door.

He had to get out of there. The dealer was crazy.

"I'll consider this to be your first payment," Lando called after him, patting his pocket. "Tell your Grandma I said hi."

Hurrying back to the Buick, Cisco drove back the way he'd come, his head filled with images of the wings branded into the girl's tender skin.

How long has Lando been branding the girls he uses to carry his deliveries? How many has he marked as his property?

Cisco's stomach was still queasy when he turned the corner onto Neptune Way and pulled into his grandmother's driveway.

He stopped and stared at the red car parked along the curb. It was one of those old models he'd seen at car shows.

He stopped in surprise as a young woman climbed out.

"Francisco Silveri?"

She sounded friendly.

"Or should I call you Cisco?"

When he didn't reply, she continued.

"I'm Special Agent Bailey Flynn with the FBI. I need to ask you a few questions. Can we talk inside?"

CHAPTER SEVENTEEN

Bailey stood next to the Camaro and stared at Cisco Silver, watching as he opened his mouth several times before closing it again. He looked younger than she'd imagined, with dark shaggy hair and faded acne scars on his thin face. Lifting a bony hand, he scratched at the light stubble on his chin.

"Cisco? Can we go inside and talk?"

The sound of the front door opening had her hand moving closer to the Glock in her holster but she relaxed when she saw an older woman step onto the porch.

"Nonna, I can handle this," Cisco said. "Go back inside."

Ignoring the order, the woman looked at Bailey.

"You're the one who called earlier asking for my grandson? The FBI agent?"

"Yes, ma'am," Bailey said. "I need to ask Cisco a few questions. Perhaps we could talk inside?"

She glanced over at Cisco, who looked tensed as if he might make a run for it at any minute.

"Please, come in," Teresa Silveri said. "I'll get you something to drink and we can talk."

Bailey nodded.

"I'd appreciate that," she said. "But I have a dog in the car, just let me make sure he's okay and I'll join you."

"Feel free to bring him, too," the older woman offered as Cisco began walking toward the house. "I like dogs."

Bailey turned swiftly back to her car and opened the door to let Ludwig out. As she did, she pulled out her phone and tapped on Fraser's number.

She was relieved when he answered on the first ring.

"Where have you been?" she asked. "No, forget that. We don't have time."

Her eyes flicked to the little house.

"Madeline matched a print from the wallet we found at Bellamy Beach to Francisco Silveri, a man with a long criminal record. He lives on Neptune and I'm just getting ready to question him. I need you to meet me here."

"Cisco Silver?"

Fraser didn't sound surprised.

"I know the guy. Stealing wallets at the boardwalk seems like something he'd do. Cisco usually keeps to small-time stuff, like breaking into cars and tipping over vending machines," he said.

"So, you don't think he's dangerous?" Bailey asked. "You don't think he could be the Stalker?"

There was a short silence as Fraser considered it.

"I guess he could have graduated to murder, but I doubt it," he said. "But wait outside until I get there just in case."

"That's not necessary. His grandmother's here and we're just going to talk until you arrive. Then you can decide if you want to bring him in for stealing the wallet."

Ending the call, she snapped on Ludwig's leash and led the dog up to the house, admiring Teresa Silveri's flowers along the path as she went.

She knocked softly on the front door and stepped inside, greeted by the smell of fresh coffee and something sweet baking in the oven.

"We're in here," Teresa called out from the little kitchen.

Once they were all seated around a polished wooden table with steaming cups of coffee and a plate of almond biscotti, Bailey cleared her throat.

"Cisco, I believe you were at Bellamy Beach last Friday."

She let the words hang in the sweetly scented air, taking a sip of the coffee as she waited for Cisco's response.

"I wasn't doing anything-"

"Tell her the truth, Cisco," his grandmother cut in. "A woman has lost her life. The person responsible must be brought to justice."

Bailey stared at the woman, her pulse jumping.

She'd been expecting a denial about the pickpocketing he'd done on the boardwalk, not a flat-out confession about Emma Walsh's murder.

Before Cisco could reply, a knock sounded at the door.

"That will be Detective Fraser with the Belle Harbor PD," Bailey said. "I think he's going to want to hear what you have to say."

Pushing his chair back, Cisco jumped to his feet and bolted toward the back door, throwing it open and racing outside as Bailey instinctively chased after him.

She stopped as she saw him struggling to climb over the

back fence, which was covered in thorny rose bushes.

"Cisco, you're ruining my flowers!" Teresa called as Fraser appeared at the back gate, his weapon drawn.

"It's okay," Bailey called out. "He's not going anywhere. In fact, he's got something he wants to tell us about Bellamy Beach last Friday night."

She looked back at Fraser.

"But I think we'd better take him down to the station," she said. "We'll talk there."

They led Cisco around the house to Fraser's Interceptor as Teresa watched with worried eyes.

Once they'd settled him into the backseat, Cisco's grandmother turned and went inside, closing the door quietly behind her.

Fraser walked Bailey and Ludwig back to the Camaro.

"He definitely saw something at the beach Friday night," she told him. "He may even be involved."

"There was only a few hundred bucks in the wallet so if we book him on the theft charge, it'll be a misdemeanor, which means he'll likely be allowed to bail out tonight," Fraser said as she opened the door. "We won't have much time to get him talking. And if he lawyers up, we're screwed."

Bailey nodded her agreement as she checked her watch.

"You get him back to the station and set him up in a room. I've got one more stop to make and then I'll join you. I'd like to watch the interview and hear what he has to say."

* * *

Bailey glanced back in her rearview mirror, watching as the Interceptor rolled out of view, then entered an address on Windhaven Way into her GPS app.

Twenty minutes later she was pulling up to a wooden security fence with a small sign.

Welcome to Ashworth Recovery Center.

She pushed a call button on a metal box by the gate.

"This is Special Agent Bailey Flynn with the FBI," she told the faint voice that sounded from the speaker.

The gate in front of her clicked and swung open, revealing a group of low buildings surrounded by a large, asphalt parking lot.

After parking the Camaro in a *Visitor's Only* space near the front, she looked back to see Ludwig dozing in the backseat.

Deciding not to wake him, she cracked the windows and climbed out of the car, unimpressed with the dreary exterior and total lack of landscaping or greenery.

As she approached the front door, she saw a sign next to it reading *Ring Bell for Entry.*

Bailey pushed the little metal button and heard nothing from within. But a few seconds later a man appeared at the door and pushed it open.

His long, dark hair was twisted into a topknot, and he wore a t-shirt with a peace sign on the front, along with baggy yoga pants and sandals.

"Hi, I'm Neil Ashworth, the facility manager," he said. "How can I help?"

"I'm Special Agent Bailey Flynn with the FBI. I was hoping to ask a few questions about-"

A loud voice called out from somewhere within.

"Neil, what are you doing? Who's at the door?"

An older woman with bottle-red hair and cat-eye glasses appeared in the hallway.

Bailey recognized her as Nigella Ashworth, a Summerset County councilwoman who owned several local businesses and sat on the boards of the biggest companies in town.

"It's an FBI agent, mother."

"Well, don't just stand there," Nigella said. "Let her in."

Forcing a polite smile, Bailey stepped in behind Neil, who waved her into the lobby.

The room was dark and gloomy with little natural lighting. It looked nothing like Bailey had expected.

She'd never actually been in a rehab center before but had imagined something along the lines of a quasi-medical facility. A quiet building with sterile white walls, bright lights, and wide windows.

Ashworth Recovery Center was anything but sterile.

The drab carpet, old-fashioned wallpaper, and dusty curtains reminded her of a dilapidated house she'd responded to back when she'd been driving patrol.

The neighbors had complained about a putrid smell, and she and Emma had forced the old lock only to find the poor woman who lived there had been dead for over two weeks.

Of course, the smell wasn't as bad, but the general feel was almost as depressing.

"Mrs. Ashworth, I'm sorry to-"

"It's *Councilwoman* Ashworth," the woman corrected with a tight smile. "And I can't imagine what the FBI wants with our little recovery center. We've never had any problems here before."

Considering the center routinely treated ex-convicts and drug addicts, Bailey found the woman's comment hard to believe but decided not to challenge her.

She would need to pick her battles with the overbearing woman carefully, already sensing that squeezing any useful information out of Nigella Ashworth would require a battle, if not a full-out war.

"Three homicide victims in Summerset County were residents at Ashworth Recovery over the last year," Bailey said. "Wren Dempsey, Tori Cabot, and Hallie Kwan were all victims of homicide over the last twelve months."

"Are you saying these three girls are the victims of the Summerset Stalker we've been hearing about on the news?" Neil asked. "I hadn't heard their names but–"

A hard look from his mother stopped the man's words.

"We are looking into the possibility that a serial killer is responsible for these homicides," Bailey confirmed. "Which is why I'm here. We need to find out as much as we can about the victims and who they were associating with so that we can find the person responsible before–"

"Let's not blow this out of proportion," Nigella cut in dismissively. "You'll get my son and the community in a panic for no good reason."

She exhaled with an exasperated huff.

"The girls you mentioned were all addicts with emotional issues," she said bluntly. "Most likely they were trying to score drugs and it got out of hand. But there's no need for normal, law-abiding citizens to be scared."

Patting her stiff hair, she shrugged.

"Maybe their deaths will even be good for the community in the end," Nigella added. "It'll put the fear of God into the young ones, that's for sure. Make them think twice about taking drugs and running around at all hours of the night."

Bailey gaped at the older woman in surprise.

"You think the death of three women is a good thing?"

"That's not what I said," Nigella protested. "At least, not exactly. I'm sure you know what I'm trying to say."

Not sure that she did, Bailey turned to Neil.

"Is there any way I can view the records you kept for these women while they were here?" she asked. "I'm sure there were notes from their counseling session and such that might be helpful in-"

"We can't provide any information without a court order or a warrant," Nigella cut in coldly. "We offer our residents complete confidentiality so they feel safe opening up."

The councilwoman turned her hard eyes on her son.

"Neil, why don't you walk Agent Flynn back to her vehicle while I get back to my very busy schedule?"

As the woman started back down the hall, Neil led Bailey back to the Camaro.

"Cool car," he said. "What is it, a '67?"

Bailey nodded, allowing the man to rub a finger along the sleek lines of the classic car.

"You couldn't tell me what you know about these young women, could you, Neil?" Bailey asked. "I can get a warrant to search, or a court order compelling you to deliver certain records, but that takes time. And there are other women out there who could be hurt in the meantime."

The man's eyes turned quickly toward the entrance as if he expected his mother to be standing by the door.

"I can't discuss any of our residents specifically," he said. "But I can tell you that the young people who come here have usually fallen into the wrong crowd. They get involved with the wrong type of people and are pulled into illegal activities to fund their habit. But once they've been released from prison and come here to kick the drugs..."

"Of course, they don't want to come here at first, but the program is part of their release conditions, so most people try to make the best of it and end up doing well. That can continue once they're out of here, as long as they stay away from bad influences."

Bailey thought of what Chad Hearst had told her.

"Speaking of bad influences...what do you know about Lando Gutierrez and the Tumba Cartel?"

Recognition lit up Neil's eyes and then was gone.

"I don't think I know them," he said to her surprise.

Before Bailey could push the issue, Nigella was walking down the sidewalk toward them.

"I've got to go," Neil said. "I hope you find the man you're looking for."

Scurrying up the sidewalk, he walked toward his mother, who stared over at the little red Camaro with unfriendly eyes before disappearing inside.

CHAPTER EIGHTEEN

As Jimmy Fraser drove toward the Belle Harbor police station in his black Interceptor, he glanced into the rearview mirror, studying Cisco Silver who was slumped against the window, his dark, shaggy hair hanging in his eyes like a sullen child. The man didn't look dangerous to Fraser.

He probably weighs about ninety pounds soaking wet.

Of course, you could never tell what someone was capable of doing just by looking at them.

He should be grateful the guy hadn't pulled a weapon when Bailey had shown up on her own to question him.

She should have had backup. I should have been with her.

But then, his morning hadn't exactly gone to plan.

Fraser had already been on his way to the station when the school nurse had called. Sasha was in the clinic at Belle Harbor Elementary with a stomach ache. The distraught fourth grader had needed to be picked up right away.

With Linette hosting an open house that morning for a real estate listing in Sun Creek, he'd had no choice but to drive straight to the school.

And by the time he'd picked up his oldest daughter and

arranged for Linette's mother to watch her until the open house was over, it had been close to lunchtime.

Now he needed to get his mind back in the game.

He would have to question Cisco Silver and find out what he knew.

They needed to identify a suspect soon.

The public was already starting to ask questions about why the murder of three young women had remained unlinked and unsolved for so long.

And the intensifying coverage of the Summerset Stalker in the press would no doubt incite panic in the community.

The worrisome thought was still at the forefront of Fraser's mind when he pulled up outside the Belle Harbor police station to see Sabrina West from Channel 3 News waiting outside.

Spotting Fraser climbing out of the vehicle, the reporter made a beeline straight toward him, shouting questions and holding up a video recorder.

As he led his detainee into the station through a side entrance, Cisco lifted his arm and tried to hide his face.

"Is it true a task force has been formed to find the Summerset Stalker?" Sabrina called out. "What's being done to protect the community?"

Pushing past her, Fraser was thankful to see Killian Rourke holding the door open for him.

As he and Cisco slipped inside, the uniformed officer stepped out and blocked Sabrina's view.

Fraser could hear Rourke threatening to confiscate the reporter's camera as the door swung shut behind them.

"We're investigating the homicide of Detective Emma Walsh," Fraser said as he led Cisco to Interview Room A and pointed to a chair. "We have reason to believe you were on Bellamy Beach the night of her murder."

"Whoever told you that was lying," Cisco said, not meeting his eyes. "I was nowhere near the-"

"You can cut the act," Fraser said. "We found a wallet in the sand with your fingerprint on it. We know you stole the wallet from a man on the boardwalk that same night."

Leaning back in his chair, he crossed his arms over his chest as if settling in for a long rest.

"Now, we can either consider you a suspect or a witness," Fraser continued. "How do you want to play it?"

Cisco pushed his shaggy hair out of his eyes.

"Okay, fine," he finally said. "I was there."

He shifted in his seat.

"I needed money, so I went down to the Bellamy Beach Boardwalk and lifted a few wallets. No big deal."

"I'd say the people you stole from might disagree," Fraser said. "And with your record, it'll get you six months in the county jail. So, why take the risk?"

The sullen expression was back on Cisco's face.

"I told you, I needed money. I owe money to a dealer...a real maniac. Lando's crazy, and if he sees me talking to the cops...if I tell you what I saw...there's no telling what he'll do to me."

Sweat had broken out on Cisco's forehead.

"But I sure the hell didn't kill anyone."

The mention of Lando had Fraser's full attention.

As did Cisco's comment.

If I tell you what I saw...

Things were suddenly getting very interesting.

They already knew there was a connection between Lando and Tori Cabot. And now there was a connection between Lando and Cisco Silver, a man whose print was on the wallet found near the scene of the latest homicide.

Connections were good. They solved cases.

Deciding to let the man stew while he waited for Bailey to arrive, Fraser left the room, walking down to the break room for a cup of coffee before peeking outside.

Relieved to see that Sabrina West's white minivan was gone, he slipped outside to wait for Bailey.

He had just drained the last drop of coffee from his mug when he saw Dalton West approaching.

"Are you and your sister working shifts or something?" he asked with an exaggerated sigh. "First she stands outside and harasses anyone coming in or out, and then when she gets tired, you take over?"

Dalton smiled.

"Sabrina told me you'd arrested someone," he said. "I was just wondering if you've got a suspect in the Summerset Stalker case."

"We haven't arrested anyone," Fraser said.

Dalton raised both eyebrows.

"So, the Belle Harbor police have no suspects in the murder of one of their own detectives?"

He tutted and shook his head.

"That'll give my sister a sensational headline."

"Off the record, I can say we are talking to a person of interest in the investigation. Although we haven't officially named anyone as a suspect. At least, not yet."

The information sparked a light in Dalton's eyes.

"So you think this person of interest knows something about the murders? Has he told you anything?"

"If he had, I couldn't tell you," Fraser said. "I've already said too much. Your sister would have this guy's name and photo all over the evening news, and he's already shaking in his boots. The poor guy thinks he's going to be killed the moment he walks out of here."

Dalton frowned.

"Why is that? Is he a witness? Did he see the Stalker?"

Fraser looked away, hoping to see Bailey's little red car, but the street was empty and Dalton wasn't ready to give up. He was like a dog with a bone.

"Look, it's my sister's job to broadcast other people's business to the world," Dalton said. "I know that, which is why I never tell her anything about the cases I work on. I can assure you, whatever you tell me will be off the record."

He stepped closer and lowered his voice.

"Tell me, Detective. What is the witness afraid of?"

"It's not what he's afraid of," Fraser said. "It's *who*."

Knowing he was probably saying too much, he couldn't resist sharing a final thought.

"All I can say is the witness thinks this guy is going to come after him if he's seen talking to the cops."

"What witness? What guy?" Dalton asked in frustration.

But a little red Camaro had pulled into the lot.

CHAPTER NINETEEN

D alton walked back to his pickup truck as Fraser ran over to the red Camaro and greeted Bailey Flynn. Climbing into the Dodge's cab, he kept his head down as Fraser and the FBI agent walked past him, their voices lowered in urgent conversation. Through the open window, he overheard a snippet of their conversation.

"Cisco Silver met up with Lando Gutierrez," Fraser was saying. "He says the man is crazy and he's scared that-"

The voices died away as they disappeared into the building, leaving Dalton sitting in the truck with a confused frown on his face.

Lando Gutierrez?

The name rang an alarm bell in Dalton's mind.

Tori Cabot's parents had overheard their daughter talking about a guy named Lando.

When he had been helping them search for their missing daughter, the distraught parents had tried to remember anything she could have said that would let them know where she might have gone.

Her mother had overheard Tori telling a friend that she was scared of someone named Lando.

It appeared she wasn't the only one living in fear of Lando. Someone named Cisco Silver was afraid of him, too.

Dalton mulled over the information.

Is Cisco in the police station right now being questioned? Does he have information implicating Lando in the murders?

This could be the lead Dalton had been hoping for.

But how can I find Lando Gutierrez?

He wasn't exactly familiar with the South Florida drug scene. And if Lando was as menacing as he sounded, Dalton couldn't just start asking around on street corners.

Maybe Sid Morley would know.

After all, the older man had been an agent in the FBI's Maimi field office for over two decades before he'd been forced to retire after losing his leg in the line of duty.

Morley had taken on some contract security and investigative work with Dalton over the last year, and he hadn't seemed to have lost any of his connections.

If Lando Gutierrez was a feared drug dealer and criminal in the area, Morley would be the one to help him dig up information on the dealer.

Or at least let me know where to start looking for the lowlife.

Starting the Dodge's engine, Dalton drove to the little house on Mariner's Trail where Morley lived.

As he parked in the driveway, Amadeus came bounding toward him. The sight of the big black German shepherd running straight for him was an intimidating sight.

But the dog only raced around him in a circle, looking for the treats he always brought with him as bribes.

Taking a treat from his jacket pocket, he held it out to

Amadeus, laughing as the dog quickly swallowed it and began sniffing at his hand, wanting more.

A second treat had already joined the first in the dog's stomach by the time Morley made an appearance in the yard.

"What are you doing here?" he asked. "I don't have a doctor's appointment today, so it must mean you're working a case and need my help."

"That's right," Dalton agreed. "I need your help finding a man named Lando Gutierrez."

Morley lifted a thick hand to scratch at his scruffy beard.

"Rumor has it that Lando works for the Tumba Cartel," he said. "They traffic any drug you could want, including Fentanyl, heroin, and cocaine. Lately, they've even been rumored to be pushing Devil's Breath."

Dalton frowned.

"What's Devil's Breath?"

"That's the street name for scopolamine," Morley said.

He saw the confusion on Dalton's face and chuckled.

"It's an odorless sedative that you can snort or even absorb through the skin. It's hard to detect, which is what makes it so dangerous.

"I think they get it off Borrachero trees in Colombia. Or maybe off the flowers on the tree. Either way, the cartels process it into a powder similar to cocaine and sell it.

"It's claimed the drug makes some people highly suggestive and compliant. The Nazis were even rumored to have used it as a truth serum during interrogations.

"In larger doses, it can cause hallucinations and

delusions, and even knock a person out for hours. It's ugly stuff in my opinion, but it's in high demand."

Bending over to give Amadeus another treat, Dalton considered Morley's words.

If Lando was the Stalker, maybe he'd tried to use the Devil's Breath on the women.

Maybe they fought back and that's why he stabbed them.

Dalton glanced up at Morley.

"Do you know where I can find Lando?" he asked.

"I just told you he's part of a dangerous cartel. Why would you want to mess with him?" Morley shot back.

Studying the frown on Morley's face, Dalton wondered if he should share his suspicions.

"I think he might have killed Tori Cabot and the other women," Dalton admitted, unable to resist. "The Belle Harbor police are questioning an associate of his right now. And Tori Cabot's parents told me she was scared of the guy. She refused to testify against him because she thought he'd retaliate. She went to jail instead."

"Okay, so he's a bad guy," Morley said. "I won't argue with you on that point. But a serial killer who's gotten away with three homicides? That doesn't sound like Lando. The guy isn't exactly the subtle type."

"Four homicides," Dalton corrected. "Don't forget Emma Walsh. And according to Cisco Silver, Lando's crazy."

"Cisco Silver?"

Morley let out a belly laugh.

"If you're getting your information from Cisco you're in more trouble than I thought," he said. "The guy's a career criminal who's spent more time in jail than out. You think you can trust him to tell you the truth about anything? Even a scumbag like Lando?"

"And what are you planning to do if you find Lando?" Morley asked. "Do you think he's going to break down and confess to you?"

"Maybe," Dalton said. "If he doesn't know who I am. I could get him talking and-"

"So now you're an undercover agent?"

Morley raised a thick eyebrow.

"You find missing people for a living," he said as if Dalton may have forgotten. "And you're good at it. Why don't you let the police and the FBI do their jobs and you stick to what you know?"

"Lately, all I've been finding are dead bodies," Dalton corrected him. "And the only thing I know for sure is that the man responsible has to be stopped."

✳ ✳ ✳

Dalton followed Morley's directions to Kennard Street and parked his truck along the curb, watching as a steady stream of people came and went from Lando's house.

Ducking down as a tall man with long, dark hair came outside, Dalton glanced over at Morley, who was sitting calmly in the passenger seat.

"Is that him?" Dalton asked.

"Yep, that's the ugly bastard in the flesh," Morley agreed as they watched the dealer walk out to a car.

Leaning into the car, he spoke to the driver, then climbed into the passenger seat.

As the car pulled away, Dalton started the truck's engine.

"What are you doing?" Morley asked.

"I'm following the guy, what do you think I'm doing?"

Ignoring the disapproving shake of Morley's head, Dalton stuck close to the little car, following it all the way to the *Up All Night Smoke Shop* near the Bellamy Beach Boardwalk.

Dalton tried to see into the windows, but they were covered with colorful advertisements and signs hawking lottery tickets.

"I'm going in," he said. "I want to see what he's up to."

Leaving Morley in the truck, Dalton pushed through the door and looked around the small, cluttered shop, trying to listen in as Lando made some sort of plans with the clerk, who had led the drug dealer into the back room.

"I got a shipment coming in on Friday," he was saying. "Jazz can drop off what you need then."

"You still using that dope head Jasmine for deliveries?" the man asked. "Last time she came in she was out of it."

"You trying to tell me how to run my business?" Lando asked in a menacing voice. "Cause my girls are my concern, not yours. You understand?"

"Okay...okay," the clerk said. "I'm just saying...I don't need any trouble around here. I'm only trying to help. Remember what happened with that other girl? What was her name? Hallie?"

Dalton inched closer to the door.

As his boot kicked a display, sending several pipes

tumbling onto the floor, the men stopped talking.

The clerk appeared in the doorway to the back room.

He stared at Dalton in surprise.

"I didn't know anyone was still in here. Something I can help you with, man?"

Dalton held up one of the pipes.

"Yes, I'll take this."

He used cash to pay for the pipe, then turned and left the shop. Risking a look back, he saw Lando Gutierrez standing in the doorway, staring after him with narrowed eyes.

CHAPTER TWENTY

Bailey sat across from Cisco Silver in Interview Room A, listening as Fraser led the self-proclaimed thief through the events of Friday night. So far, all he had admitted to was his trip to the boardwalk, where he'd pickpocketed a half-dozen wallets before heading home.

"Only, you didn't head home, did you?" Fraser asked. "You couldn't have because we found one of those wallets, still loaded with cash and credit card, in the sand dunes where Emma Walsh was found."

He banged both fists on the table.

"Now, if you weren't there, how'd that wallet get there?"

"I must have dropped it," Cisco said, crossing his arms over his chest. "Someone else could have picked it up."

Bailey groaned and stood up, stretching her back.

"This is a waste of time," she said. "Let's just book him on theft and throw him in jail."

"Yeah, and we can make sure his photo is plastered all over the news," Fraser said. "Everyone in Summerset County will know he was talking to the police."

Standing up beside Bailey, he headed toward the door.

"Wait a minute," Cisco said. "I haven't said anything.

Nobody can say I've been grassing anyone up."

"No one out there knows what you've said in here," Fraser reminded him. "You better hope your friend Lando assumes you kept your mouth shut."

Cisco balled his hands into fists.

"Fine, I'll tell you what happened Friday night," he said in a low voice. "But you have to grant me immunity. And you have to put me in witness protection."

Looking over at Fraser, Bailey lifted an eyebrow, but she didn't interrupt as Cisco continued.

"I want to go somewhere nice. Not some dump," he said. "And my Nonna would have to come with me."

"We can't make any promises about witness protection or immunity right now," Bailey admitted. "Not without hearing what it is you have to say."

She watched as Cisco's face fell.

"But if you help us find the person responsible for killing Detective Walsh, and if you agree to testify if needed, Detective Fraser and I will do whatever we can to keep you and your grandmother safe," she added.

Holding her breath, she waited as Cisco stared up at her.

"Okay, fine."

He exhaled and shook his head.

"I *was* on Bellamy Beach Friday night," he conceded. "I was looking for a house Lando had told me about. He said the guy who lived there was loaded and was out of town."

"I found the house with no trouble, but then I heard someone coming and I hid, but I could see that it was Detective Walsh."

Adrenaline shot through Bailey at his words.

He was there. He saw what happened. He saw her killer.

"I thought she was coming after me, but then I overheard her talking on the phone. It sounded like she was planning on meeting someone there. She was telling them to hurry."

"Then this guy came out of nowhere. He had a knife. Detective Walsh tried to pull out her gun, but the guy stopped her. He chased her and...I didn't know what to do."

His breath was coming fast as he continued.

"I thought if I called the police, I'd get in trouble for being out there, but I decided to go after them anyway. I thought maybe I could help."

He dropped his eyes to his fisted hands.

"But when I found her, she was already dead."

The room fell silent for a long beat, then Cisco looked up.

"Just don't name me in the press," he said. "Lando will kill me if he thinks I'm talking to you guys about him."

Bailey's ears perked up at his use of the name.

Now we're really getting somewhere.

She looked over at Fraser and saw the gleam in his eye.

"Tell us about Lando," Fraser said. "Tell us what you know about him so we can get this guy off the street."

"I know he's crazy," Cisco said. "I know he sells drugs and uses young girls as couriers. Only he calls them *mules*."

Cisco shook his head in disgust.

"And I know he brands them. I saw this girl at his house with something burned into her skin. Lando said he does it to mark his *property*. Said he does it to protect them and claims it's easier than a tattoo."

He looked back and forth between Bailey and Fraser.

"That's got to be illegal, right?"

"It sounds like he's using scarification," Fraser said. "That's where you burn or carve a design on skin. It's definitely not legal if it was done against someone's will or if they were coerced into complying."

Bailey held back a shudder as she thought of the autopsy photos she'd seen of the Stalker victims, picturing the patch of flesh cut from their backs.

"You said this mark was burned onto her back?"

Cisco nodded.

"And when and where did you see this girl?"

"This morning, at Lando's house on Kennard Street."

It was the information Bailey had been waiting for.

"Okay, I think that's all for now," she said, trying to hide her eagerness to act on the lead he'd provided. "We'll continue the interview later."

After she'd called in Officer Rourke to take Cisco away, Bailey immediately turned to Fraser.

"Let's go get Lando."

"I'll drive," he agreed, already heading toward the parking lot. "Cisco said Kennard Street, right?"

Fraser drove quickly, but when they arrived outside the little house, there were no cars in the driveway and all the windows were covered.

And when they knocked on the door, no one answered.

CHAPTER TWENTY-ONE

A fist pounded on Lando Gutierrez's front door as the Stalker stood just inside. Leaning back against the cheap, scarred wood, he kept an arm wrapped around Jasmine Blake's emaciated body, pinning her against his chest. A big hand was clamped firmly over her mouth. The idea that Lando had returned home sooner than expected flitted through the Stalker's mind before the voice inside his head dismissed it.

Don't be stupid. Why the hell would he knock on his own door? It must be someone looking to score. Or maybe-

"Mr. Gutierrez?"

A woman called out from the other side of the door.

"This is Special Agent Bailey Flynn with the FBI. I need to ask you a few questions."

The words roused Jasmine, who momentarily resumed her struggle against the Stalker's grip, then fell still again.

Another firm knock caused the wooden door to vibrate. The Stalker felt it tremble against his back just as Jasmine was trembling against his chest.

He jumped as a man called out.

"Lando? Open up, man. We need to talk to you."

There was a moment of silence, then more shouting.

"You really gonna make us come back with a warrant?"

Holding his position, the Stalker leaned his head back against the door and squeezed his eyes shut, listening as boots crunched over gravel and a car door slammed.

Then an engine started.

The Stalker eased his grip and turned to look through the peephole. A black Interceptor was backing onto the street.

"They're gone," he said into the quiet room as he turned his attention back to Jasmine. "Now, where were we?"

"You were just about...to let me go," Jasmine gasped as his hand fell away from her mouth. "When Lando hears about this, he'll...kill you."

He knew her bravado was artificial. A product of the drugs she'd been fed continuously for weeks if not months.

She didn't have enough brain matter left to know that she was in trouble and that he would never let her go.

Not after she had recognized him.

Not after she'd threatened to tell Lando.

Besides, if she was out of the way, all the drugs in the house could be his for the taking.

"Where's the Devil's Breath?" he asked.

Keeping his arm wrapped around her, he held her tight against his chest.

"Tell me where the powder is, and I'll let you go."

"Lando would kill you," she said. "Then he'd kill me."

The thought of the drug dealer *was* unsettling. The man was a violent thug, who would offer up a much fairer fight than the young women the Stalker usually targeted.

But he doubted it would ever come to that.

There was no need for Lando to ever suspect he had been in his house or that he'd stolen his supply.

And of course, there were always more foolish young girls out there willing to act as couriers for Lando.

Jasmine won't be missed for very long and-

The thought was cut short by a sharp elbow in his ribs.

Twisting free from his grip, Jasmine lunged out of reach.

She moved faster than the Stalker had anticipated, racing down the hall to the kitchen, and heading for the back door.

Her hand had already closed around the doorknob when the blade of his father's combat knife sank into her back.

Hot blood spilled over his hand as Jasmine crumpled onto the dirty linoleum. His eyes fell onto the angel wings burned into her back.

A fourth skin for my collection.

Yanking the knife smoothly from her still-warm flesh, he gave a grunt of satisfaction, then lifted the serrated blade and began to carve.

CHAPTER TWENTY-TWO

Zach Walsh sat at the desk in his comfortable study, nursing his second glass of whiskey, despite the early hour. He'd been up all night reviewing Emma's phone records and credit card statements, determined to find a clue as to why she'd been on the beach Friday night.

What did she do to get herself killed?

From what he could see, there were no suspicious calls and nothing to suggest she'd been seeing someone else.

Of course, he'd heard the rumors about her supposed affair, and he'd felt the shift in their relationship.

But all marriages had their ups and downs, didn't they?

With a sigh, he stood and stumbled into the living room, turning on the television to block out the terrible silence that had settled over the house ever since he'd gotten back from his camping to find Emma gone.

That Sunday night had been the worst.

He'd lain awake in their bed, not knowing where she was, not able to reach her on the phone.

Imagining her with another man, he'd tortured himself over what he could have done to make her stray.

Once her body had been found the following night, and

he knew she was lying in the morgue, it had been somehow easier to bear. He'd even managed a few hours of sleep.

But that had been three days ago, and the initial shock was starting to seep away, leaving a cavern of emptiness and silence that he didn't know how to fill.

As she sank onto the sofa, a familiar voice on the television drew his attention.

Sabrina West from Channel 3 News was standing in front of the Belle Habor police station.

"...person of interest has been taken in for questioning in the murder of Detective Emma Walsh, who was found Friday night at Bellamy Beach. Sources tell us..."

Zach grabbed the remote and raised the volume.

"...possible that Detective Walsh was a victim of the Summerset Stalker who is thought to have killed three other local women in the last twelve months."

Jumping to his feet, he began to pace the room, wondering who the police had taken in for questioning.

He stopped abruptly as a loud knock sounded at the door, sending his whiskey sloshing over the rim of his glass.

When he opened the door, his father stood on the step.

"I've been trying to call you all morning," Gavin Walsh said, pushing past him into the house. "Are you okay?"

"No I'm not okay," Zach muttered. "I'm a widower."

Grabbing the whiskey from his son's hand, the judge carried it to the kitchen and poured what was left of the liquid down the sink.

"What are you doing?" Zach called out. "I need that!"

"You don't need to be drinking whiskey at eight o'clock

in the morning," his father protested. "Now, get cleaned up and get dressed. We need to make arrangements."

Zach shook his head.

He was in no mood to make funeral arrangements.

"They've arrested someone for Emma's murder," Zach said. "Do you know who it is?"

Before his father could answer, there was another knock, and then the front door swung open and Tony Brunner strode into the room.

"It smells like crap in here, Zach," he called out as he crossed the room to open a window. "And you look like..."

Catching sight of Zach's father, he hesitated.

"Sorry, Judge Walsh. But I wanted to stop by and check on Zach. He needs to stop wallowing and get back to work."

"I heard they've arrested someone for Emma's murder," Zach said again, this time to Brunner. "Do you know who?"

His partner shook his head.

"I haven't seen the news this morning."

As Zach began pacing again, his father reached out and grabbed his arm, forcing him to stand still.

"I signed a search warrant this morning," the judge said. "For a man suspected of dealing drugs. The police think he may have something to do with Emma's death."

The words struck Zach like a blow.

"Drugs? They think she was killed..."

Suddenly a memory fell into place in his mind. He remembered what Emma had been working on.

It all made sense.

"Emma had been investigating a girl's murder," he said

slowly. "She thought some dealer might be involved."

"Yes, the warrant was for a man named Lando Gutierrez," the judge said. "He's a person of interest."

Brunner frowned at the name.

"Are you sure?" he asked. "I represent Lando and he hasn't called me to say he's been picked up."

Judge Walsh stared at him in dismay.

"You represent a violent drug dealer?"

"He's got a lot of liquid assets," Brunner said unapologetically. "And he pays his bills on time."

Sniffing in disapproval, the judge turned toward Zach.

"Well, I just signed the warrant so I imagine the police won't serve it or pick up Lando for another few hours," he said. "Now, why don't you get in the shower and-"

Zach backed away, pointing toward the door.

"Please just leave, both of you," he said. "I appreciate your concern but I can shower and get dressed by myself. Once I've done that, I'll come see you."

His father started to protest, but Zach steered him toward the door, assuring him he would be alright.

Once his father and his partner were gone, Zach raced back into the study. Sitting in front of his laptop, he signed into the law practice's billing system.

He typed in *Lando Gutierrez.*

Once the client record was displayed on the screen, he jotted down the address and then went upstairs to change.

Before he left his room, he unlocked his gun safe and removed a small Ruger that fit into his jacket pocket.

Hurrying out to his car, he headed west, arriving at

Lando's house on Kennard Street at ten minutes after nine.

He patted the Ruger in his pocket as he walked up to the door, ignoring the rain that had started to sputter, and knocked with a shaky hand.

When no one answered, he tried the knob, but it was locked. Walking around the side of the house, he looked for an open window, stopping when he reached the backyard.

The kitchen door hung open, swinging slowly back and forth in the drizzle, revealing the dim interior within.

Zach slowly walked forward as his hand settled around his gun. Then he stopped and stared down at the thick pool of blood on the kitchen floor.

He stood there for a long beat, then backed away, and pulled out his phone.

CHAPTER TWENTY-THREE

Bailey stood at the edge of Summerset Park Pond, staring across the murky water at Ronin Godfrey. Her bullet had missed its mark this time, and the man was walking toward her on the water, his eyes open, his hands reaching for her. Opening her mouth, Bailey prepared to scream, but then suddenly Godfrey was gone and her phone was buzzing on the bedside table.

Blinking away the remnants of the nightmare, Bailey sat up and looked around the dark room with wide eyes.

The blinds in Cate's study were still drawn and rain was pattering against the window. As she reached for her phone, Bailey saw that it was after nine o'clock.

I must have forgotten to set the alarm.

She glanced down at the phone's display, surprised to see Zach's number. Clearing her throat, she pressed *Accept* and held the phone to her ear.

"I think I found a crime scene," Zach said, sounding far away. "The door was open and there's blood on the floor."

Swinging her legs off the sofa, she felt Ludwig's soft body at her feet. The German shepherd had slept in, too.

"Where are you, Zach?" she asked.

Managing to slide past Ludwig, she opened the blinds.

"I'm on Kennard Street," he said.

She frowned, watching the rain stream down the window as she tried to remember why the name sounded familiar.

Then it hit her.

"You found out about the warrant," she said, knowing his father must have told him. "You went to Lando Gutierrez's house."

"But I didn't do anything," he said. "The blood...it isn't because of me. I didn't do anything."

Trying to think, she flipped on the light switch.

"Wait in your car," she said as she opened her suitcase. "I'll be there as soon as I can."

In the suitcase, she managed to find a pair of black pants and matching jacket that weren't too wrinkled and paired them with a hunter-green blouse.

Strapping on her holster, she made sure her Glock was in place before slipping on the same muddy black boots she'd been wearing all week.

Her hair was beyond help, so she brushed it back into a ponytail and secured it with a rubber band she found lying on the desk in Cate's study before shrugging on her FBI raincoat.

By this time Ludwig was waiting by the door, eager for a chance to go outside. She sheltered under the awning and called Fraser as the dog took care of business.

"Zach Walsh called and said he's at Lando Gutierrez's house on Kennard Street. Claims he discovered what he referred to as a *crime scene*."

Fraser muttered a curse under his breath.

"I'm heading over to the house now," she said. "We've got the warrant so..."

"So, I'll meet you there," Fraser finished for her.

Ending the call, she called to Ludwig and waited for him to get into the tiny backseat, then set off for the highway.

When she turned onto Kennard Street, she saw Zach standing beside his black BMW, his blonde hair wet from the rain, his eyes wide and red-rimmed.

"I didn't do it," he said as soon as she climbed out.

Bailey pulled up the hood of her raincoat as he led her around the side of the house.

She smelled alcohol on his breath as he stopped in the backyard and pointed to the open door

"There's blood...a lot of it...in there."

Footsteps crunched over leaves, coming around the side of the house, and Bailey reached for her Glock.

She dropped her hand when she saw a fair-haired man in a sturdy jacket and boots come around the corner.

Dalton West stopped when he saw Bailey and Zach peering into the kitchen.

"What are you doing here?" Bailey asked.

"I'm a private investigator," he said, sounding offended. "I came here to investigate a lead Sid Morley passed me and I saw your empty car parked out front. I was worried."

She was tempted to ask him what lead he'd been investigating but didn't want to have the conversation in front of Zach, who looked shaky.

"I need both of you to go back to your vehicles," she said.

"This is a matter for law enforcement. In fact, I have a BHPD detective on his way, and he's bringing a warrant."

Dalton raised an impressed eyebrow.

"You sure there's nobody in there?"

"Just the opposite," Bailey said. "Based on the pool of blood I see on the kitchen floor, I'd say there is definitely a body in there. Either that, or someone's taken it away."

She slid her Glock from the holster and nodded toward the side yard.

"Please, see that Zach gets back to his car and tell Detective Fraser I'm back here when he arrives," she said. "I don't want to wait to go in and check the premises, in case there's someone hurt inside."

"You can't go in there without backup," Dalton said.

With the nightmare of Ronin Godfrey still fresh in her mind, Bailey glared over at him.

The look was enough to get Dalton moving backward.

"Alright, whatever you say."

He motioned to Zach.

"You come on with me," he said. "We'll go wait for the police like good little boys."

As the two men disappeared around the corner, Bailey held the Glock up in a ready position and crept steadily toward the kitchen door.

Holding the gun out in front of her, she stepped into the room and cleared it, before taking a long look at the drying puddle on the linoleum.

She knew it only took a loss of about half a gallon of blood to be fatal and estimated there to be substantially more than that on the floor.

Ludwig growled low in his throat as he tried to follow her into the room, his nose twitching in response to the sharp, metallic scent that filled the room.

"Stay, Ludwig," Bailey called out as she inched around the sticky puddle. "Stay back."

Several thick smears of blood led toward the hall, and a stained strip of material had been discarded on the floor.

Moving further into the house, she cleared all the little rooms without finding a body, then returned to the kitchen.

She jumped as she saw a figure standing in the doorway.

"You should have waited for me to go inside," Fraser said, lifting both hands until she'd lowered the gun.

"There's enough blood here to indicate a serious injury," Bailey said. "I just wanted to make sure..."

Her voice trailed off as she saw the look on Fraser's face.

"Whoever left that puddle is no longer breathing and we both know it," he said. "Nothing we can do to change that."

Bailey nodded, then pointed to the scrap of material.

"Looks like someone lost part of their shirt during the attack," she said. "Maybe Ludwig can help us find them."

"Madeline and her CSI team aren't going to like you picking that up or bringing that dog in here," he said.

But Bailey was already calling to the German shepherd.

"Come here, Ludwig," she called, gesturing to the material on the floor. "Scent, boy."

The dog had been trained to work crime scenes. And he carefully stepped around the puddle, before lowering his head to sniff at the stained strip of silk.

Lifting his head into the air, he stood still and sniffed.

"Go find it, Ludwig," Bailey said, stepping back to give him access to the open kitchen door.

It seemed most likely that the attacker had carried the body out the back, leaving the door open behind him.

But Ludwig trotted down the hall and stood just past the bathroom door. He barked and turned in a circle.

"What's wrong with him?" Fraser asked.

The dog barked again and looked up at the ceiling.

Following his gaze, Bailey saw the outline of the trap door leading into the attic.

Stepping forward she flipped on the light in the hall and stared up. A single smear of blood was visible on the faded white wood of the door, which had no string attached.

"Help me open this!" Bailey called, suddenly sure someone was up there and alive. "We've got to open this!"

Her voice rose in panic as the image of a small pink shoe floated behind her eyes.

"Hurry! Get help!"

Fraser disappeared from the doorway, returning minutes later with Dalton West, who was carrying a folded ladder from the back of his truck.

Propping the ladder against the wall, Dalton held it in place as Bailey climbed up and pushed the trap door open, sticking her head into the dark, musty space that smelled of death and decay.

"Use this," Dalton said, handing her up a flashlight.

She turned on the flashlight and aimed it into the dark, revealing the stiff, discolored face of a young woman.

The woman's body had been wrapped in a white sheet and shoved into the attic crawl space.

For one heart-stopping moment, Bailey thought she was looking at Dolores Santos, then her eyes focused and she saw that it was another young girl. A girl with dark, blue-tipped hair and royal blue eye shadow.

Another girl who hadn't been saved.

Working with Fraser and Dalton, she managed to lift the dead girl down and lower her to the floor.

Fraser gently lifted her left shoulder.

Only a raw patch of blood, skin, and bone remained where Lando's mark had been.

CHAPTER TWENTY-FOUR

Mason Knox turned the big medical examiner's van onto Kennard Street and pulled up to the curb behind a Belle Harbor PD cruiser with a bar of flashing lights. He could see the medical examiner's van parked further up the road, but as of yet no reporters or news vans were on the scene.

"Let's go ahead and take the gurney up to the house," he said to Finola, who was pulling on her protective coveralls and adjusting a cap over her coppery hair.

"From what Detective Fraser said, the body and scene have been disturbed, so we may not be here long."

Once the body had been moved and the scene trampled, it was impossible to fully evaluate the body in situ.

They would have a quick look around, take a few photos, and then get the body back to the office for autopsy.

As they rolled the gurney up the driveway, Officer Rourke opened the front door and waved them inside.

"There's blood evidence in the kitchen," he explained. "So, it's best to roll the gurney through this way."

Moving into the living room, Mason saw Fraser and Bailey Flynn standing beside a body wrapped in a sheet.

"We've got a fingerprint," Bailey said as soon as she saw him. "It's up there on the trap door. We found her up in the attic crawl space and lifted her down."

Mason looked up to a bloody smudge on white wood.

"So, the Stalker has finally left us some evidence," he said with obvious satisfaction.

"Let's just hope there's a match in AFIS," Bailey said, her eyes bright with angry anticipation. "If so, we'll know who the Stalker is within the next twenty-four hours. Although I'm pretty sure we've got our guy."

Moving toward the body, Mason knelt and used a gloved hand to pull back the sheet.

"Her name is Jasmine Blake," Bailey said. "She had a school ID in her pocket. Poor girl is only eighteen."

With Finola's help, he turned the victim over, revealing a familiar-looking stab wound in her back, as well as a missing patch of skin.

"We interviewed a witness yesterday who said he'd seen a brand on the left shoulder of a girl in this house," Bailey told him in a quiet voice. "We got a warrant based on that information and look what we found."

"A brand? Like a brand you put on livestock?" he asked.

Bailey nodded.

"Our witness claimed a design that looked like angel wings had been burned or carved onto her back. Said that our suspect called it *scarification*."

Now Mason understood why she looked so angry.

"Apparently, the guy said he was putting his mark on his couriers to *protect* them."

As Mason tried to absorb the information, he heard an angry shout outside. He jumped to his feet as the front door flew open to reveal a tall, rangy man with long, dark hair and small, mean eyes.

As he stood in the doorway, staring at the body on the floor, Bailey pulled out her Glock and aimed it at his heart.

"Just give me a reason to pull this trigger, Mr. Gutierrez," she said, her blue eyes cold as ice. "I won't hesitate to put a bullet through your heart, just as you put a knife through this girl's heart."

"What the hell is going on here?" Lando demanded.

He turned to see Officer Rourke aiming a gun directly at his head.

"Lando Gutierrez, you're under arrest for the murder of Jasmine Blake," Fraser said. "Officer Rourke will cuff you and escort you to the cruiser."

"This is insane!" Lando shouted as Rourke roughly pulled back his hands and snapped on handcuffs.

Before he knew what he was doing, Mason dropped down on one knee and pulled back the sheet covering Jasmine Blake's body.

"No, what's really insane is stabbing a young woman in the back and cutting flesh off her body," he yelled in a deep voice that reverberated around the small room.

Lando stared at Mason in shock, then lowered his eyes.

"I didn't do...*that*," he said, his voice cracking. "I wouldn't have done that to Jazz. She was my...my girl."

"I thought she was your *mule*," Bailey said as she slid her Glock back into her holster. "Or was she your *property*?"

Her blue eyes blazed.

"Isn't that why you branded her?"

She stepped toward Lando, staring up into his face.

"But why did you cut off the brand?" she said. "Were you trying to hide who she was? Or was that your way of saying you were done using her?"

The drug dealer shook his head.

"Sure, I put my mark on her," he said, his voice now sullen and defensive. "But I didn't kill her or anyone else."

He nodded toward a chest of drawers.

"You can see my mark in that drawer," he said. "It was no big deal. Just something I won at the Summerset County Fair a few years back."

Fraser crossed to the drawer and slowly pulled it open as if he thought something might jump out at him.

Reaching inside, he pulled out a heavy brass belt buckle in the shape of wide wings.

"As soon as I saw it I knew it would make a good branding iron," he said. "You know, to make sure everyone knows who these girls work for, just in case they get any big ideas about double-crossing me."

"So, you admit you mutilated Jasmine Blake with this?"

Lando shook his head, sending his dark hair, still damp from the rain, flying around his face.

"It's not mutilation, it scarification," he said indignantly. "Some dealers use tattoos, but that takes too long and it's too much of a hassle. With that buckle, all you have to do is hold the metal over an open flame for five or ten minutes and you're good to go."

Mason stared at the man in disgust and confusion. He'd mutilated Jasmine, that was clear. But had he killed her?

If so, why had he looked so shocked? And why kill someone who's making you money if you're a dealer?

Studying Lando, Mason noted there was no blood on his clothes or shoes. No blood on his hands or under his nails.

And why come back to the scene of the crime if you know the charge for getting caught would be serial murder, and the penalty would be death?

Something just wasn't adding up.

"Put him in the cruiser," Fraser ordered. "And be sure to read him his rights. We'll take him to the station and question him there."

As Rourke led Lando out of the room, Mason and Finola lifted the body onto the gurney and rolled it to the van.

Mason was closing the back door to the van, glad to see that the rain had finally stopped when Cate Flynn ducked under the crime scene tape.

"Where's my sister?" she said. "Bailey called and told me what happened. Where is she?"

The prosecutor's eyes fell on the police cruiser and the man in the back seat.

"Is that him?" she asked. "Is that the Stalker?"

Suddenly, Mason wasn't so sure.

"Lando Gutierrez is definitely a psychopath," Mason said. "But I'm not convinced he killed that girl in there...or any of the others. And I'm not convinced he's the Stalker."

CHAPTER TWENTY-FIVE

Cate stared at Mason Knox in surprise. Based on everything Bailey had told her, she'd been sure they had their killer. After all, the latest victim's body had been found in Lando's house, and he had admitted to branding them with his own belt buckle. How much more evidence did Mason need?

She followed Mason toward the front of the van.

I don't know how you can doubt they've got the right guy," she said. "It's obvious Lando removed the angel wings he'd branded on those poor women to try to hide their identities."

She spoke slowly as if speaking to a small child.

"And he didn't want anyone to connect the girls back to him. He even tried to hide his latest victim in the attic until he could throw out her body. But he didn't count on Ludwig."

She looked around for the German shepherd, wanting to give him a hug. When she looked back at Mason, he was frowning over at the police cruiser.

"It's a logical conclusion," he admitted. "But the bloody fingerprint will tell us if it's the right conclusion."

He cleared his throat, knowing he was probably wasting his breath, but willing to give it a try.

"It's just that I didn't see blood on Lando's hands, or his clothes, or shoes when they arrested him," he said. "It was a lot of blood. It'd be hard to get it all off."

"And when Lando first saw Jasmine...when he saw the skin missing, he seemed genuinely shocked."

The comment earned an eye roll from Cate.

"Ok, maybe he's a great actor," Mason said. "But what's his motivation? Why kill the women who work for you?"

Cate hesitated, not sure how much she should say. She had promised Judge Walsh she wouldn't share the information in the victims' files outside the task force. But then Mason was the medical examiner.

She lowered her voice, thinking of the disturbing details uncovered during the Offender Review Commission investigations.

"All the women previously worked for Lando Gutierrez as couriers," she said. "They were his victims long before their deaths. Then, when they left him and tried to rebuild their lives, he hunted them down and killed them."

The crease between Mason's dark eyes told her he still wasn't convinced.

"So, you really don't believe he's our guy?" Cate asked. "You don't think Lando is the Summerset Stalker?"

Mason shook his head.

"No, I don't," he said. "Although I hope I'm wrong."

"Why is that?"

"Because if Lando isn't the man who killed these women,

then I can expect more victims on my dissecting table."

"You performed the autopsies on all the others?"

He nodded.

"And now I need to go prepare for another one."

Cate watched him climb into the van and pull away, while also keeping one eye on the cruiser where Lando Gutierrez was staring out with hate-filled eyes.

Turning around, she saw Madeline Mercer coming toward her. The CSI team leader wore protective coveralls and a cap over her dark hair.

"She must have followed you over here," Madeline teased as she nodded toward Sabrina West, who had pulled up in a Channel 3 News van.

"Is this another Stalker victim?" the reporter called out. "Can you give us her name?"

Madeline ignored the reporter as she stepped closer to Cate and lowered her voice.

"Have you seen Fraser?" she asked. "I've been trying to reach him. Digital forensics say they've gotten what they can from Emma Walsh's burner phone."

"Burner phone?" Cate asked with a frown.

"Yep, she had an unregistered phone in her pocket," Madeline said. "Fraser's been after me to find out who Emma called the day she died."

Cate raised her eyebrows.

"Okay, so who'd she call?"

"According to the examiner, she made two calls just before midnight on Friday night. Those were likely the last calls before her death."

"One call was to an unregistered burner phone. The other call was made to a number registered to Anthony Brunner."

"Why would Emma be calling her husband's business partner in the middle of the night?" Cate murmured. "You don't think she could have been..."

"Could have been what?"

Bailey had appeared at her shoulder.

"According to Madeline, Emma made two calls the night she died using a burner phone," Cate admitted. "One of those calls was to Tony Brunner. So, I was just wondering if he could be the man she'd been seeing on the side."

CHAPTER TWENTY-SIX

Bailey was still turning Cate's words over in her head as she followed Fraser into the Belle Harbor Police Department. Had Emma really been sleeping with Zach's law partner? And if it was true, had Zach known about the affair? Could his wife's infidelity be considered a motive for murder?

As Fraser led her down the hall to the interview room where Lando Gutierrez was waiting, she pushed the disturbing question to the back of her mind.

"Mr. Gutierrez, I'm Detective Jimmy Fraser with the Belle Harbor PD, and this is Special Agent Bailey Flynn with the FBI. We'll be interviewing you today in connection to the homicide of Jasmine Blake."

Sinking into a chair across from the dealer, Bailey studied the man's close-set eyes and long, uneven nose, which she suspected had been broken more than once.

"This interview is being recorded," Fraser added. "Now, do you have any questions before we get started?"

Lando's wide mouth twisted into a nasty sneer, revealing a set of sharp, tobacco-stained teeth.

"Yeah, I want to know why you all were in my house," he

said. "Cause when I left there last night, Jazz was alive. I come back today and find the place swarming with cops and she's dead."

He glared at Bailey.

"Something doesn't add up."

Before Bailey could respond, he added the words she'd been hoping not to hear. At least not before they'd gotten a chance to get Lando's story out of him.

"You all are trying to set me up, but I know my rights, and I'm not saying anything else without a lawyer."

Fraser met Bailey's eyes over the table.

"Officer Rourke allowed Lando to make a call to his attorney," he said. "I believe Mr. Brunner is on his way."

A knock sounded on the door before she could reply and Rourke stuck his head in.

"Tony Brunner's here to meet with his client," he said. "You want me to show him in?"

Nodding reluctantly, Bailey leaned back in her chair as Brunner was led into the room and sat beside his client.

"Mr. Brunner, hopefully, you've had a chance to review the charges against your client," Fraser said. "He's being charged with one count of first-degree murder."

"As our investigation continues, the charges may very well expand to include murder charges for four other homicide victims in Summerset County, including Wren Dempsey, Tori Cabot, Hallie Kwan, and Emma Walsh."

"And we'll be considering adding trafficking and felony battery charges based on the information discovered over the last twenty-four hours."

Nodding gravely, Brunner steepled his hands.

"My client vigorously denies all charges," he said. "And we have serious concerns about the legality of the warrant issued, considering the judge who signed it is the father-in-law of a supposed victim of my client."

Bailey stared at Brunner with contempt.

"With or without the warrant, we were in the house legally," she said. "We were there responding to a call for medical help at your client's residence."

"Someone called 911?" Brunner asked.

He flashed her an innocent smile, making it clear he already knew that Zach had made the call.

"No, not exactly," she admitted. "I was contacted directly by a concerned citizen."

Brunner raised a surprised eyebrow.

"Someone called your personal phone about a medical emergency?"

He seemed intrigued.

"Are you a doctor?"

"Stop the games," Fraser said, slapping his hand on the table. "Who called who about what doesn't matter. Police responded to your client's house and found the dead body of a woman your client admitted to mutilating and trafficking."

Lifting a long finger, Brunner wagged it in the air.

"Oh, I disagree," he said. "It's all very relevant. Because my client obviously feels as if he's been set up."

"Who would want to set you up, Lando?" Bailey asked. "You think someone broke into your house and killed an innocent woman just to get at you?"

The dealer glared back at Bailey and his nostrils flared with anger as he met her eyes.

"Someone probably wanted my stash and Jazz was just collateral damage. They tried to make it look as if I killed her so I would be banged up and couldn't come after them."

"When you say *stash*, are you talking about drugs?"

Brunner held up a hand before Lando could answer.

"My client is not saying there were drugs in the house. However, someone might have assumed there would be."

"And who would this person be? The one who assumed there were drugs and killed Jasmine Blake?" Bailey asked.

Leaning forward, Lando spit out the name.

"Cisco Silver."

He banged a fist on the table.

"That little punk came by and tried to chat up Jazz the other day," he said. "And he doesn't have enough cash to buy pills and –"

"And he probably made an assumption there may be pills at Lando's house," Brunner finished for him.

Tired of the lawyer's word games, Bailey sighed.

"We have a fingerprint from the scene," she said. "A fingerprint in the victim's blood. Once we get that tested, we'll know if Lando left the print or if Cisco Silver or some other perp did. It won't be long before we have answers."

Fraser nodded his agreement and turned to Brunner.

"In the meantime, we'll be holding your client on charges related to the large quantity of illegal substances found in his residence during today's search."

Lando started to protest but Fraser called in Rourke, who quickly led the dealer away.

As Brunner stood and prepared to follow his client out, Bailey cleared her throat.

"We'd like you to stay and answer a few questions," she said. "Questions related to Emma Walsh's homicide."

* * *

Brunner sat stiffly in the chair across from Bailey and Fraser, his amused, sardonic attitude slipping a little as a drop of sweat rolled down his permanently tanned face.

"We know about the call you received from Emma Walsh on Friday night," she said. "Your partner's wife was calling you using a burner phone."

Looking down at a printout on the table, Bailey frowned.

"It seems she called you just before she was killed."

She hesitated, waiting for an explanation. When he didn't offer one, she continued.

"So, we're curious to know why she called you and what you talked about."

More beads of sweat had formed on Brunner's forehead and he lifted a hand to wipe them away.

"Don't you have anything to say?" Fraser asked. "Or would you like to call a lawyer?"

Before Brunner could respond, there was a knock on the door and Madeline Mercer stuck her head inside.

"Sorry to bother you, Agent Flynn. Can I have a word?"

Bailey nodded and joined the CSI team leader in the hall,

closing the door behind her.

"Sorry to interrupt you, but I thought you'd want to know as soon as possible," Madeline said. "The bloody print lifted from the Jasmine Blake scene doesn't match Lando Gutierrez."

The words caused Bailey's stomach to sink.

"Then whose print could it be?"

"I don't know," Madeline admitted. "There was no match found in AFIS. Whoever the Stalker is, it looks as if he doesn't have a record."

Turning glumly on her heel, Bailey went back into the interview room, where Brunner was looking pale.

"Listen, this is a delicate matter," he was saying to Fraser. "Zach is my partner. I never meant to hurt him."

"So, in order *not* to hurt him, you slept with his wife?" Fraser said.

Bailey gaped at Brunner.

"You admit it? You were having an affair with Emma?"

"I think the word *affair* is a bit too grand a word for what was going on," Brunner said. "We were simply having some fun. It was no big deal."

He shifted in his chair.

"In fact, we were already having problems," he admitted. "She was mad at me for representing Lando when she was investigating him in relation to a case she was working on."

"What case?" Bailey asked, instantly suspicious. "What did she think Lando was guilty of?"

The lawyer wiped more sweat from his forehead.

"As Lando's attorney, I'd prefer not to say," he replied

stiffly. "But I'm sure the details are in Emma's files. Suffice it to say she didn't think Lando was a good man. And she was angry he was using the beach house."

"The beach house?"

Both Fraser and Bailey said the words at the same time.

Brunner nodded.

"There's a beach house not far from the boardwalk. It's owned by one of my former clients. He lets me use the house when he isn't in town.

"Use the house for what?" Bailey asked.

The lawyer shrugged.

"To socialize and party," he said. "Emma and I met there sometimes. Then she got mad because I let Lando come over and hang out while we discussed his case."

"I bet you did," Fraser said. "He probably brought a few of those young girls he has working for him, too."

Brunner shook his head.

"It wasn't like that," he said. "But Emma had been acting weird. I thought she was still mad about Lando. We were planning to meet there Friday night, but then she called and canceled our plans. I never heard from her again."

Falling silent, he dropped his eyes to his hands.

"Did Emma tell you why she canceled?" Bailey asked

"She said she'd gotten a new lead on that homicide she was working on and wanted to follow up," Brunner said.

Fraser sighed and shook his head.

"Why didn't you tell us any of this earlier?" he asked. "It looks bad. It looks like you have things to hide."

"I didn't say anything because I'm a good guy," Brunner said. "I didn't want to break Zach's heart. Not when the information wouldn't help find Emma's killer."

Leaning forward, Fraser stared directly at Brunner.

"You didn't worry that sleeping with his wife would break the guy's heart?"

"It was either me or someone else," Brunner said as he shifted in his chair. "Emma was a damaged woman. I've known women like her before. Always looking for someone to fix whatever's broken inside them. But no one man can ever do the trick."

Balling her hands into fists, Bailey felt her anger and outrage growing.

"I always thought that was why Zach was attracted to her in the first place," Brunner went on. "He liked it that she needed him. At least, until she decided he wasn't enough. That's when she turned to me. She would have moved on eventually. Women like her always do."

He shrugged his shoulders.

"In fact, I figured that's what she'd been doing Friday night," he said. "I thought the bit about the lead on her case was just an excuse. I figured she'd found her next fix."

Bailey exhaled slowly, trying to control her temper.

"Are you done disparaging the victim?" she asked in a cold voice. "Because we need to move on now and collect your prints and DNA."

The lawyer seemed startled by the request. He studied her clenched jaw and hard eyes, then sighed.

"Look, I'm sorry. I shouldn't have said any of that. But I

didn't do this," Brunner said, reaching out to touch her arm. "I would never have hurt Emma. I give you my word."

"I don't need your word," Bailey said, jerking her arm away. "I need your fingerprints and a DNA sample. Oh, and an alibi for Friday night would help, too."

Brunner's back stiffened and he started to shake his head in automatic denial.

"If you refuse, we'll request a warrant," Bailey told him as she got to her feet. "I'm sure Judge Walsh will grant the request once he hears you were the last person his daughter-in-law called the night she died."

CHAPTER TWENTY–SEVEN

Fraser didn't try to stop Bailey as she left the room, banging the door shut behind her. He couldn't blame her for being upset and emotional after hearing Brunner's story. And Emma's death must be causing her all sorts of conflicting emotions. How could it not? First Bailey's fiancé had left her for Emma, her best friend, and then she found out Emma had betrayed them both.

Turning his eyes back to Brunner, Fraser sighed.

"Is there anything else you can tell me about Emma?" he asked. "Anything that would further the investigation?"

The lawyer hesitated as if struggling with his conscience.

"Emma did share certain details about the investigation she had conducted into Tori Cabot's death," he finally said. "She'd discovered a connection to her own past."

He sucked in a deep breath.

"You see, Tori Cabot wasn't the only one who had a sealed record. Emma confessed that she'd also gotten into some trouble as a teenager, although she wouldn't tell me what kind."

Fraser raised an eyebrow as Brunner continued.

"She just said that she could understand girls like Tori,"

he added. "The case seemed sort of...*personal* to her."

As if reading the skepticism on Fraser's face, Brunner sighed and sat back in his chair.

"I'll give you my prints and DNA," he declared. "I don't want you wasting time on me or Lando when the person who killed Emma is still out there."

His voice softened.

"She was a complicated woman, but I did care about her. And I do want you to find out who killed her. Zach deserves to have at least that. He deserves closure."

Fraser thought of Zach and sighed.

Emma's husband would expect an update. And he would have to be told about Brunner and Emma's affair. It was bound to come out sooner or later. The man's grief was about to be complicated by betrayal.

Deciding that could wait for now, he picked up the phone and called Madeline Mercer.

"Tony Brunner is ready to give us a DNA sample and prints," he said. "I could use your help."

"You've got it," Madeline said. "I'm on my way."

* * *

After Madeline had taken Brunner away, Fraser called Linette, bracing himself for his wife's disappointment.

He would be late again.

"I'll be home as soon as I can," he assured her.

"I've heard that before," she sighed. "Oh, and Sasha still has a stomachache. I told her you'd stop at the drugstore on the way home and bring her some Pepto-Bismol."

When he hung up and turned around, Madeline had opened the door and was standing behind him.

"I've taken Brunner's prints and DNA," she said. "We should have results on the prints back tomorrow."

"Thanks, Madeline."

Instead of walking away, she hesitated.

"I'm not sure if you knew, but Emma and I had been friends," she said. "We're the only ones who still smoke, so we ended up talking out in the back. I guess it'll just be me out there from now on."

"I didn't know Emma was still smoking," Fraser said. "I thought she'd quit a long time ago."

Madeline's mouth turned up in a half smile.

"She asked me not to tell you," she admitted. "She didn't want you to be disappointed in her. She said you'd been a good mentor. She was determined to earn your respect."

Her smile faded.

"She told me she figured pretty much everyone else at work hated her. That they either thought she was a home wrecker or that she'd slept with the chief to get her promotion."

"That's not fair," Fraser protested. "She was good at her job. Real good. She deserved that promotion."

Madeline nodded.

"I agree. But Emma was insecure. I think she just felt as if she didn't deserve the promotion. Or her marriage for that matter," she said. "She worried Zach felt as if he'd made a mistake by marrying her instead of Bailey. She didn't want kids, you see. And he'd started talking to her about having a family."

Her voice turned wistful.

"Though she didn't want kids of her own, she always said what lovely girls you had. But she knew you were getting grief from your wife about never being home. I know she tried to handle after-hours calls by herself if she could. So you wouldn't have to come out."

Fraser felt a pang of guilt.

Had Emma been trying to follow up on a lead without him so he could keep the peace with Linette?

Was that why she'd been out there on her own?

If he'd been there, would she be alive now?

"Anyway, I'm going to go home," Madeline said. "I just wanted to let you know you aren't the only one around here who cared about Emma. Sure, she made some mistakes, but she was a good person and a good detective."

Once Madeline had gone, Fraser walked out to his Interceptor and headed home, stopping off at the drugstore on the way to buy the Pepto-Bismal.

When he walked into the house, Linette was in the kitchen making dinner, still wearing the suit she'd worn to her last showing of the day.

"Take that medicine to Sasha," she called out.

Sasha was lying on her bed, staring at the wall when he walked into her bedroom.

"I brought you something," he said. "Mommy says it'll make you all better."

Turning to stare up at him with wide, brown eyes, his

daughter shook her head.

"That won't help."

"Why not?"

She was silent as he sat next to her on the bed.

"What is it, Sasha? What's wrong?"

"I'm scared, Daddy," she said, suddenly sitting up and wrapping her thin arms around him. "The play is tomorrow night, and I have to get up on stage in front of everyone."

Her little body shivered in his arms.

"What if I mess up?"

The soft words were muffled by his shirt, but he suddenly understood.

"You're scared of getting on stage?"

Nodding solemnly, her eyes flicked toward the door.

"Don't tell Mommy," she said. "She thinks I'm brave."

Tears stood in her eyes.

"You are brave," Fraser said. "But being brave isn't what most people think it is."

Taking her hand in his, he sighed.

"My father always told me that being brave doesn't mean you aren't scared of doing something. It means you're scared but you do it anyway. It means you're strong enough to face your fears."

"Are you scared sometimes?" Sasha asked.

"Yeah, I am," he said. "But don't tell Mommy."

The words prompted a giggle.

"And, you know what? It's easier to be brave when you have someone else with you," he said. "So, how about tomorrow night, if you get scared, you look out into that audience and know I'm there and that you're not alone."

"Okay," she said as she gave him another tight hug. "But, Daddy? You won't have to work late, will you?"

Fraser returned the hug.

"Not tomorrow, honey."

"You'll be there? You promise?"

He hesitated for only a moment, then nodded.

"I promise."

CHAPTER TWENTY-EIGHT

Sabrina stood on Kennard Street, pacing up and down the sidewalk, keeping an eye on the house where the Summerset County CSI team was still working. Based on Bailey Flynn's earlier presence at the scene, Sabrina was convinced the Summerset Stalker had killed again, but so far they'd released no information about the latest victim.

Checking her watch, she knew she couldn't wait any longer. Otherwise, she'd be late for the interview she'd scheduled with Tori Cabot's parents.

Paul and Robin Cabot had agreed to sit down for an on-camera interview as part of a special Sabrina was producing on the Summerset Stalker.

She found the grieving parents sitting on the front porch watching the sun go down when she arrived and quickly captured the poignant moment to use in the segment.

"Thank you both for being part of this special," Sabrina said as she attached the video camera to a tripod and focused it on the couple. "Why don't you tell our viewers about Tori? Tell us what happened to your daughter."

Dabbing her eyes with a tissue, Robin Cabot nodded.

"Tori was always such a sweet child," she said. "And

very well behaved. But then in high school, she started hanging with the wrong crowd."

Her mouth tightened at the memory.

"She started experimenting with drugs and ended up spending time at the county detention center. But then she went through rehab and we thought she'd finally turned her life around."

Sabrina continued to record as Robin started to cry.

"When she went missing, we knew something bad must have happened. She wouldn't leave home willingly despite what the police suggested."

Putting an arm around his wife's shoulders, Paul cut in.

"That's when we called West Investigations. They tracked down our daughter. They used phone records and even search dogs. Never charged us anything."

Robin nodded beside him.

"Mr. West helped us bring home our little girl and lay her to rest," she said. "Although, we still don't know who did this terrible thing to her or why."

Holding out a tissue box, Sabrina arranged her face into a somber expression.

"I know it must be upsetting to talk about, but do you know why the Stalker would target your daughter?"

Dabbing at her eyes, Robin shrugged.

"I keep thinking she must have met someone at Ashworth who lured her away. The place was bad news. She wouldn't talk about it but I got the impression she had a terrible time there."

Sabrina frowned.

"Ashworth?"

"That's the rehab center she was assigned to after she left the detention center," Robin said. "The Ashworth Recovery Center is where most offenders in Summerset County go after they've served time for a drug offense. It's court-mandated so they don't have a choice."

Making a mental note to look into the place, Sabrina continued asking questions and providing tissues for another ten minutes.

When she had enough footage, she thanked the tear-stained couple for their time and climbed back into her van.

As she merged back onto the highway, she called Dalton. Her brother picked up on the second ring.

"Hey, little sister, what's up?"

"I just wrapped up an interview with Tori Cabot's parents," Sabrina said. "They mentioned Tori stayed at this rehab facility called Ashworth Recovery that she hated. They think she may have met the person who killed her there."

"So, I want to visit the place tomorrow and try to find out what happened to Tori. Her parents said almost all drug offenders in the county end up there. I'm thinking maybe the other Stalker victims were in there, too."

"It sounds dangerous," Dalton said.

"That's why I'm taking my big bro with me," Sabrina said in her sweetest little sister voice. "We'll leave at nine."

* * *

Dalton called at nine o'clock sharp and asked Sabrina if

she was ready for him to come pick her up.

"Yep, I'm ready," she said, grabbing her camera bag.

Two minutes later, he was knocking on her door, freshly showered, and wearing his usual gun and holster under his jacket.

It didn't take long to walk across the courtyard from his apartment to hers. They'd been neighbors for over a year now, although it hadn't necessarily been Sabrina's choice.

Three years earlier, when she'd been an entry-level reporter at a small station in Willow Bay, Florida, she'd accepted a position with Channel 3 News thinking a move to Miami would provide her with greater opportunities for excitement and advancement.

At the time, her brother had been living with their ailing father in Dallas, using their childhood home as a base for his bounty-hunting business.

She hadn't expected that her father would die so soon, or that his dying wish would be for his two children, the only family he was leaving behind, to reconnect and watch out for each other once he was gone.

Arriving in Miami without warning six weeks later, Dalton had taken his father's wish seriously, moving in next door to Sabrina at the Armory Apartments in order to start rebuilding the brother-sister relationship that had been on pause ever since Dalton had joined the military fresh out of high school.

While Sabrina had stubbornly vowed to continue living her life just as she had before, she had to admit she had gotten used to having a big brother nearby.

It was actually kind of nice to have someone to talk to when she got home from work or to help out when needed.

And the fact that Dalton was ex-military with a background in security, bounty hunting, and search and rescue operations, meant he was more than qualified for the mission she had planned for today.

"We'll take your truck," she said, looking over at the Dodge. "It'll be less conspicuous than the news van."

"Are we on a covert operation?" Dalton asked, amused.

"Yes, it's so secret that I can't tell you about it until we get there," Sabrina shot back. "Now, shut up and drive."

Twenty minutes later Dalton steered the big truck onto Windhaven Way. The Ashworth Recovery Center sat in a cul-de-sac at the end of the street.

A wooden security fence surrounded the property. As they approached in the Dodge, the gate swung open and a car exited, giving Dalton a chance to roll through before it closed behind them.

There were no trees, bushes, or flowerbeds to soften the harsh lines of the squat, single-story building.

Sabrina read the *Ring Bell for Entry* sign, then tried the handle anyway. After finding the door locked, she decided to knock. When she got no response from inside, she gave up and rang the bell.

A man with thick, shoulder-length hair appeared at the door wearing a loose cotton caftan over wide-legged pants. The flip-flops on his feet appeared to be made out of cork.

Sabrina wondered if his feet were cold as she produced a wide television-ready smile.

"Good morning, I'm Sabrina West, a reporter with Channel 3 News, and I'm producing a special on local heroes in the community."

The man stared at her blankly, demonstrating none of the instant enthusiasm people usually showed when they thought they might get on TV.

"I was hoping to interview Nigella Ashworth for tonight's segment," she said, thinking back to the research she'd done on the center the night before. "I understand she owns the center?"

"She's not here," the man said. "I'm Neil, her son. I manage the facility."

He looked over her shoulder to where Dalton was standing and raised an inquisitive eyebrow.

"Oh, that's just my colleague," Sabrina said. "He's helping me conduct the interviews for the segment."

Suddenly, she clapped her hands as if she'd just had a wonderful idea and turned to Dalton.

"I know, why don't you interview Mr. Ashworth here for our segment?" she said. "If he runs this place he's as much of a hero as his mother is. You could interview him out here where it's so nice and...scenic."

Looking around for something that looked remotely scenic, she settled on a concrete bench under the overhang.

"You two sit here and I'll work the video camera," she said, setting up the tripod. "Go ahead and get started, the camera is already recording."

She backed up and smiled as Dalton asked Neil Ashworth how long the facility had been open.

"That's perfect," Sabrina said. "You two keep going. I'm just going to use the ladies' room."

Hurrying into the building, Sabrina walked past the sign for the ladies' room and continued down the hall until she found a door with *Manager's Office* on the nameplate.

She opened the door and stuck her head inside, quickly crossing to the desk, behind which a life-sized portrait of Nigella Ashworth hung on the wall.

The councilwoman, whom Sabrina had met many times before and didn't like, seemed to be watching her from the portrait, following her with cold and calculating eyes as she sank down into the chair in front of the computer.

Clicking on an icon labeled *Resident Registration*, Sabrina typed in Tori Cabot's name, followed by Hallie Kwan, and Wren Dempsey. Just as she suspected, all three women had been court-ordered residents at the center.

They'd all completed the rehab program and checked out as scheduled without any apparent incidents.

Sabrina stood to leave, then impulsively sat back down.

Maybe all the Stalker's victims came here...

Typing in Emma Walsh's name, she pressed *Enter*.

No record was found.

Of course not. She was a cop. She couldn't have a record or they wouldn't have hired her. Unless...

She typed in Emma's maiden name.

Emma Kaminski.

She was astounded to see a record. Emma had been a court-ordered patient in the facility a dozen years earlier.

Hearing footsteps in the hall, Sabrina jumped up and

hurried out of the office, expecting Neil Ashworth or his mother to be standing there threatening to call the police.

But the footsteps belonged to a young woman with wide, haunted eyes who froze in place as she saw Sabrina as if she'd been caught somewhere she shouldn't be, then turned and fled in the other direction.

Walking back outside, Sabrina saw Neil and Dalton still talking on the bench. When she approached, she heard her brother saying something about transcendental meditation as his benchmate listened with rapt attention.

"I just got a call from the news station," she said. "Unfortunately, we've got to go. But I'll let you know if we can use your footage on the segment."

As Dalton escorted her back to the truck, Sabrina told him what she'd found out in a furtive whisper.

"Emma Walsh used to be a court-ordered resident here," she hissed. "Only back then she was Emma Kaminski."

As she climbed into the passenger seat, she noted a familiar disapproving expression on her brother's face.

"You weren't supposed to be searching through those records without authorization," he reminded her. "It's illegal, not to mention dangerous. If you really think the person who killed Emma is involved with Ashworth Recovery, you could be putting yourself in danger."

Sabrina thought of Nigella Ashworth's cold eyes.

The woman is certainly not a local hero.

But was she or someone at the rehab center a serial killer? Of that, Sabrina couldn't be sure.

CHAPTER TWENTY-NINE

Bailey ran behind Ludwig in the Friday morning sunshine. It had been a full week since Emma had gone missing, and Bailey wasn't sure they were any closer to finding the man who'd killed her. Now that she knew Lando Gutierrez wasn't a match to the bloody print they'd found near Jasmine Blake's body, she was doubtful the drug dealer was the Stalker after all.

Her phone buzzed in her pocket just as she and Ludwig were walking back into Cate's apartment, both breathing hard from the run.

Madeline Mercer's name appeared on the display.

"The print lifted at the Kennard Street crime scene isn't Brunner's," she said. "We're still waiting for the DNA results to see if he matches blood recovered at the scene."

"Okay, thanks for letting me know."

Ending the call, Bailey wasn't sure if she was disappointed or relieved that Emma's lover and Zach's law partner wasn't the Stalker.

Of course, he could still have killed Emma. There could still be two different killers out there...

As she followed Ludwig into the kitchen, she saw Cate

sitting at the table, still wearing her robe, cradling a steaming cup of coffee in both hands.

"Who was that on the phone?" Cate asked with a yawn. "And what were they letting you know?"

Realizing she'd never updated her sister as to her interview with Tony Brunner the night before, Bailey sank into a chair at the table and sighed.

"Turns out Tony Brunner was the man Emma was seeing behind Zach's back," she said. "Based on that, and his connection with Lando, we tested Brunner's prints and DNA, just to eliminate him as a suspect."

Cate stared over the rim of her coffee mug with wide green eyes and Bailey braced herself for a cutting comment about Emma and her infidelity.

She was relieved when, for once, her sister kept her opinion to herself. Perhaps Cate had realized it was bad luck to speak ill of the dead.

Though I speak ill of the dead all the time. At least in my head.

The thought brought with it a vision of Ronin Godfrey's leering face and the gaping bullet hole between his eyes.

Godfrey's terrible deeds and his violent end were never far from Bailey's mind, nor was the rage that always came with her memories of that day, despite her assurance to everyone else that she'd let go of the anger and moved on.

She'd taken a man's life, but felt no remorse, only fury.

Is there something wrong with me?

She thought back to the day she'd visited Morley in the Summerset Medical Center after he'd lost his leg.

After she'd admitted she'd never shot anyone before,

much less killed a man, Morley had reached out a weak hand to grip her wrist and had spoken aloud what she hadn't allowed herself to think.

"Some men deserve to die. Godfrey was one of them."

The words echoed in her head now, as she watched Cate stand and carry her coffee cup to the sink.

Shaking away the old memories, she cleared her throat.

"I'd better get ready," Bailey said, checking her watch. "I'm meeting with the task force this morning at the Miami FBI field office. Now that the guilt of our prime suspect has been called into question, we need to decide what we're going to do next."

After showering and dressing, she strapped on her underarm holster and Glock, as well as the small Ruger she usually wore around her ankle when working a case.

She'd arranged to meet Fraser at the Belle Harbor Police Department so they could drive over to the Miami field office together.

When she pulled up outside the station, Dalton West was standing in the parking lot, leaning against his truck.

"I was hoping to see you," he said, circling around to open the passenger side door for Ludwig.

Bailey climbed out and stood looking up at him as he smiled down at her, thinking for a moment he was planning to ask her out on a date.

"I have information about Emma that I thought you'd want to know," he said. "To help with your investigation."

She pushed back a faint pang of disappointment.

"Oh...okay, what is it?"

"Emma went to court-ordered rehab at the Ashworth Recovery Center when she was a teenager," he said. "And all the other victims went to rehab there, too."

She nodded slowly, thinking of the information Brunner had shared the night before.

"And you know this...how?" she asked.

"I can't reveal my sources," he said with an apologetic grin. "But I can assure you, it's credible information."

Just then Fraser's Interceptor pulled into the lot.

"Thanks for letting me know," Bailey said. "But my ride's here and Ludwig and I have to get to a task force meeting."

Reaching into her pocket she pulled out one of the cards she usually left with witnesses after interviews.

She held it out to him.

"In case you get more information."

Bailey's cheeks grew warm as he took the card and studied it, then looked up with another apologetic smile.

"I actually don't have any cards with me today," he said. "But if you can hold on just a minute..."

Walking back to his truck, he dug around in his glove box, eventually managing to find a slip of paper and a pen.

He wrote down his number and handed her the paper.

"In case you need anything, at any time."

She smiled and shoved the paper into her pocket as Fraser appeared on the sidewalk.

He nodded a greeting to Dalton, then looked down at the Camaro, his eyes flicking to the tiny backseat and then at Ludwig, who returned the stare.

"Looks like I'll be driving."

Bailey laughed and turned back to say goodbye to Dalton but he was already gone.

* * *

Special Agent Aisha Sharma led them into a conference room where Ramsay Ford sat, along with several agents Bailey recognized from her time working at the field office.

Photos of the five presumed victims of the Summerset Stalker were taped to a whiteboard on the wall, and Bailey studied the photos before taking a seat.

There were no obvious physical similarities between the victims, although all but Emma had been painfully young.

Wren Dempsey's hair was blonde and fair, contrasting with Tori Cabot's reddish tint and the darker shades of the other three victims.

The Stalker doesn't seem to be looking for specific physical characteristics...unless you consider the angel wings.

The thought was jolting.

Other than Emma, each victim had borne Lando's mark.

Did Lando stab them in the back? Did he remove his mark when he finished with them? Or did someone else carve the skin off the girls? And whose bloody print is on the attic door?

The questions and doubts circled inside her head as Agent Sharma stood in the front of the room.

"An analyst with the Behavioral Analysis Unit in Quantico will be joining us via conference call," she said.

Bailey recognized Special Agent Argus Murphy's ginger

hair and glasses on a monitor beside the whiteboard.

"Agent Flynn, would you like to fill us in on the investigation status?" Sharma asked. "I understand there have been several recent developments."

Bailey nodded, trying to organize her thoughts around everything they'd discovered over the last four or five days.

"Based on the Summerset County M.E.'s reports and our investigation, we believe Wren Dempsey, Tori Cabot, and Hallie Kwan were all killed by the same unknown suspect over a twelve-month period leading up to Detective Emma Walsh's death last Friday night on Bellamy Beach."

"We know Emma was a detective with the Belle Harbor PD and that she was investigating Tori Cabot's murder, although we don't believe she knew about the other victims."

Sucking in a deep breath, Bailey looked around at the gathered faces to see if there were any questions thus far, but everyone appeared to be listening intently.

"Emma made two calls prior to her death. One of the calls was to Tony Brunner, a local lawyer and her husband's partner, with whom she'd been having an affair.

"Upon questioning, Brunner said they'd planned to meet that evening. He claims that Emma was getting close to finding Tori's killer and that she canceled the meeting they'd arranged the night she was killed.

"According to Brunner, Emma had been angry at him for defending a local drug dealer named Lando Gutierrez, whom she considered a suspect. He insists that was the last time he ever spoke to her and has no idea who killed her."

"And the other call?" Ramsey asked.

"The other call was placed to an unregistered burner phone. Digital forensics is still trying to trace it."

The SAC nodded and Bailey continued.

"The Stalker struck again Wednesday evening. Eighteen-year-old Jasmine Blake was working as a courier for Lando Gutierrez. She was found dead at his house yesterday morning. A bloody fingerprint was found at the scene.

"So far we've eliminated Lando and Brunner as matches for the print, and there was no match for the print in AFIS. Luckily, the Belle Harbor PD was able to detain Lando on other charges while we continue the investigation."

"What do we know about the victims?"

It was Ramsey again. He was taking notes.

"Wren Dempsey, Tori Cabot, and Hallie Kwan were all involved in the local drug scene and had spent time at the Summerset Women's Detention Center and the Ashworth Recovery Center.

"We believe the three girls were victimized and exploited by Lando Gutierrez, who admitted to branding them with what he called his *mark* in the weeks and months leading up to their deaths."

Bailey gestured to the autopsy photos on the table.

"The brand he used was a metal belt buckle in the shape of angel wings. The brand was then sliced off of the victims' bodies after they were attacked and killed with a single stab wound to the back."

As she ended her summary, she sighed.

"So far, the only physical evidence the unsub left behind

is a single bloody fingerprint."

"Are you thinking Emma managed to track down the man who killed Tori?" Sharma asked. "You think he killed her in an attempt to silence her? With her out of the way, he went on to kill the next victim on his list, Jasmine Blake?"

"That's the most likely scenario," Bailey agreed.

Fraser cleared his throat.

"It's also possible that Emma wasn't killed by the same perp responsible for the other homicides," he said. "If someone had enough information about her investigation into Tori Cabot's case to make it look as if it was the same perp, we could have two different killers on our hands."

"And who would have that information?" Ramsey asked.

Everyone in the room was now staring at Fraser.

"Maybe Emma gave details about Tori's murder to her husband or to Brunner," he said. "The whole love triangle drama could be considered a motive for either of the men."

Agent Sharma nodded.

"And Tony Brunner was also Lando Gutierrez's lawyer," Sharma reminded them. "If Emma had been investigating Lando, maybe she shared details. Or Lando could have even confessed to his lawyer and-"

"And we need to keep our minds open," Ramsey cut in. "Despite the print at the last crime scene not matching any of our suspects, I think we need to keep Brunner and Lando on the list."

Writing the men's names on the whiteboard, Sharma hesitated and then added Zach Walsh.

"Emma's husband can't be eliminated as a suspect yet,

either," she said. "I know he's offered an alibi, but he could have followed Emma before he left on his camping trip. Or he could have hired someone, knowing he'd be out of town, so he'd have an alibi."

"It's possible," Bailey admitted. "Of course, we need to investigate Zach and anyone else who may have a personal motive toward any of the victims. We'll have to consider all possibilities."

"Including the possibility these killings were perpetrated by a psychopath who selected his victims based mainly on proximity and opportunity," Argus added, speaking up for the first time. "Perhaps something about each of these victims triggered him."

All eyes in the room turned to the monitor.

"So, we may be looking for a random psycho?" Fraser asked with a grimace. "If that is the case, do you have any ideas on where we might find him, Agent Murphy?"

"I've already started working with Agent Sharma," Argus assured him. "We've been adding all available data from the case to a shared investigation database.

"I've been adding data as Bailey's been talking, and I've run a preliminary geolocation algorithm, which analyzes data about the victims' activities and frequented locations to determine our unsub's predicted location.

"Based on what we know so far, or at least what we've had time to input in the database, the algorithm has identified a probable area where the unsub lives, works, and/or commutes on a regular basis. It's where he most likely encountered his victims."

Bailey stared at Argus' screen, which he'd shared with the task force. It showed a map of Summerset County.

Red lines formed a triangle around the heart of the county. Points of interest labeled on the map included Ashworth Recovery Center, the Summerset County Courthouse, and Lando Gutierrez's house.

Agent Sharma pointed to the shaded area on the screen.

"This is where the investigation should be focused."

On the monitor, Argus nodded his agreement.

"We've also created a POI database. That is a *person of interest* database that includes possible witnesses, suspects, and other potential victims.

"All data about the people who frequent the businesses or places the victims were known to frequent or who had other relevant connections to the victims will be added.

"So far, the database includes all known data about courthouse employees, recovery center employees and residents, and local offenders with drug records, as well as violent offenders in the area."

Illuminated by the monitor, Sharma's face was grim.

"The unsub may have committed other crimes. Serial killers rarely start out with murder. They usually work their way up from burglary, stalking, assaults, or other crimes."

"And there could be other homicide victims we haven't identified yet," Fraser added. "I mean, victims outside Summerset County we don't know about."

"Absolutely," Sharma agreed. "Which is why I made sure all relevant details about the known victims were properly entered into CODIS. But there weren't any immediate hits.

No other homicides in the system match the profile of the murders attributed to the Summerset Stalker."

"So, what is the next step?" Fraser asked, looking wary. "Are you saying we need to interview and investigate all the people in the POI database? How many are there?"

Argus leaned forward, his face filling the screen.

"There are hundreds of people in the database."

The analyst adjusted his glasses as a murmur passed through the room.

"We know you won't have time to interview them all, not if you want to find this guy before he kills again," Argus said. "Which is why I recommend you try to get a geofence warrant as quickly as possible."

Bailey nodded. She'd seen the method work before.

"The warrant would require Google to provide phone location data for all of the people who were near the scene around the time of Emma's murder," Argus explained.

"We would then compare the data from the geofence warrant with the data in our POI database to identify anyone included in both databases. Those people, if there are any, are the people you would interview first."

An agent in the back raised a hand.

"What if the unsub carried a burner phone?"

"That's always a possibility," Argus admitted. "Which is why you'll still need to interview as many people as you can and enter all relevant data collected during the interviews.

"The collection of new data and identification of connections will narrow down the list of possible suspects. It's just a matter of statistics."

"Statistics?" Fraser asked with a grimace. "That was never my best subject in school."

"It's pretty straightforward," Argus assured him.

The analyst's voice was suddenly animated.

"Just think about it. What would you normally do if you interviewed a credible witness who said they saw a blue Honda speeding away from a crime scene around the time a homicide was committed?"

"I'd query the DMV database to find owners of blue Hondas in the area," Fraser said. "Which would give me tons of names to wade through."

"Exactly," Argus said. "But by running that list through a POI database, you can quickly identify the blue Honda owners who have a relevant connection to the victim or who meet certain characteristics of the killer's profile."

"That'll narrow down the number of people you need to investigate further," Argus continued. "Once you narrow your list down far enough, you're bound to find the killer."

"Argus is right," Ramsey said. "Roger Calloway up in the Washington Field Office assured me that his algorithms and databases have helped his team identify and capture more than one serial killer over the last few years."

Looking around at the task force members in the room, Ramsey stood and hooked a thumb at the door.

"Okay, let's get going with those interviews," he said.

Bailey's phone buzzed in her pocket as she followed Fraser to the door. Mason Knox was calling.

"You want a second shot at observing an autopsy?" the M.E. asked. "I'll be starting on Jasmine Blake after lunch."

CHAPTER THIRTY

Mason Knox was waiting in the quiet lobby of the Summerset County Medical Examiner's office when Bailey arrived with Ludwig in tow. Looking down at the German shepherd, Mason's forehead wrinkled into a worried frown. A dog's sense of smell was much stronger than a human's, and most humans had a hard time handling the smells of an autopsy suite.

"Why don't we have this big guy wait in my office?" he suggested as he led Bailey into the back. "I don't think Ludwig would appreciate being in the autopsy suite while we're working on Jasmine Blake."

"That's probably a good idea," she agreed, following him down the hall. "Although, he might be a bit of a nuisance if left on his own."

She grimaced as Ludwig began sniffing at a bag on Mason's desk which contained the remainder of the breakfast sandwich he'd gotten on his way to work.

"Here, let me help you," he said, opening the bag and pulling out a bite of egg and cheese.

As he fed the leftovers to the eager German shepherd, Bailey smiled and rolled her eyes.

"You're just like my father," she said with a laugh. "He can't resist giving Ludwig half his food, either."

It was the first time Mason had seen the agent laugh, and she looked suddenly young and carefree. It made him think of the young woman waiting for them in the autopsy suite.

Jasmine Blake would never laugh again.

A soft knock at the door was followed by Finola's head as she peered into the room.

"I've got everything prepped when you're ready."

"Thanks, Finola, we'll be right there."

He turned to Bailey.

"You ready to do this?"

The agent's smile faded as she nodded and followed him to the prep room where they put on protective coveralls.

Mason pulled on an extra set of gloves and positioned his face shield as he led her into the autopsy suite.

Standing next to Jasmine Blake, who was lying on the dissecting table under a white sheet, Mason hesitated.

"Are you ready?" he asked quietly.

Bailey nodded silently behind her mask.

The medical examiner pulled down the sheet, revealing a small, thin woman with a mass of dark, blue-tipped hair.

As Finola clicked on the recorder, Mason began to speak.

"The decedent is a white female measuring sixty-one inches and weighing ninety-eight pounds. She was eighteen years old at the time of her death...which came too soon."

He examined the dead girl's body from head to foot, before he and Finola turned her over, exposing the angry wound in her back and the raw tissue on her shoulder.

"Now we know the killer was removing the scarred skin from her back," he said, as Finola took photos.

He motioned for Finola to turn off the recorder and stared over his mask at Bailey, his dark eyes blazing.

"So, Lando Gutierrez branded her in a sick attempt to mark his property," he said. "But did he kill her?"

"We don't know," Bailey admitted. "But Lando is in jail now, and he is still a prime suspect."

Meeting her green eyes over her mask, Mason saw doubt.

"You don't sound very confident that he's the Stalker."

She shrugged.

"The print we found at Lando's house isn't his."

Mason wasn't surprised as he recalled Lando's reaction to Jasmine's body. He'd had doubts at the scene.

Now, he was sure.

Someone else was responsible for putting Jasmine Blake on his table, and the killer could be out there even now, ready to do it again.

"So, the official cause and manner of death is the same as the others?" Bailey asked.

He nodded

"Yes, it's homicide by knife wound to the back," he said in a grim voice. "Just like the others."

He finished the rest of the autopsy quickly, then removed his protective clothing and led her back to his office, where Ludwig had settled into the corner for a nap.

"Did Madeline Mercer share the information I gave to her about the knife?" he asked.

"Not yet," Bailey said. "But I'm behind on email."

Opening a folder on his desk he pointed to the report he'd prepared for the crime scene team.

"I analyzed the stab wounds using optical microscopy and CT scans," he explained. "That allowed me to measure the length of the surface injury and the depth of penetration into the tissue."

He slid the printout toward her.

"I've determined the blade length and characteristics and confirmed a serrated edge was used based on the tool marks on the bone. It's all there."

Baily stared down at the paper.

"I believe the knife used in the murders closely matches a combat knife regularly used by marines in Vietnam," he explained. "And whoever killed these young women did it with one stab of the knife."

His throat constricted, and he reached for his coffee.

"That indicates the killer is likely fit and strong," he said. "Most soldiers who were in Vietnam would be too old to fit the profile. I guess the weapon could have been bought somewhere. Maybe online or something, but..."

He hesitated, not sure if his theory would make sense to anyone else but him.

"I was thinking the weapon might have some sort of special meaning to the killer. Maybe it was passed down from a father or even an uncle. Why else use an old knife?"

Bailey cocked an eyebrow.

"So, you think we have a sentimental psychopath on our hands?" she asked, her mouth twitching.

Suspecting she was suppressing a smile, Mason's cheeks

flushed with embarrassment.

"What? Does that sound crazy?"

"Not at all," she said. "In fact, I think you might have something there. I'll ask our behavioral analyst in Quantico if there's a way he can match our POI database against the military service records database."

She sounded hopeful.

"It may be a longshot, but Argus has been known to do some pretty amazing things when it comes to data."

Mason raised an eyebrow.

"Who is Argus? And what is a POI database?"

"Argus Murphy is an analyst and profiler with the FBI's Behavioral Analysis Unit," she said. "He created a person of interest database to identify pools of suspects."

As Bailey stood to leave, he remembered something else.

"We're ready to release Emma's body to the family," he said. "I'll be calling her husband once I get out of here."

He cleared his throat.

"I just thought you'd want to know."

"Thanks, now I'd better get back to my investigation."

Mason frowned as the words conjured a memory.

Emma Walsh had said the very same thing to him the last time they'd spoken about Tori Cabot.

He watched as Bailey and Ludwig left the room, hoping she'd be more careful than her former partner had been.

CHAPTER THIRTY-ONE

The Stalker waited for Bailey Flynn to come out of the medical examiner's office, his thumb ceaselessly rubbing at the edge of the combat knife blade, his eyes scanning the area to make sure he hadn't been followed. As he dry-swallowed his fifth benzo of the day, a butterfly flitted past the window, capturing his attention.

He smiled, recognizing the broken pattern of orange, yellows, and browns on its tiny wings. It was a Painted Lady, known in Latin as *Vanessa cardui*.

Tempted to get out of the car and catch it, his hand reached for the net he always kept under the front seat, then pulled back.

I can't risk being seen outside the M.E.'s office running around with a butterfly net. I can't risk being seen by Bailey Flynn.

Not for such a common prize.

The Painted Lady was the most common butterfly and he already had several pinned up on his wall at home. As much as it pained him, he'd have to let this one fly away.

Catching movement out of the corner of his eye, he turned to see Bailey Flynn emerge from the medical examiner's office, heading toward her red Camaro, leading the sharp-tooth German shepherd behind her.

For a minute, the Stalker's vision blurred, and the FBI agent appeared to flicker in and out of focus, just like the butterfly wings. His eyes were playing tricks on him again.

Or maybe Bailey Flynn's the one playing tricks. Maybe she knows I'm here and she's trying to get me to make a mistake.

Rage began to expand his chest as he watched her climb into her car and back out of the parking space.

Shaking his head, trying to think, he wondered if he'd inhaled too much of the Devil's Breath the night before.

It was making him see things again. And forget things.

He couldn't remember much of the evening but had woken feeling anxious, knowing he needed to stop Bailey Flynn before she stopped him.

As he followed the red Camaro, he stayed at least two or three cars behind until she pulled into the Sanctuary Apartments where her sister lived and went inside.

Waiting outside, keeping watch on the little red car, he checked the news on his phone, tapping on the latest video that had been uploaded to the Channel 3 News website.

Sabrina West was standing in front of the courthouse, giving the latest update on the Summerset Stalker. Photos of four young women suspected to be his victims were displayed on the screen.

"Questions are still being asked about Detective Emma Walsh's death and the connection to the Stalker's killings."

A photo of Emma popped up on the screen, causing the Stalker to grit his teeth.

This is all Emma's fault.

He pictured her heart-shaped face as it had looked that night in the moonlight, recalling the shine of terror in her wide, brown eyes.

She had caused all this.

No one had even cared about any of the fallen angels he'd taken until Emma had gotten herself killed.

Little did they know that the detective had been one of the fallen. She'd sinned just like all the others.

He'd had no choice but to send her into the darkness along with the others. Not after Emma had forced his hand by calling him that night, demanding to see him.

The only reason she hadn't taken him in for questioning before was because he had known her little secret.

He had threatened to expose her if she did.

She had known that if the Belle Harbor PD found out about her juvenile record of drug possession with the intent to distribute, she might lose her job.

And while she had her suspicions about him, she hadn't been sure he'd been the one who'd taken Tori.

If she had known for sure, she never would have met me there. She would have been more careful.

Turning at the sound of a door slamming, he saw Bailey head back to the Camaro. Seconds later, the little red car was heading onto the highway with the Stalker in pursuit.

He stayed behind her all the way to the Ashworth Recovery Center, fuming as he watched her go inside.

Bailey Flynn is getting too close. She'll have to be delivered into darkness like the others, and it will have to happen soon.

CHAPTER THIRTY-TWO

Bailey pulled out her FBI credentials as Neil Ashworth opened the door and waved her inside the dreary lobby. The facility manager's thick dark hair had been pulled back into a low man-bun, and he wore a flowing white cotton caftan over faded jeans.

"I'm here to see your mother," Bailey said, holding up the credentials in hopes they would make her visit seem more official. "It's vital that I speak to her."

"Sure, she's in the back office," he said, leading her down the hall. "She might be kind of busy..."

He stopped and waved her into another dreary room, this one with a window covered by heavy blinds and a life-sized portrait of the center's founder on the wall.

The overall impression was gloomy.

"Agent Flynn, I thought we might see you back here," she said. "I told my son the last time you stopped by that we hadn't seen the last of you."

The woman at the desk stood and crossed to Bailey, her too-bright red hair stiff and unmoving around her head as she produced a crocodile's smile.

"I'm sorry to bother you, Councilwoman Ashworth, but I

need to ask you a few questions about a past resident," she said. "A woman named Emma Kaminski."

She registered surprise in the older woman's eyes.

Nigella hadn't been expecting the question or the name, but she recovered quickly, shrugging her rounded shoulder in a dismissive gesture.

"I can't remember the name of all our residents," she said as if Bailey had been foolish to think otherwise. "And we can't give out confidential resident information in any case, as I told you last time you were here."

"You might better know her as Emma Walsh," Bailey said, watching the woman's eyes. "She came here asking you about Tori Cabot during the last few weeks, didn't she? Can you tell me what you two talked about?"

Nigella's voice was cold as she walked back to her desk.

"I think this might constitute harassment, Agent Flynn," she said as she sank back into her chair. "I might just have to call your superior at the Bureau and file a complaint."

"That's your choice, of course," Bailey said.

It was an empty threat and they both knew it. Neither Roger Calloway nor Ford Ramsey would be intimidated by a county commissioner, no matter how stern her tone.

"You're Jackie Flynn's daughter, aren't you?" Nigella said with a sudden gleam in her eye. "She's got a client asking the Commission to put a halt to that new Greenbelt project over by Sun Creek. She's been trying to get a meeting with me for weeks. In fact, there's a council meeting about it this afternoon."

Bailey stared at the woman in surprise.

Before she could respond, there was a knock on the door behind her. Neil Ashworth stood in the doorway.

"Mother, the mayor's on the phone. He says he's been trying to get hold of you for–"

"Yes, please transfer the call, Neil."

Turning icy eyes on Bailey, she waved an impatient hand toward the door.

"I'll let you see yourself out, Detective Flynn."

Neil was waiting for Bailey when she stepped out of Nigella's office and closed the door behind her.

"I'm sorry about my mother," he said as he walked with her toward the door. "I know she can seem like a hard woman but she's done a lot of good, both for me and for this community. And now I'm trying to do a good thing for the people who come here hoping to start a new life."

"If you want to do a good thing, you'll tell me what you know about Emma Walsh," Bailey said. "She stayed here as a resident about ten years ago. Help me figure out who might have wanted her dead."

"I wish I could," Neil said, looking toward the door as if he expected his mother to stick her head into the room at any minute. "But I was still in school back then. I've only been working at the recovery center for a couple of years."

He opened the door, and as she stepped through, Neil lowered his voice, issuing a soft warning.

"Be careful. You don't want to get on Mother's bad side."

* * *

Bailey left Ashworth Recovery in a foul mood.

It wasn't the right kind of mood to be in if you had to share bad news with a grieving widower.

But she knew she had to talk to Zach. Had to tell her ex that Emma and Brunner had been having an affair.

She couldn't leave it up to Fraser. That wouldn't be fair. It was her burden to bear. But her heart sank as she turned onto Waterman Way and saw Zach's car parked outside.

Parking along the curb, she stared up at the large, two-story home with a warm stone façade and gripped the steering wheel.

This might have been my house. The man inside might have been my husband. Emma stole this life from me.

Baily waited for sadness or anger to wash over her, but instead, she felt a strange sense of relief.

She'd had it all wrong.

Emma didn't steal this life. She saved me from this life.

The thought was a revelation.

Bailey didn't want the house or the man inside. She'd only been doing what was safe. What had been expected.

If she'd married Zach as planned, she never would have applied to the FBI Academy. She never would have trained with Ludwig. She would have a different life.

It would have been all wrong.

As she sat there, she noticed a car pulling up behind her.

Looking in the rearview mirror, she saw Gavin Walsh step out and walk up to the house.

Telling herself that Zach's father would provide a calming presence and a witness, she followed him inside.

"The M.E. already called and told me Emma's body would be released later today," Zach said in a surly voice when he saw her standing in the doorway.

"I know," Bailey said. "But that's not why I'm here. I have something I need to-"

"Don't tell me you're here to question him again," Judge Walsh said. "Because he's told you everything he knows."

"That's right," Zach said. "And Tony advised me not to talk without him present."

"Actually, I need to talk to you about your partner," she said. "He's sort of why I'm here. You see, we found out Emma called Tony Brunner the night she was killed. It came out during the interview that Tony and Emma were...*involved*. I thought you would want to know before the press picks it up."

The blood drained from Zach's face.

"You must be enjoying this," he said. "After I canceled the wedding and ran off with your best friend. This must feel like vindication to you."

His tone wasn't bitter. He just sounded resigned.

"It's karma, isn't it?" he said. "I've only gotten repaid for what I did to you. I got what I deserved."

He swallowed hard as Judge Walsh started to protest.

"Emma is the one who-"

But Zach held up a hand to stop him.

"Emma didn't deserve to die like that, no matter who she was seeing," he said in a hoarse voice.

His red-rimmed eyes met and held Bailey's.

"And, if I'm honest with myself, I knew she wasn't

233

happy. I knew she'd already checked out of our marriage. I didn't want to believe it, but I...I didn't want this to happen either."

"I know," Bailey said. "Neither did I."

Zach stared at her for a long beat.

"I always knew you'd be alright," he said. "You never really needed me. Not like Emma did."

His face twisted with pain.

"But in the end, I wasn't able to give her what she needed and...now she's gone."

"I think it's time for you to go," Judge Walsh said, taking Bailey by the arm and steering her toward the door.

She looked over to see an angry flush on his face.

"What did Emma expect would happen if she made a habit of playing with people's hearts and lives?" he said between clenched teeth. "Some people will say that she got what she deserved."

"Those people will be wrong," Bailey said. "Emma was damaged. I know that now. She tried to hide it, even from me. Even from Zach. But in the end, she died trying to do the right thing. She was trying to catch a killer."

The judge just stared at her as if surprised by her passionate reply. The anger in his eyes was starting to fade.

Bailey turned to leave, then remembered what she had wanted to ask the judge.

She turned back around.

"What do you know about Nigella Ashworth and the Ashworth Recovery Center?" she asked. "It seems odd that three of the victims in our investigation were sent to the same facility when there must be dozens of similar places in Summerset County. Could Nigella have pressured the courts to send her these offenders and boost business? Could someone have wanted to hide that arrangement?"

"Not that I'm aware of," the judge said indignantly. "She's certainly never pressured *me*. Of course..."

He lowered his voice as if someone might be listening.

"Everyone knows Nigella has the mayor's ear, so I guess it's possible she's using her influence with someone over at the Offender Review Commission to get offenders assigned to her program. But that would be highly inappropriate."

"I'd say *illegal* is a more accurate description," Bailey corrected. "And I'll be sure to look into it. I have a contact at the Commission who may be able to help."

As Bailey pushed through the door, Judge Walsh called after her. She looked over her shoulder.

"Don't let Nigella know you're investigating her," he cautioned. "She's not someone you'd want as an enemy."

Bailey's phone buzzed before she could respond.

The call was from her mother.

Bailey walked back to the Camaro before she answered.

"Your father's been wondering where his car is," Jackie said in a reproving tone. "He said you could use it for a few days and it's been almost a week now."

"Fine," Bailey said. "I'll get a car from the Bureau's pool and bring the Camaro back tonight."

"And you can stay for dinner," Jackie said, sounding slightly mollified. "We haven't had a chance to catch up since you came back to Belle Harbor. I'm still waiting to hear all about your new job. It sounds dangerous and your father and I want to discuss possible-"

"I've got to go, Mom," Bailey said. "I'll see you tonight."

CHAPTER THIRTY-THREE

Jimmy Fraser walked into the courthouse, checked the directory, then headed over to Judge Walsh's office, impatient to submit the request for the geofence warrant they needed as quickly as possible. The judge's signature would ensure a lot less shoe leather would be required to narrow down their suspect list.

"Judge Walsh is taking a personal day," Inez Flores told him as he stepped into the outer office. "But luckily, Judge Ingelbert is back in chambers today. I'll see if he can consider the warrant request before he leaves."

Fraser's heart fell.

He knew Inglebert had no stake in the case and would be less inclined to sign a blanket geofence warrant without asking for more information.

But there was nothing he could do, so he thanked Inez and left the building, knowing he should be out conducting interviews, although the number of persons of interest in the database was overwhelming.

Thinking of what Argus Murphy had said about narrowing down the list of potential suspects, he decided what he needed was an eyewitness.

Someone who'd seen the killer firsthand and who could give him something useful to go on. And as he checked his watch, he knew he needed to find a witness fast.

Sasha's school performance was scheduled for seven o'clock. His daughter had been practicing for weeks and after their conversation the day before, he couldn't miss the show. He only had a few hours to find a hot lead and break open the case before he'd have to report for daddy duty.

Getting back in the Interceptor, he opened his notebook and scanned through the notes he'd taken thus far.

Staring down at a name he'd written in blue ink and circled twice, he hesitated.

I should be talking to more people and collecting additional information. Not running in circles.

Ignoring his own advice, he started the engine and headed toward the Summerset County Jail. Walking inside, he waved at the uniformed officer manning the front desk.

"I need to see one of the prisoners," he said. "I need to speak to Cisco Silver as soon as possible."

Thirty minutes later he was sitting across from Cisco in one of the little rooms the jail normally used when a prisoner met with their legal counsel.

The repeat offender was slumped in a plastic chair. His pale, thin face was framed by dark, greasy hair, which hung over eyes that watched Fraser warily.

"I need more information about what you saw the night Emma Walsh was murdered," he said bluntly.

Cisco was hesitant.

"Shouldn't I have a lawyer here?"

"That's one option," Fraser agreed. "But getting a public defender assigned could take a while, and Lando Gutierrez was checked in just last night. He's down the hall in solitary confinement and might be released into general population at any time."

Fraser frowned.

"He seemed pretty mad at you. He even suggested you were the one who killed Jasmine Blake. He's blaming you for his arrest, too, from what I can tell."

"That's why I need to get out of here," Cisco said. "You told me you'd put me into witness protection if I helped you catch the Stalker."

"That's just it," Fraser said. "We haven't caught the Stalker yet. This is why I need you to tell me everything you remember about the night Emma Walsh died."

He leaned forward and looked into Cisco's scared eyes.

"If you can tell me something that helps me find Emma's killer, you just might get out of here."

Cisco shook his head.

"I don't know. I've been going over it in my mind again and again. It's like I told you before, I was walking down the beach, looking for the house Lando told me about.

"I found the house but then I heard a woman's voice. I hid under the stairs, and that's when I realized it was Detective Walsh. She was on the phone. And then this man came out...he said something and then..."

His voice wavered as if he didn't want to remember.

"Think," Fraser said. "What exactly did he say?"

Sweat popped out on Cisco's temple as he closed his eyes

and tried to concentrate.

"You think I had something to do with that dead girl, don't you? I know you've been watching my house. I saw you parked across the street last night. Did you think I wouldn't recognize you? Do you think I'm a fool?"

Fraser frowned.

"Are you sure that's what he said? The exact words?"

Fraser's heart began to thump in his chest as the thief nodded.

"Yeah, every part of that night is burned in my mind."

Thinking he might have gotten the information they needed to narrow down their list, he jumped up from the table and called the guard.

As Fraser left the jail, he called Bailey, but she didn't answer the phone. Ending the call, he tried Argus.

As soon as the analyst answered the phone, Fraser repeated the words Cisco had heard on the beach.

"We need to trace the activity and location of Emma's phone the night before she died," he said. "If we determine her phone was outside the residence of someone in our POI database, we'll have a prime suspect."

"I'll get to work on it," Argus said.

Ending the call, Fraser suddenly felt lighter.

Yes, you get to work, and I'll get to Sasha's performance.

CHAPTER THIRTY-FOUR

Cate walked out to the red Camaro wearing her favorite red jacket with a matching pencil skirt and heels. Sliding into the passenger seat beside Bailey, she smiled as she realized that even the car she would be driving today was color-coordinated.

Her sister had finally arranged to get a car from the Bureau's pool of vehicles and Cate had agreed to drop Bailey off at the FBI's Miami field office and then drive the Camaro back home to her father.

When they reached the towering glass FBI building, Cate climbed out and circled around to the driver's seat, waving to Bailey and Ludwig as they disappeared inside.

She was halfway back to Belle Harbor when she looked down and saw Bailey's phone in the footwell. It must have fallen off the dashboard or out of her sister's pocket.

Slipping the phone into the glove compartment, she assured herself she would give the phone back to her sister when they saw each other that evening for dinner.

But first, she wanted to stop by the courthouse to see how the county commission hearing was going.

Her mother was scheduled to speak to the commission

about the proposed Greenbelt project, and Cate wanted to be there to support her.

Suspecting the meeting had already started, Cate parked the Camaro in the metered spaces along the curb and hurried inside, crossing to the main meeting room.

The entire county commission was in attendance, as was a large group of concerned citizens and county staffers as Jackie Flynn stood at the head of the room and made an impassioned plea.

Cate looked at the crowd, trying to judge their reaction, and her eyes fell on Nigella Ashworth, who was staring at her mother with hard, angry eyes.

What has Mom done to get on Nigella's bad side?

Once the hearing was over, Cate followed the crowd out to the lobby, where Nigella allowed herself to be interviewed by a variety of reporters.

Cate watched, then turned away in disgust as the woman explained why she planned to vote for the Greenbelt project.

Bumping into a man as she turned away, she excused herself and went back to her office, gathering the files she needed to work from home over the weekend.

As she went back down on the elevator, she stepped out to find Nigella talking loudly to Jackie.

"It seems your daughter is pursuing some sort of vendetta against me."

At first, Cate thought the woman was talking about her, thinking she must be deluded. Then she realized Bailey must have done something to piss her off.

"She had the nerve to contact an investigator at the

Offender Review Commission and ask him some very impertinent questions about me."

"Apparently she believes I may be using my influence to pressure their investigators into assigning drug offenders to the Ashworth Recovery Center."

"I'm sure that isn't the case," Jackie said, her eyes darting around the room as if searching for escape. "You must be mistaken."

"I'm not mistaken," Nigella replied with unflinching conviction. "My sources within the Commission are very reliable."

Cate finally stepped forward, determined to put her mother out of her misery one way or the other.

"I'm sorry, Ms. Ashworth, did you say sources inside the Commission have shared confidential information about an ongoing federal investigation with you?" Cate asked.

She spoke loudly, making sure her voice carried through the marble-floored lobby, drawing startled looks from several bystanders, including Sabrina West, who held a microphone with a large Channel 3 News logo on the front.

"Maybe that's why the FBI suspects you're wielding undue influence over the Offender Review Commission."

Nigella drew herself up to her full height.

"Come on, Neil. Let's go."

As the county commissioner turned on her heel and headed toward the exit, a leanly muscled man in a white linen tunic and black yoga pants followed after her.

The man, who had his shoulder-length hair pulled back into a low ponytail, looked back over his shoulder, then quickened his step when he saw Sabrina West heading in their direction.

"You think Nigella Ashworth and her son will be on the news tonight?" Cate asked as she turned to her mother with a self-satisfied smile.

Jackie wasn't amused.

"Nigella may be a pain in the *you-know-what*, but she can single-handily derail my client's case," she hissed.

Smarting at the reprimand, Cate told her mother she would bring the Camaro home shortly.

"You've got the Camaro?" her mother asked in surprise.

Cate nodded.

"Bailey asked me to drop it off," she explained.

"Make sure you fill the gas tank first," Jackie sniffed. "Your father won't like it if he finds it on empty."

As soon as Cate walked outside, she saw Sabrina West pacing along the sidewalk with her microphone in hand, looking for her next victim.

Striding quickly away, before the reporter could ask her any questions about Nigella or her mother, she climbed back into the red Camaro.

She started the engine, heading for her parents' house, still keyed up and angry at Nigella Ashworth, and irritated by her mother's attempt to placate the awful woman.

Looking in the rearview mirror, she noticed a black sedan following close behind her just as the glove compartment buzzed. A call was coming in on Bailey's phone.

Cate dug out the phone, noting the name Argus Murphy on the display as she pushed the *Accept* icon.

"This is Bailey Flynn's phone. She's not here right now."

"Oh...well, I was hoping to speak to Bailey," a hesitant voice said. "I'm an analyst with the Behavioral Analysis Unit at the FBI. Do you know if there's another way I can reach her?"

Before she could reply, he hastened to explain.

"There's been an important development in a case, and I actually tried to reach Detective Fraser, as well, but he's not answering his phone, so..."

"Sorry...I have Bailey's phone," Cate said. "I'm her sister and she left it in the car when I dropped her off. But I can let her know you called when I see her."

Assuring her he'd already left a message on Bailey's voice mail, the analyst ended the call and Cate slid the phone back into the glove box.

She was driving toward Haverfield Road when she noticed the black car was still following her.

But as she pulled into the gas station, which sold the only grade of gas her father allowed in the classic car's rebuilt engine, she was relieved to see that the black car was nowhere in sight.

I must be getting paranoid with all this talk about the Stalker.

Filling up the tank, she looked down to see the back tire was flat.

"Now, how did that happen?"

Driving the Camaro slowly to the side of the building, Cate stepped out and approached the air machine, not sure how many quarters she'd need.

Suddenly the black car was pulling in beside her, and the

driver was walking toward her, holding a white cloth.

Before she could react or scream, he grabbed her arm and pressed the cloth over her mouth and nose.

As the world started to spin around her, she heard him whisper in her ear.

"It's the Devil's Breath. It makes me do bad things."

CHAPTER THIRTY-FIVE

ailey climbed into the dusty Ford Expedition she'd borrowed that morning from the Miami field office and reached into the pocket of her jacket, intending to call Fraser. Coming up empty, she frowned and tried the other pocket. The phone was gone.

Turning to look back at Ludwig, she saw the dog had settled comfortably into the backseat by the window.

"You're the search and rescue expert," she said with a sigh. "So, where did I leave my phone?"

The German shepherd stared at her with what she suspected was a mixture of reproach and disappointment.

"That's okay, I'll just use the locator app on my computer to find it," she said as Ludwig turned his dark eyes toward the window. "Oh...but my computer's back at Cate's place."

As she started the engine, she contemplated swinging by Cate's apartment on her way to her parents' house, then reluctantly decided against it.

It was getting late. She could already see the sun sinking into the horizon in her rearview mirror and knew her mother would be pacing the floor by now, especially if she couldn't reach her on the phone.

Jackie Flynn had always been a worrier, but after Bailey's shoot-out with Ronin Godfrey and subsequent move to the special crimes task force in DC, her mother had become downright paranoid, expecting a fateful call at any minute informing her that her youngest daughter was gone.

Pulling onto the highway, Bailey headed east.

She turned onto Claremont Street thirty minutes later, expecting to find the red Camaro parked in her parents' garage, but the car's usual spot was still empty.

Cate wasn't home yet.

As she walked into the house, Jackie emerged from the kitchen wearing her usual frown.

Drying her hands on a dishtowel, her mother didn't offer a greeting as Bailey started to take off her jacket.

"I thought you said you'd be home in time for dinner."

"Have you heard from Cate?" Bailey replied, ignoring her mother's petulant statement. "She said she'd bring the Camaro home before dinner."

Waving away the question with an irritable hand, Jackie lifted her silk-clad shoulders in a shrug.

"Your sister probably just stopped to get gas. I told her to make sure she didn't bring the car back empty."

"How long ago was that?"

Jackie pursed her lips and looked down at her watch.

"Over an hour," she admitted. "Maybe closer to two."

Picking up her phone, Jackie tapped on the display.

"I'll call her and see what's keeping her."

She held the phone to her ear, then lowered it and glared

at the display.

"It went straight to voicemail."

Her green eyes met Bailey's.

"Do you think something could have happened to her?" she asked, her voice raised in sudden alarm. "Do you think she had an accident? I'm always telling her to slow down, but does she listen? No, of course not."

"Nothing's happened," a voice called out from the kitchen. "Everyone just calm down."

Appearing in the doorway, Chris Flynn held up his phone and began tapping on the display.

"There's no need to panic," he assured them. "I put a new GPS tracker on the Camaro a few months ago. I'll just check and see where Cate is."

He tapped a few more times, then nodded.

"Yes, she's at that gas station on Haverfield Road," he said, sounding relieved. "It's a bit out of the way but it has the gas I like to use for-"

"Why would it take her two hours to get gas?" Bailey asked, shrugging her jacket back on. "Something's not right. I'm going to look for her."

She plucked the phone out of her mother's hand.

"And I need to borrow this," she said as she headed toward the door. "I lost my phone somewhere and I need to be able to keep in touch with Dad in case the car moves."

Ignoring their questions and protests, Bailey hurried back to the Expedition, suddenly convinced something had happened to Cate.

She opened the door to allow Ludwig to jump into the

backseat of the SUV before heading toward Haverfield Road.

As she raced along the highway, she lifted worried eyes to the darkening sky ahead. The weather forecast had warned of overnight thunderstorms in Summerset County, and they appeared to be moving in earlier than expected.

Nerves on edge, she turned into the gas station fifteen minutes later, relieved to see the Camaro parked beside the air pump. Her relief turned to concern when she pulled alongside the car and noted the dark, empty windows.

Jumping out of the Expedition, Bailey circled the little red car, then turned and surveyed the surrounding area.

The gas station lot was practically deserted.

There was no sign of Cate as she and Ludwig hurried into the little store and crossed to the cash register.

A young man in a Miami Heat baseball cap sat behind the counter. He didn't look up as they approached, his attention firmly fixed on a little television mounted to the wall.

Clutching her mother's phone, Bailey scrolled to a picture of Cate and held it up, along with her FBI credentials.

"Excuse me," she called out.

The clerk turned toward her with bleary eyes.

"I'm looking for this woman. Have you seen her?" Bailey asked. "She was in that red Camaro out there."

The clerk frowned and sat forward, squinting at the smiling image of Cate, before looking through the window at the little red car.

"I was just about to call for a tow truck," he said, scratching at his chin. "That car's been parked there for over an hour. It's getting in the way of paying customers."

Bailey looked into the dark lot, which was completely empty, unable to see anyone having to wait.

"Have you seen this woman?" she repeated.

The man shook his head.

"No, can't say that I have."

His eyes flicked down to Ludwig.

"And we don't allow dogs in the store."

Ignoring the comment, Bailey walked to the door marked *Employees Only* and pushed through.

"Hey, you're not allowed back there!" the clerk cried out.

Bailey saw at a glance that the small room was empty except for a metal desk and several long shelves of boxed inventory. She turned back to the store and tried to think.

Her eyes fell on the television behind the counter, which was turned to Channel 3 News, where one of the nightly anchors was introducing a report on the proposed Greenbelt project in Summerset County.

"...conducted an interview early this afternoon inside the courthouse with councilwoman Nigella Ashworth."

Video footage of Sabrina West inside the Summerset County courthouse began to play on the little screen.

"Turn up the volume," Bailey said, walking forward. "I need to hear that report."

With a shrug of his thin shoulders, the man picked up a tiny remote and jabbed at a button with his thumb until Sabrina's voice was clearly audible.

As the reporter questioned a smiling Nigella Ashworth about her plans to vote for the Greenbelt project, Bailey was watching a graceful figure in red visible in the background.

"That's Cate," she murmured.

On the screen, her sister turned away from the camera, accidentally bumping into a man who'd been standing behind her as she made her way through the crowd.

Bailey's eyes narrowed as she saw the man immediately turn and follow Cate out of view.

Something about the man looked familiar, but he'd been wearing a hat and glasses, and he'd been standing too far from the camera for her to get a good look.

She watched as Sabrina signed off and the anchor moved on to the weather forecast, warning of possible flooding.

Turning toward the exit, Bailey pushed through the doors and stepped outside, her mind churning with questions as rain began to patter onto the pavement around her.

Who was that man? Was he following Cate? Where is she now?

A terrifying range of possible scenarios played through her mind, fueled by disturbing images of the violent crimes she'd investigated in the past.

She needed to find answers. She needed to know what had happened to Cate after she'd turned and walked away.

Maybe Sabrina West has more footage of Cate at the courthouse. Maybe she saw the man who followed her.

Looking down at her mother's phone, she saw Cate's smiling image again and felt the first stirrings of panic.

With a deep inhale, she urged herself to calm down.

Just call Sabrina West and find out if she remembers seeing Cate at the courthouse. Ask for any extra footage.

How could she get hold of the reporter quickly?

Perhaps I can call the station or maybe her brother can help.

She remembered the slip of paper in her pocket. Dalton West had given her his number and it should still be there. The private investigator was bound to know how to reach his sister.

Reaching into her pocket, Bailey pulled out a few crumpled tissues, a ballpoint pen, and a scrap of paper.

Dalton West's number was written on it in blue ink.

With a numb finger, she tapped on the display, not quite sure what she was planning to say, hoping he would accept a call from an unfamiliar number.

Her tight grip on the phone relaxed as Dalton's deep, reassuring voice sounded in her ear.

"This is West Investigations."

"Dalton? This is Bailey Flynn."

She tried to keep her voice steady.

"I need your help. My sister's gone missing and I think your sister has footage of the last time she was seen."

"When was she seen?" Dalton asked. "And where?"

Relieved he wasn't wasting precious time with irrelevant questions, Bailey exhaled.

"Cate was last seen at the Summerset County courthouse this afternoon around five p.m. when your sister was interviewing Nigella Ashworth," she said. "I saw footage on Channel 3 News just now showing Cate walking away. A man was following her and...now she's missing."

Her throat constricted around the words.

"Ok, I'll call Sabrina and get any footage she has," Dalton said without hesitation. "And I'll find out if she saw anything unusual. I'll call as soon as I know anything."

After ending the call, Bailey decided to try Fraser again, but his phone rang a few times and then rolled to voicemail.

Running through the rain to the Expedition, Bailey ushered Ludwig inside and slammed the door shut.

Rain drizzled down the windshield as she tried to decide what to do. Should she go home and check her computer in hopes she could find her phone?

Maybe Cate's left me a message and this is all a waste of time.

A small flame of hope flickered in her chest at the thought, then grew brighter as she realized she could check her messages remotely.

So much for being a hotshot FBI agent.

Within minutes she was listening to the barrage of messages that had been left for her over the last few hours, but her hope was extinguished when she realized none of them were from Cate.

The only messages of interest were the two left by Argus Murphy. She immediately tapped to play the first.

"Bailey, this is Argus. I've been trying to reach Detective Fraser with an important development on the Summerset Stalker case but he's not answering his phone. Can you call me back?"

The second message began to play automatically after the first. Argus was beginning to sound stressed.

"It's me again, Bailey. I just remembered your sister told me you left your phone in her car, so you probably don't have a callback number for me either."

He proceeded to recite his phone number, including country code and area code.

Grateful for the analyst's attention to detail, Bailey

immediately tapped in his number.

Argus picked up on the first ring.

"It's Bailey Flynn," she said. "You left me a message. You said you've spoken to my sister?"

"Yes, I called earlier," Argus confirmed. "Your sister-"

"When?" she interrupted. "When did you speak to Cate?"

There was a startled pause before Argus replied.

"It's been two hours and sixteen minutes," he said. "I just checked the time stamp on my call."

"I see," Bailey said, unable to hide her disappointment. "It's just that she never came home. I tried to call, but she didn't answer, so I tracked her car to a gas station, but she's not here. I don't know where she could be."

Or if she's even alive.

Shaken by the unbidden thought, Bailey forced it away.

"I'm sorry, Argus, but I've got to go."

Her hands were starting to tremble as the realization of what was happening sank in.

"Cate's missing and I have a terrible feeling that whoever killed Emma might have taken her."

"Don't hang up," Argus said before she could end the connection. "I was calling you earlier to tell you we think we may have identified the Stalker."

Bailey's hand gripped the phone tighter as he continued.

"Detective Fraser went out to the Summerset County Jail this afternoon and conducted a second interview with Cisco Silver," Argus quickly explained. "Cisco claimed the man who attacked Emma told her he'd seen her outside his house the night before she died.

"So we used historical cell-site location information to piece together the various locations where Emma's phone had been the night before her death. One location matched the home address of a person of interest in our database. Someone who had contact with the three original victims."

Argus sounded pleased with himself.

"We figure he's the prime suspect in the Stalker case."

The words sent a shiver down Bailey's spine.

"Who is he?' she asked. "Who's the suspect?"

"His name's Chadwick Hearst," Argus said. "He's an investigator with the Offender Review Commission."

Closing her eyes, Bailey replayed the image of the figure in the courthouse. The man who'd followed Cate.

"Yes, that's him," Bailey said with a catch in her throat. "That's the man I saw behind Cate at the courthouse. I knew I'd seen him somewhere before..."

Her voice broke as she pictured the investigator's face.

She had added him to the POI database herself because he was the county employee who had referred three of the victims to Ashworth Recovery Center.

But I never really thought he could be the one. If only I had...

But Argus was talking again and she forced her mind to focus on what he was saying.

She couldn't afford to get caught up in self-recrimination now. Not if she wanted to find Cate in time to save her.

"When I couldn't get hold of you or Fraser, I called the Miami field office," Argus explained. "Ramsey dispatched agents to Hearst's house. They intended to bring him in for questioning, but he wasn't home. Neighbors saw him leave with a suitcase this afternoon. He appeared to be alone."

Bailey's stomach twisted as she tried to think.

"Do you know if Ramsey has a trace on Hearst's phone?" she asked. "He gave me his card...I have his number."

"We'd need a warrant for that," Argus reminded her. "It's Friday night. I'm not sure what judge is going to-"

"I'll get the warrant," she said. "You just tell Ramsey to have resources ready to run the trace."

Realizing she didn't have the number she needed stored on her mother's phone, she tapped in a number she still knew from memory, exhaling in relief when her call was answered on the second ring.

"Zach, I need to speak to your father," she said without preamble. "I think we've identified the Stalker but need an emergency warrant to trace his phone."

Bailey struggled to keep her voice from breaking.

"I think he has my sister."

* * *

Bailey was still sitting in the Expedition ten minutes later when her mother's phone buzzed in her hand.

Special Agent Aisha Sharma's voice sounded far away.

"Judge Walsh just signed the warrant to trace Hearst's phone," she confirmed. "We've already got resources working on getting the real-time cell-site location."

"Thank God," Bailey said, releasing the breath she'd been holding. "Please, tell them to hurry."

Agreeing to keep her updated, Sharma ended the call as

Bailey stared out of the Expedition's rain-streaked window.

Her eyes settled on the Camaro and she sighed. She might as well make use of her time while waiting for Sharma to call back with a location.

Maybe Cate or Hearst left some sort of evidence behind.

Lightning flashed overhead as she pulled up the hood of her raincoat and stepped out into the storm.

Crossing to the Camaro, she opened the driver's side door with a gloved hand and stared into the car's interior, careful not to touch the steering wheel or upholstery, not wanting to contaminate what would surely be designated a crime scene once the responding police arrived.

As rain pattered against the windshield, Bailey heard something buzz in the Camaro's glove compartment.

Her pulse quickened as she opened it to see her phone nestled safely inside. Wherever Cate was now, she hadn't taken Bailey's phone with her.

Fraser's number appeared on the display as the phone buzzed again. Bailey grabbed for it and pressed *Accept*.

"Where have you been, Fraser?"

She regretted the question before she could stop it. What did it matter where he'd been or what he'd been doing?

All that mattered now was finding Cate.

"I was at Sasha's play," he said. "Just saw your messages from earlier, as well as a dozen from Argus Murphy."

"It seems your talk with Cisco paid off," Bailey said. "They tracked Emma's phone the night before she died. She was outside the house of an investigator for the Offender Review Commission. A man named *Chadwick Hearst*."

Her jaw tightened as she said the name.

"We suspect this guy Hearst is the Summerset Stalker," Bailey added. "And we think he has Cate."

Fraser inhaled sharply.

"The Stalker *took Cate*? Do we know where?""

"Judge Walsh signed an emergency warrant," Bailey said. "Sharma's already got resources tracing Hearst's phone."

As if on cue, Bailey's pocket began to vibrate.

Pulling out her mother's phone, she glanced down.

"That's Agent Sharma texting now."

Heart thudding, Bailey opened the text. Sharma had forwarded GPS coordinates along with a brief message.

This is Hearst's current location.

Fraser's anxious voice sounded in her ear.

"What did she say? Do they know where Hearst is?"

"His phone's been located on the coast, looks like he's just north of Bellamy Beach," Bailey said. "It's not far from where Emma's body was found. Just past the Belle Harbor Lighthouse. I'm fifteen minutes away."

She sucked in a shaky breath, wondering if Cate was with Hearst. If so, why had he taken her to the old lighthouse?

What is he planning to do with her? Is she still alive?

Bailey pushed the question away, refusing to let her mind go there. Unwilling to contemplate what she might find.

"I'll forward you the location and meet you there."

She was already moving back toward the Expedition.

"It'll take me at least thirty minutes," Fraser said, sounding as if he too was now on the move. "Promise me you won't confront Hearst on your own."

"Just meet me there as fast as you can," she said.

Ending the call, Bailey saw an alert on her phone.

Her heart stopped as she read the text message that had been sent from Cate's phone.

Meet us at the lighthouse. Come alone or she dies.

Spinning around, she started back toward the Expedition, where Ludwig was waiting, then froze as a bright blue Tesla pulled into the gas station and headed straight for her.

As the car rolled to a stop beside the Expedition, Bailey's mother jumped out, followed by her father.

"You didn't answer our calls," Jackie said, opening an umbrella against the rain. "We were getting worried."

"Where's Cate?" Chris asked, looking into the interior of the Camaro with a frown. "Did the engine overheat again?"

With both of her parents staring at her in confusion, Bailey started again for the Expedition.

"I don't have time to explain," she said, knowing that if Jackie found out what was really going on, she would dissolve into full-blown hysterics. "I'm going to get Cate, and I need to go now. Take the Camaro home and wait for us there. The keys are in the ignition."

"Is Cate alright?" Jackie asked, her voice in high-pitched pre-panic mode. "Has something happened to her?"

"All I know for sure is she needs my help, Mom."

Bailey caught and held her mother's scared green eyes, which appeared to be a mirrored reflection of her own.

"Trust me...just this once," she implored her.

Before her mother could respond, Bailey climbed into the Expedition and started the engine.

Both Jackie and Chris stood silently, watching with worried eyes as she pulled onto Haverfield Road and headed east toward the ocean without looking back.

CHAPTER THIRTY-SIX

hadwick Hearst gripped the steering wheel with both hands as the black Lexus sedan sped through the rain. He'd bought the car ten years earlier and it was in need of some repair. The engine had been known to overheat, and the back left tire had a slow leak, so he kept the speed down to sixty.

He was heading up the coast toward Bellamy Beach, not far from where Emma had agreed to meet him the week before after he'd threatened to reveal her little secret.

She'd told him she was visiting a friend's house on the beach and he'd offered to come to her.

"It's probably best to talk where no one can listen in. I doubt you'll want anyone at the station to hear what I have to say."

He hadn't given her a chance to say very much.

Her investigation into Tori Cabot's murder had led her to his office several months earlier. The pretty, young detective had remembered him from her own encounter with the legal system when she'd still been a minor.

Back then Hearst had pressured a teenage Emma to score drugs from her old dealer, claiming she'd owed him for requesting that her files be sealed.

The ploy usually worked with the younger offenders he'd been assigned to investigate, and he often targeted young women who were still struggling to get sober.

"You can pay back my kindness with some of your own," he'd tell them. "Unless you want me to change my recommendation. Maybe you'd like to go back inside?"

Plenty of the girls caved in, bringing him drugs, and agreeing to his other demands, fearful his implied threat of retribution would end in further time locked up at the Summerset County Women's Detention Center or spent at Ashworth Recovery.

Hearst had never expected the messed-up teenager he'd known as Emma Kaminski to reappear in his life as cool, confident Detective Emma Walsh.

She'd told him she was working a homicide. A young offender named Tori Cabot had gone missing. The girl had ultimately been found stabbed and mutilated behind a rest stop in Bonneville.

"You must know the place," Emma had said, watching his reaction. "There's lots of drug activity around there."

Hearst had seen the suspicion in her eyes as she'd left his office, and he had sensed it wouldn't be the last he'd hear from the detective.

Deciding to be proactive, he had followed her around for weeks, watching as she conducted a not-so-secret affair with Tony Brunner, a high-profile lawyer who had worked with plenty of the same offenders and dealers Hearst had investigated and exploited in the past.

When Emma had contacted him for a second interview,

Hearst had threatened to reveal her past, saying he would destroy her career by leaking her sealed record to the press and her boss, the Belle Harbor chief of police.

When he'd suggested they should discuss the matter privately, she'd foolishly agreed, even suggesting they meet up outside the luxury home of one of Brunner's associates.

And when he'd seen how close the beach house was to the lighthouse, where he'd spent so much time as a child, it had all seemed like fate.

He would take her out just like he had the others. It was no big deal. And at first, everything had gone to plan.

That was until Bailey Flynn had come back to town.

He'd known from the first time he'd seen the FBI agent that she would be a problem, and he had quickly come to realize that killing a police detective had been a mistake.

One he wasn't sure he could correct.

But then, just that morning, when he'd seen Cate at the courthouse, he'd had a brilliant idea as to how he might be able to fix everything after all.

He would use Bailey Flynn's sister as bait.

And when he got the agent where he wanted her, he'd take her out, along with her sister, using his father's trusty combat knife to silence them both for good.

Slowing down as he approached the Belle Harbor Lighthouse, which stood like a silent witness on the dark horizon, he pulled onto a poorly maintained gravel road, confident the part-time keeper was gone for the day.

He drove the sedan toward the ocean, steering the car past the boarded-up lightkeeper's house, before turning onto a narrow dirt road, which was half-hidden from view by an overgrown sand dune willow.

Following the road toward the water, Hearst remembered the last time he'd taken this same route with his father.

They'd come out to the coast looking for treasure many times, and he could still hear his father's words in his head.

"They named this beach after old Samuel Bellamy. He was the richest pirate there ever was, boy. Some say he drowned off the coast up north, but others think he sailed off to Florida where he buried his treasure. If it's around here, we're gonna find it."

The remembered voice faded as Hearst brought the sedan to a stop in front of the ruins of a small house. Leaving the headlights on to illuminate the crumbling stone walls, he dragged Cate out of the car, making sure her hands were still securely tied behind her back.

She swayed on her feet, dizzy from the Devil's Breath he had sprinkled onto the gag before tying it over her mouth.

He'd used the supply he'd taken from Lando Gutierrez's house after he'd killed Jasmine Blake, knowing from past experience that the drug would make the prosecutor compliant and unlikely to fight back.

Forcing her to walk across the uneven ground, he steered Cate toward the remains of what had been a caretaker's house, back when the small graveyard beyond had provided a final resting place for residents of the coastal community.

Stumbling and disoriented, Cate tripped and almost lost a shoe as Hearst propelled her forward, not stopping until they were sheltered under the caretaker's sagging roof.

As rain dripped through cracks in the ceiling, Hearst

released Cate's arm, letting her slide to the ground, her arms still bound awkwardly behind her back.

The gag, now wet and soggy, fell down around her neck.

"You're the one who killed them, aren't you?" she said in a hoarse voice. "You killed those girls. And Emma."

She glared up at him.

"Why'd you do it?" she asked, her words slurring. "What did they ever do to you?"

His jaw clenched as he met her accusatory gaze.

"They defiled my mother's memory," he said, adopting a soft, dangerous tone. "And they defied God's will."

A flash of lightning lit up the sky, filtering through the bare windows and the cracked ceiling.

Bending down, he spoke close in her ear.

"Those *angels* had fallen," he said with a scornful sneer. "And so I did what needed to be done. I sent them to hell."

His sneer turned into an angry laugh, and Cate stared up at him with wide, dilated eyes.

"You *are* the devil," she gasped, sagging against the wall.

Her words were followed by a roll of thunder and then a blast from the lighthouse's horn.

The fog was rolling in.

Hearst cursed loudly as a stream of cold rainwater trickled down the back of his neck.

Thinking of his warm, safe house sitting empty only miles away, he felt his frustration and anger grow.

If they discover my secret, I can never go back home.

For all he knew, the police could be there now, searching through his things, waiting for him to arrive.

266

Luckily, he had packed his collection of wings in his suitcase, along with some clothes and other essentials.

He'd known Bailey Flynn and the FBI task force had been investigating the connection between the fallen angels and the Ashworth Recovery Center.

Bailey had gotten Nigella Ashworth all riled up with her questions and accusations and, according to Sabrina West's latest report on Channel 3 News, the FBI had assigned agents from the Miami field office and the Bureau's Behavioral Analysis Unit in Quantico, Virginia to help the local police solve the Summerset Stalker case.

Hearst knew it would only be a matter of time before the task force discovered he was the one common denominator between all the Stalker's victims.

They'd eventually figure out that he'd been assigning the majority of his offenders to Ashworth Recovery Center for over a dozen years, and that Nigella Ashworth had made it worth his while financially, allowing him to make enough money on a government worker's salary to support his expensive drug habit.

And of course, it would come out that he had pressured the more vulnerable, easily manipulated offenders into supplying him with drugs, even though he'd known what he was doing could technically be called coercion.

But lowlifes like Lando Gutierrez do the same and worse all the time and they get away with it. Can they blame me for taking advantage of the situation like everyone else?

Thinking back on it, he decided that everything had been just fine up until a year ago. The real trouble hadn't started until he'd gotten the idea to use Devil's Breath as a chaser to the benzos he took by the handful.

A Colombian dealer who regularly supplied him with cocaine had shown Hearst the fine white powder.

"They call this Devil's Breath, although it comes from flowers on the Borrachero trees called Angel's Trumpet."

He'd laughed as if he'd just told a joke.

Suppliers back home get the locals to crush up the seed pods and then they sell it along with cocaine."

He'd left Hearst with a solemn warning.

"The effects can be dangerous, so you have to be careful. Take it only when you're alone. It can make you do bad things."

The dealer had been right.

The Devil's Breath had messed with his head.

Past and present, good and evil, had all gotten distorted somehow. He'd started having dreams and hearing voices.

Just as the dealer had predicted, it had made him do bad things. Like when he'd encountered Wren Dempsey and had seen her angel wings. That night he'd lost all control.

It was time to take it back.

Sensing that the rain was stopping, Hearst lifted the gag back into place and tightened it over Cate's mouth before jerking her to her feet.

As he pushed her forward, he used the low rumble of crashing waves to guide him in the right direction.

They'd only covered a few yards of uneven ground when his phone buzzed in his pocket.

Stopping abruptly, he pulled out his phone. Was Bailey Flynn calling in response to his text?

He accepted the call, silently holding the phone with his free hand as a deep, unfamiliar voice spoke in his ear.

"Hello? Is this Chadwick Hearst?"

The foghorn on the lighthouse blew again as Hearst quickly ended the call, not interested in talking to anyone but the woman he was planning to meet.

Moving ahead, he steered Cate into a thick growth of coastal scrub, pushing aside the prickly fronds of a saw palmetto to reveal the old stone archway straight ahead.

Bellamy Beach Burial Ground – Est. 1896

As he let the wide fronds fall back into place behind them, the branches blocked the sedan's headlights, throwing Hearst and his captive into shadowy darkness.

Lifting the phone in his hand, he activated the flashlight, illuminating the old graveyard beyond, revealing a scattering of tilted headstones and an above-ground crypt he remembered well from previous trips with his father.

There's more than treasure buried around here, boy.

His father's harsh laughter echoed through Hearst's head, filling him with a growing sense of urgency.

There isn't much time left. Soon Bailey Flynn will arrive.

Drawing his father's knife from the sheath at the small of his back, he approached the rusted iron door that blocked entry to the crypt and used the tip of the sharp, serrated blade to jimmy the old lock.

Hearst wrenched the door back, wincing as it screeched open. Peering into the rough stone vault, he nodded with satisfaction, ignoring Cate's muffled scream of alarm.

Little had changed since the last time he'd been there. It

was just as he remembered. Nothing had been disturbed.

The crypt would serve nicely as the final resting place for the Flynn sisters just as he'd envisioned.

Of course, there was still one sister missing.

And in order for his plan to work, he'd need Bailey to meet him at the lighthouse as he'd instructed.

And she'd better be alone.

CHAPTER THIRTY-SEVEN

Dalton West looked over at Sid Morley, who sat beside him in the pickup's cab. Before he could ask where the next turn was, Amadeus' head appeared between the seats. The German shepherd's tongue lolled out of his mouth as he surveyed the dark road ahead with interest, and Dalton noticed that the fur around his muzzle was starting to fade from black to gray.

"Are you sure we're not on a wild goose chase?" Morley asked as he leaned forward to peer around the dog's snout.

Turning his eyes back to the highway, Dalton shrugged.

"I'm not sure of anything," he admitted. "But you saw that footage Sabrina took outside the courthouse. The guy in the black Lexus was definitely watching Cate Flynn. And he pulled out right behind her when she left."

The sedan's license plate had been clearly visible once Sabrina had zoomed in on it, and Morley had called in a favor with one of his contacts at the DMV to link the tag to a name and address, which he had immediately forwarded to Bailey Flynn, along with a message asking if there was anything else he could do to help.

When she hadn't responded after a solid ten minutes, he

hadn't been able to resist doing a little more digging.

He was a natural-born investigator after all, unable to resist an unanswered question or an unsolved mystery.

In this case, it had only taken a simple Google search to come up with a phone number, which Dalton had promptly called. Although he hadn't been sure what to say when the phone had been answered on the second ring.

Are you the Summerset Stalker? Did you abduct Cate Flynn?

Neither option seemed appropriate, so he had settled on something more generic.

"Hello? Is this Chadwick Hearst?"

Dalton's hesitant question had been followed by the long, mournful wail of a foghorn, unmistakable in its intensity.

The call had been abruptly disconnected, but the sound of the big horn had continued to echo in his head, convincing him that he and Morley should go take a look around the old Belle Harbor Lighthouse.

"It's right next to Bellamy Beach, close to where Emma's body was found," he'd told Morley. "Maybe Hearst has taken Cate there, too."

However, now that they were nearing the coast, with a thunderstorm roiling overhead, he was beginning to wonder if the person on the other end of the call had in fact been the man in the black sedan, and if the horn he'd heard had really been as close as he'd estimated.

Maybe it was all just wishful thinking.

"Turn in there," Morley said, pointing toward a gravel road. "The lighthouse will be straight ahead."

As the Dodge made the turn and began bumping over the

uneven ground, its headlights fell on a house with boarded-up windows.

"That's the old lightkeeper's house," Morley explained as if he were a tour guide on duty. "No one lives on the property anymore. It's no longer necessary now that the lantern and foghorn are all automated."

Dalton steered the pickup toward the big white tower, impressed with its size as they drew nearer.

"The city retains a part-time keeper who maintains the equipment," Morley was saying. "But it doesn't look as if anyone's here now."

The older man dug two flashlights out of the bag at his feet as Dalton brought the Dodge to a stop in the middle of the grounds, just past the keeper's house.

After taking a flashlight from Morley, Dalton checked his holster, making sure his Glock was secure.

"Are you going to be alright out there?"

He nodded toward his companion's prosthetic leg.

"It's pretty muddy and wet."

"I think I can manage," Morley said with a shrug. "If it gets too much, I'll take a rest. And one thing's for sure..."

He hooked a thumb toward the lighthouse.

"I won't be going up all those stairs. From what I remember, there's over two hundred of them."

Opening the door before Dalton could respond, Morley climbed out of the truck, allowing Amadeus to jump down after him. The dog immediately began running through nearby puddles and sniffing the soggy ground.

"The rain strengthens the scent of just about everything

out here," Morley said as Dalton switched on his flashlight and joined him beside the truck. "It gets him excited. Better put on his leash or he'll be...oh, there he goes now."

The German shepherd darted toward a thick line of scrub that led down toward the water. He barked and turned in a circle as Dalton aimed the flashlight in his direction.

Squinting into the shadows, he couldn't see what had caught the dog's attention. Moving closer to get a better look, he saw a patch of something red.

"Is that a *shoe*?"

Dalton hurried toward Amadeus, ignoring the dirty water his boots kicked up as he went, aiming his flashlight at the ground ahead. The beam illuminated a red high–heeled shoe, halfway submerged in a muddy puddle.

Bending over, he picked up the leather shoe by the heel and turned to Morley, who was walking toward him with careful, deliberate steps, obviously trying to keep his balance over the muddy terrain.

"Cate Flynn was wearing a red suit in that video your sister took outside the courthouse, wasn't she?" Morley asked as he smoothed back his thinning hair, which was now wet with rain and plastered to his head. "Do you remember if she was wearing matching shoes?"

Dalton nodded slowly, mentally replaying the video footage he had seen earlier that evening.

"Yes, I believe she was," he said, his pulse quickening as he studied the sodden shoe. "Which means she might have been here. Could *still* be here. Hearst could be here, too."

A sense of foreboding spread through him as he turned

and used the flashlight to check his surroundings.

"Did you bring a weapon?" he asked as his hand moved to rest on the butt of his gun.

"I never leave home without it," Morley assured him.

The retired agent patted the shoulder holster strapped under his jacket. His eyes scanned the keeper's house then moved on to the ground around the lighthouse.

"I don't see any other sign of them," he said, belatedly pulling up the hood of his jacket. "But let's see what Amadeus can find."

Calling the black German shepherd to him, Morley snapped the leash onto his collar.

He held out the muddy shoe.

"Let's get to work," he told the dog, allowing him to sniff eagerly at the shoe. "You got the scent?"

Smiling to himself as Amadeus barked with excitement, the older man loosened up on the leash.

"Find it!" he encouraged. "Find it, boy!"

Amadeus barked and held his nose up, testing the cool, wet air, before lowering his head to the ground.

His tail wagged back and forth as he scurried forward, heading toward a messy overgrowth of shrubs that masked the entrance to a narrow dirt road.

Quickening his gait to try to keep up with the dog, Morley followed him onto the road, while Dalton brought up the rear. Soon they were cutting across scrubland and dunes toward the ocean, their booted feet sinking ankle-deep in wet sand and dune grass.

Dalton kept an eye on Morley's uneven gait, watching it

become more and more erratic as they went.

When the older man's prosthetic leg got caught up in a flowering railroad vine, Dalton reached out and steadied him just before he could topple into a knee-high prickly pear cactus growing along the side of the road.

Concerned for his companion, and worried they were in fact on a wild goose chase as Morley had suggested, Dalton was just about to suggest they turn back when he saw the ruins of an old house up ahead.

"What's that?" he asked, surveying the caved-in roof and crumbling stone walls. "And what's it doing out here?"

His question was answered as Amadeus pushed past a wide palmetto frond to reveal an old stone archway.

Century-old words had been etched into battered stone.

Bellamy Beach Burial Ground – Est. 1896

Moving under the arch, Dalton shone the flashlight around what appeared to be an old graveyard.

Weathered headstones sat at odd angles around an above-ground stone crypt. Two wide stone steps led up to its rusty iron door, which hung slightly ajar, allowing Amadeus to stick his snout inside.

Immediately the German shepherd backed away, then turning to Morley, he began to bark.

"Okay, boy, I hear you," Morley said, tugging on the dog's leash to pull him back. "Let's see what you found."

Before Dalton could step forward to take a look, Morley held out a hand to stop him.

"Wait, we've got prints."

He pointed down to the stone steps.

Boot prints were visible next to the muddy paw prints Amadeus had left behind. And another set of prints, too.

"What about that shoe we found?" Dalton asked as his eyes met Morley's. "Is it a match to the print?"

Both men were silent as they compared the pointed toe and small rounded heel of the red shoe to the muddy prints.

"Yep, it's a match," Morley said.

Glancing toward the iron door, he swallowed hard.

"You think Cate Flynn is dead in there?"

Dalton hesitated, then shook his head.

"You're holding a left shoe, and that's a left print," he said, pointing to the stone step. "So, whoever was wearing that shoe, must have lost it after they made that print."

His logic seemed to confuse Morley.

"Why would Cate Flynn be walking around a graveyard on a rainy night?" he asked. "And where is she now?"

"I'm guessing she and Hearst came out here first for some reason, then circled back to the lighthouse," Dalton said. "Doesn't make much sense to me either, but it must have something to do with whatever's in that crypt."

Stepping forward, he gripped the iron door and pulled.

The door creaked open a few more inches, releasing a high-pitched shriek of rusted metal.

A fetid scent of decay greeted him as he leaned forward and aimed the beam of the flashlight into the tomb, bracing himself for an unpleasant view of old, dusty remains.

Unprepared for the sight that met his eyes, Dalton staggered backward with a horrified cry.

He lost his footing on the bottom step and almost

277

brought Morley down with him as he fought to regain his balance, terrified he might fall into the nightmare within.

Even as he squeezed his eyes shut, he could see the stacks of bones along the walls, and the pile of skulls arranged on the raised platform in the middle of the tomb.

The flashlight had revealed every disturbing detail, lighting up the top skull, which still had strands of hair attached, and a skeletonized corpse, still clothed in jeans and a sweatshirt, its hands fastened behind its back with shiny metal handcuffs.

Forcing the images away, he turned to Morley.

"Call the police," he said in a shaky voice. "Call 911."

"Should I ask for an ambulance?"

Dalton quickly shook his head.

"It's way too late for that."

Then his eyes fell on the red shoe in Morley's hand.

Looking toward the lighthouse, he frowned.

"Or maybe not. Maybe I can still get there in time."

CHAPTER THIRTY-EIGHT

B ailey kept the gas pedal pressed to the floor of the Expedition, refusing to slow down until the calm voice of the GPS app on her phone instructed her to take the next turn. Her destination was on the right.

Pulling onto an uneven gravel road, she instinctively turned off the SUV's headlights, not wanting to alert Hearst that she'd arrived just yet.

The storm had picked up again in the last few minutes, making it necessary for Bailey to turn on the windshield wipers as she strained to see the road ahead, using only the glow from the lantern one hundred and fifty feet above her to light the way.

A streak of lightning flashed overhead as the Expedition rolled silently forward, revealing a boarded-up building, which Bailey assumed must be the lightkeeper's house.

A Dodge pickup was parked nearby, and she put one hand on her Glock as she brought the Expedition to a stop beside the truck, straining to see through the rain and the fog.

Was Hearst in there? Was Cate?

Her heartbeat quickened, then settled again as another flash of lightning illuminated the empty cab.

She looked into the Expedition's backseat to see Ludwig staring through the window, watching the churning sky with worried eyes that mirrored her own unease.

As the lighthouse's fog horn blew overhead, they both jumped and looked up at the glowing beacon.

"I know we're not supposed to go out there and look for Cate without back-up," she said, remembering Fraser's warning. "But we can't just sit here and wait, can we?"

Ludwig cocked his head as if he was considering the question but wasn't quite sure of the answer.

"Fraser should be here soon," she murmured, reaching for the door handle. "But maybe not soon enough."

She was thinking of Sid Morley now.

If I'd arrived even a few seconds later that day, Ronin Godfrey would have killed him. If I'd waited for backup then, Morley would be dead now. Just like Dolores Santos.

A memory of the little girl's pale, lifeless face flashed through Bailey's mind, followed by an image of the grisly bullet hole between Ronin Godfrey's bulging eyes.

The hated images had been burned into her brain that day. They had lived in her memory and haunted her dreams ever since, despite all her efforts to make them go away.

Morley lost a leg and Dolores lost her life because I wasn't there to save them. If I wait now, what will happen to Cate?

A shiver rolled up Bailey's back at the thought, and she shook her head, trying to dislodge the fear and doubt that threatened to take hold.

She couldn't just sit in the car and wait for help to arrive when Cate was at the mercy of a madman.

No, she and Ludwig needed to get out and search for her sister. They needed to find Cate before it was too late.

But her hand fell away from the handle and she once again turned to Ludwig.

"But I don't have anything of Cate's. Nothing to help you pick up her scent," she said, looking around the interior of the Expedition. "Nothing of Hearst's either."

The German shepherd tensed upon hearing the word *scent* and stared at Bailey with dark, expectant eyes, sensing a search was about to begin.

"Or maybe I do have something," Bailey murmured, thinking of the day she'd interviewed Hearst and hoping she'd kept the business card he'd given her.

Pulling out the pocket-sized wallet where she kept her credentials and credit cards, she found the slightly wrinkled card and held it up with trembling fingers.

The card had been stored in Hearst's pocket, but would his scent still cling to the thick paper stock? And would Ludwig be able to pick up on the scent after it had been in Bailey's wallet for several days?

A dog's ability to pick up a scent was supposed to be a thousand times stronger than a human's.

But, even if the German shepherd could detect Hearst's scent, would he be able to track him in the wind and rain?

"I know you can do this, Ludwig," she said, her legs numb and her hands shaky as she checked her Glock and pulled up the hood of her jacket. "I have faith in you."

Opening the door, she stepped out into the rain, instantly on alert, one hand on her Glock as she waited for Ludwig to jump down onto the muddy ground.

As she snapped on his leash, she scanned the area for any sign of Hearst or Cate, but the buildings and surrounding grounds were dark and silent.

Holding Hearst's business card out toward Ludwig, she allowed the German shepherd to rub his nose across the smooth paper, willing him to pick up the killer's scent.

"That's it, boy," she praised as the dog sniffed the card. "Have you got it? Have you got the scent?"

Ludwig recoiled as if he'd smelled something he didn't like, but the wagging of his tail grew more frantic.

Bailey stepped back with leash in hand, hoping the card would be enough. Praying the dog would pick up the scent.

"Find him!" she said. "Go find him, Ludwig!"

The German shepherd immediately lowered his nose to the ground. Keeping his head down, he walked around the Expedition, then turned and headed toward the lighthouse.

Bailey's stomach dropped as the dog circled the area again and again, then stopped and lifted his nose into the air. Looking back at her, he blinked against the raindrops that continued to fall, unable to pick up the scent.

Holding the end of the leash in one hand and keeping the other hand on the butt of her gun, Bailey moved quickly over the muddy ground, deciding they needed to take cover.

We can't just stand out here in the open and wait.

She began circling the sturdy brick and granite base of the lighthouse but could see no way to get inside.

As she looked up at the white tower, which rose one hundred and fifty feet overhead, she was reminded of the fairytale that had always frightened her as a child.

If Cate was a princess locked away in this tower, then the evil villain would be waiting up there with her, right?

The foghorn sounded overhead just as Ludwig barked and yanked against the leash, pulling her behind him, signaling that he had finally picked up the scent.

Following the dog along the curved wall to the other side of the tower, Bailey saw a narrow set of steps leading up to a small landing.

Ludwig barked again as he came to a stop outside a large, weathered wooden door, then looked back at Bailey as if impatient for her to open it.

With little hope the lighthouse door would be unlocked, Bailey reached for the huge metal handle and pulled. The heavy door swung open with a groan of wood and metal, revealing the tower's ground floor.

Slipping the Glock from her holster, she held the gun out in front of her as Ludwig scrambled inside.

Bailey followed closely behind the dog, hesitating at the bottom of the spiral staircase, looking up toward the top with a mixture of awe and dismay.

During a field trip to the lighthouse when she was still in middle school, she'd been told there were over two hundred stairs leading up to the lantern room and the widow walk that surrounded it, as well as ten landings along the way.

Based on Ludwig's eagerness as he headed up the stairs, she suspected Chad Hearst could be on any one of the landings waiting for her right now.

Staying close to the metal banister, she ascended the

stairs, holding her Glock up, keeping the barrel trained on the next landing, bracing for the possibility that Hearst could appear above her at any moment with a knife in hand.

Bailey's legs were aching and she was sure she must have already climbed close to two hundred stairs when they reached the floor that housed the watch room, where the lighthouse keeper maintained logs of weather conditions.

Stopping to rest her trembling legs, she took a peek over the banister, looking down the way they had come, wanting to make sure no one was sneaking up behind them.

A wave of vertigo washed over her as her eyes dropped to the ground floor below. She swayed toward the rail, sure she was about to fall to her death below.

Instead, she took a quick step back, leaned against the sturdy stone wall, and lowered the Glock to her side.

As she closed her eyes and inhaled deeply, Bailey felt Ludwig's warm nose press against her hand.

He nuzzled her fingers, eager to get her attention, anxious for her to follow as he led her to a metal door with the words *Service Room* stenciled across it.

Using both paws, he scratched at the door, his body rigid and tense, his tail wagging with excitement.

So this is where Hearst is waiting.

The thought sent a burst of adrenaline through her.

Cate might be right behind that door.

Leaning forward, Bailey turned the handle and eased open the door, quietly stepping inside with her gun raised.

She'd been braced for Hearst to jump out at her, but the room was empty as Ludwig followed her inside and crossed the floor, pulling impatiently on his leash.

Keeping her weapon at the ready, Bailey's eyes strained to see into every shadow as she surveyed the room, which was filled with cleaning supplies, spare parts, and tools.

She jumped as Ludwig barked and began pawing frantically at a heavy iron door on the far wall.

Bailey knew the door must lead out to the gallery deck, which circled the tower just below the lantern and the widow's walk.

"Quiet, Ludwig," she whispered, coming up behind him.

But the dog barked again, then turned back to scratch even more enthusiastically at the door as if wanting to make sure she knew he'd found the scent.

The dog's clear signal could mean only one thing.

Hearst was waiting somewhere beyond the door.

And Cate might be there, too.

Knowing she could afford to wait no longer, Bailey nudged Ludwig out of the way, pushed open the door, and swung her Glock up as a gust of wind swirled into the room.

Adrenaline shot through her as she peered out at the open-air deck, where keepers of the past had stood above the churning ocean, watching for approaching ships while the giant beacon glowed in the lantern room overhead.

Ludwig barked behind her and tried to wiggle past.

"Sit, Ludwig," she ordered in a shaky voice. "Stay."

Reluctantly, the German shepherd sat.

Stepping out onto the wide metal platform, Bailey quickly closed the iron door behind her, ensuring that Ludwig would remain safely inside the tower.

Wind immediately swirled around her, picking up her hair and whipping dark blonde strands against her face.

Holding the gun out in front of her, Bailey took a small step, keeping close to the sturdy wall of the tower, grateful for the waist-high guardrail that separated her from a fatal drop to the sand and rocks below.

The deck was empty so far as Bailey could see, but it circled around the entire tower, which meant Hearst could be waiting for her just around the curve.

Or maybe Ludwig got it wrong this time.

The thought was disconcerting, but it was possible.

Maybe he didn't pick up on Hearst's scent from the card after all. Maybe I'm here in the wind and storm while Cate is-

Her doubts ended abruptly at the sound of a soft cry somewhere nearby. The cry had been muffled by the wind, but she knew the voice.

"Cate?"

Clutching her Glock in both hands, Bailey stood motionless on the deck, listening intently, hoping for another sound that would let her know Cate was still alive.

As the ocean churned behind her and the lights of Belle Harbor glowed in the distance ahead, Bailey sensed movement. And then a figure stepped into view.

Chad Hearst was standing on the deck, illuminated by the rotating beacon overhead, one arm pinning Cate to his chest, the other holding a knife to her throat.

"We've been waiting for you," he called out, his voice loud enough to be heard over the wind and surf.

Instinctively, Bailey took a step forward, aiming her gun

at the man's thick thatch of dark hair.

"Drop the weapon and back away!" she ordered.

But Hearst just shook his head.

"We both know you won't shoot. Not when you might hit Cate," he said coldly. "So, unless you want me to slit your sister's throat..."

He made a menacing move with the knife.

"No!" Bailey cried out. "You don't have to do this. Just let my sister go and you can leave. No one else has to get hurt."

She took in Cate's glassy eyes and slack mouth, as well as the gag that had fallen down around her neck. Hearst had obviously drugged her with something.

There was no telling what he'd given her.

"Please, my sister needs help. She..."

Bailey's voice faltered as she saw the red and blue lights over Hearst's shoulder. They were flashing in the distance, coming closer. Help was on the way.

All she had to do was stall for time.

"She needs to see a doctor," she managed to say, trying to think fast. "And so do you."

Swallowing hard, she ignored the sneer on Hearst's face.

"I mean, anyone who did what you did to those girls must need help," she continued, trying to sound concerned. "You must be sick. You can see a doctor. You can get the help you need and–"

"Oh, I don't need a doctor," he cut in. "I didn't kill those girls because I was sick. I killed them because they deserved it. And because of the Devil's Breath."

He grinned as he met Bailey's eyes.

"It makes me do bad things."

Inching closer, he looked down at Cate's lolling head.

"I gave your sister some, too. To keep her in line," he said. "Only, she can't handle it like I can."

A flash of lightning lit up the sky as he laughed.

"Those girls I killed were no *angels*," he said, his voice dripping with scorn. "Not like my mother. She was the angel. But those girls? They had all sinned. And so I did what needed to be done. I sent them to hell."

An evil gleam now blazed from his eyes.

"What about Emma?" she asked weakly. "Why kill her?"

Hearst took another step forward, his arm tightening around Cate as he cocked his head in mock contemplation.

"Oh, she wasn't who you thought she was," he snarled, growing suddenly impatient. "She was a sinner, too. Even worse than the others. And she knew what I had done. She was going to turn me in. I couldn't have that."

Nodding toward the Glock in Bailey's hand, Hearst spoke again before she could reply.

"Now, I said to drop the gun."

As Bailey looked down at the Glock, a shadow moved on the widow's walk above. A dark figure was creeping along the narrow platform that circled the lantern room.

"Hurry up," Hearst barked, pushing the blade into the soft skin below Cate's chin. "Drop the gun."

As Bailey laid the Glock on the deck, Hearst scoffed and nodded toward the guardrail.

"When I said drop it, I meant over the side."

Moving slowly, she bent to pick up the gun, stalling for

time, mentally calculating how quickly she could get to the little Ruger in her ankle holster.

"Either the gun goes over now or your sister dies," Hearst said. "It's up to you."

Lifting her hand, Bailey threw the Glock over the rail.

Hearst watched it spin out of view, then abruptly released Cate, letting her drop heavily to the deck.

He raised the combat knife in front of him and lunged toward Bailey, who dodged the blade of the knife as it slashed the air only inches from her face.

Losing his balance, Hearst fell to one knee, giving Bailey the chance to turn and run. She needed to get Hearst away from Cate before she attempted to counter his attack.

As footsteps sounded behind her, Bailey looked over her shoulder, knowing she had little room to maneuver.

If she went much further around the circular deck she'd end up back where Cate had collapsed, and Hearst would once again have the advantage.

Bending over as she ran, Bailey reached for the ankle holster that held her little Ruger. Managing to get a hand on the gun, she spun around to face Hearst, but he was already upon her, charging forward, knife in hand.

She braced for impact just as a deafening crack sounded overhead. Dropping to the ground, Bailey rolled toward the wall, thinking a bolt of lightning must have struck the lighthouse, wondering if she'd been hit.

But as she looked up, she saw Hearst staggering backward, one hand clutching his chest and the other hand gripping his knife. Someone had shot him.

Whoever was on the widow's walk must have a gun.

As Hearst began to stumble back the way he'd come, Bailey looked up, but the widow's walk was empty.

Gripping the Ruger in her hand, she raced after Hearst, knowing he would kill Cate or use her as a human shield if given another chance.

As she passed the iron door, Bailey could hear Ludwig barking on the other side as if urging her on.

"Do you think your mother would be proud, Hearst?" she shouted. "If she knew about the wings?"

He stiffened at the words, then stopped and turned.

Blood dripped from the hand on his chest, staining his white shirt a dark crimson. He swayed on his feet.

"What do you know about the wings?" he asked, his words slurred. "Or about my mother?"

"I know some of the women you killed had been branded with wings," she said. "And I know you were sick enough to carve them up and keep the wings as souvenirs."

She shook her head in genuine disgust.

"If your mother is an angel like you say, she'd be ashamed of you. Of what you've done."

Bailey aimed the Ruger at Hearst just as a man swung down from the widow's walk above, landing softly on the deck behind him.

She had time to register Dalton West's fair hair and broad shoulders before Hearst came charging toward her, his knife raised in a bloody fist, his face twisted with rage.

Dropping backward onto the deck, Bailey squeezed the Ruger's trigger seconds too late, missing Hearst by inches as he crashed past her into the guardrail.

The old metal gave way with a deafening screech, sending him tumbling off the deck, his roar of fury quickly swallowed by the roar of the wind.

Crawling to the edge of the deck, Bailey looked down to where Hearst's body was sprawled on the rocks below, his white shirt fluttering like a sail in the dark, windy night.

She turned to see Dalton West moving toward Cate, who lay crumpled on the deck shivering. Her sister's favorite red suit was soaked and streaked with mud. One of her red shoes was missing.

Jumping to her feet, Bailey hurried to Cate's side, watching with worried eyes as Dalton untied her hands and checked her pulse before covering her with his rain jacket.

As she knelt beside her sister, he pulled a red shoe from the pocket of the jacket and slipped it on Cate's foot.

"I think she lost this down there by the keeper's house," he said. "Or maybe she kicked it off on purpose. Maybe she hoped someone would find it."

Just then footsteps sounded on the stairs and the door swung open. Bailey turned to see Ludwig barking and Fraser coming through the door, gun drawn. Aisha Sharma came in fast behind him.

"It's okay. Hearst is dead," Bailey said, nodding toward the broken guardrail. "But we need an ambulance. He dosed Cate with Devil's Breath and she's having a bad reaction."

"An ambulance should be on the way," Dalton said, getting to his feet. "Morley called 911 from the graveyard."

Bailey frowned up at him.

"What graveyard? And what's Morley doing here?"

"It's kind of a long story," Dalton said as two paramedics appeared in the doorway. "And based on what I saw in that graveyard, the FBI and the Belle Harbor PD are going to want to hear all about it very soon."

He pushed a soggy strand of hair back from his eyes.

"But that can wait until after Cate gets to the hospital," he said. "She'll need you there when the drugs wear off."

Dalton backed away, making room for the paramedics beside Cate, and Bailey joined him by the door.

She bent to hug Ludwig, scratching the still-damp fur behind the dog's ears.

Looking up, she caught and held Dalton's gaze, noticing again what kind blue eyes he had.

"Thanks for coming to find us," she said, feeling suddenly awkward. "You saved my life...and Cate's."

"It's my job to find people in need," he said with a shrug. "Just like Ludwig there. And who knows, maybe one day you'll return the favor."

Bailey studied his handsome face, noting the faint flush that now colored his cheeks, and nodded.

"You could be right," she agreed. "You never know what might happen. After tonight, I'd say anything's possible."

CHAPTER THIRTY-NINE

Cate Flynn slid two pieces of wholewheat bread into the toaster before turning to the refrigerator. Opening the door and peering in, she smiled as she saw the glass of freshly squeezed orange juice Bailey had been preparing for her on a daily basis ever since she'd gotten home from the hospital.

As she carried the juice and toast to the little breakfast table, she heard the front door open.

Seconds later, Bailey and Ludwig appeared in the doorway, still breathing hard from their morning run.

"You're up early," Bailey said, running a suspicious eye over Cate's slim gray pants and matching jacket. "You aren't going back to the office already, are you?"

"You sound just like Mom," Cate said, unable to resist the barb. "And yes, I am going to the courthouse today. I got the all-clear from the doctor and I'm feeling fine."

She dropped her eyes as Bailey studied her.

"Well, maybe not *fine*," she admitted. "But I'm okay. My first session with Dr. Chung went well. She said it's normal not to be able to remember everything that happened, although, in time, some of it will come back."

Cate took a bite of the toast and slowly chewed.

In truth, the new psychotherapist she was seeing had been alarmed to find out she'd been subjected to an unknown dosage of scopolamine, telling her the drug was well known for its psychoactive effects, causing hallucinations, delirium, and harmful behavior.

Based on the nightmares she'd been having, Cate wasn't sure she wanted to remember anything about Hearst or the terrible night at the lighthouse anyway.

Sometimes it's better to just forget and move on.

Looking down at Ludwig, who had come to sit beside her, Cate slipped him a piece of her bread.

"Did you ever get the results back from the vet?" she asked, wanting to change the subject. "Is Ludwig okay?"

She turned worried eyes to Bailey, who had rushed the dog to the veterinarian in a panic after she'd gotten a call from the FBI lab, where Hearst's business card had been tested for prints and trace evidence.

A trace amount of scopolamine had been detected, which meant that Ludwig had likely inhaled some of the substance when he'd sniffed the card to pick up on Hearst's scent.

"Yes, the test came back yesterday," Bailey said as she sank into a chair across from Cate. "There was no trace of scopolamine or anything else suspicious in his blood."

She shot a relieved look at the German shepherd, who had wandered over to his empty food bowl and was looking back at Bailey with a hurt expression.

"You'd better give Ludwig his breakfast," Cate said.

Pushing her chair back from the table, she stood up.

"I've got to get to the office. I've got a meeting this morning with my team. We're preparing to file bribery charges against Nigella Ashworth."

Bailey's eyes followed Cate with interest as she took her plate and cup to the sink.

"You think the information we collected from Hearst's computer will be enough to convict him?" she asked.

"For a serial killer and a drug addict, he kept meticulous records," Cate confirmed. "We found itemized details of the payments he received from Nigella. It goes back over a dozen years."

She didn't add that Emma Kaminski had been one of the first teenagers Chad Hearst had assigned to Ashworth Recovery Center. She didn't want to see the miserable expression that fell over her sister's face whenever she spoke of her late friend.

"And what about Nigella's son, Neil?" Bailey asked. "Will he be included in the indictment?"

Cate shook her head.

"As far as we know, Neil Ashworth wasn't in direct contact with Hearst, and we have no evidence indicating he was aware of the arrangement his mother had made."

Filling her thermos with fresh coffee, Cate headed toward the door, then stopped and turned back.

"Oh, and by the way. My afternoon meeting concerns the additional charges we'll be filing against Lando Gutierrez."

She flashed a grim smile.

"Unfortunately, since he managed to make bail and then immediately skipped town, he won't be here to face them."

An angry flush colored her cheeks as she thought of the drug dealer and his recent disappearance.

"We also plan to bring human trafficking charges against Lando based on his exploitation of Wren Dempsey, Tori Cabot, Hallie Kwan, and Jasmine Blake," she added. "And the mutilated skin found in Hearst's suitcase will be used as evidence to support charges of felony battery."

She checked her watch and grimaced.

"That reminds me, I need to make a stop on the way to work, so I'd better go. I don't want to be late for my first day back at the office."

"Don't forget about the memorial service for Emma," Bailey called after her. "It's at sunset on Bellamy Beach."

* * *

Cate smoothed back her auburn hair and adjusted her suit jacket as she stepped into the lobby of the Summerset County Medical Examiner's office.

Wrinkling her nose at an underlying odor she couldn't quite identify, she stepped up to the counter and saw that the chair behind it was empty.

"You're early," a deep voice said. "We open at nine."

She turned around to see Mason Knox standing behind her. The medical examiner wore a pair of light blue scrubs under a white lab coat. He offered Cate a smile as he pushed a dark curl off his forehead.

"I almost didn't recognize you without your protective mask and cap," she said as he led her into the back. "I appreciate you meeting with me on such short notice."

"It's no problem," Mason said as he waved her into his office and took a seat behind his desk. "You wanted to discuss the autopsies I performed on the Stalker victims?"

Sinking into the chair across from him, she nodded.

"I'm preparing a case against Lando Gutierrez," she said. "As you know, he mutilated four of the women who ended up as victims of the Summerset Stalker, whom we now know was Chad Hearst."

Her voice filled with frustration.

"But if I want to get a conviction against Lando, I'm going to need physical evidence."

Mason leaned back in his chair and frowned.

"I'm glad to hear you're charging Lando," he said. "He needs to be held to account for what he did to those women. But what kind of evidence are you looking for?"

"We found women's skin in Hearst's possession," she said. "It was skin from the victims Lando had branded."

Swallowing hard, Cate forced herself to continue in a matter of fact, businesslike voice.

"Hearst had dried the skin, mounted it, and put it in a frame, as a collector might do with butterflies or moths."

She saw Mason's clean-shaven jaw tighten.

"I'm hoping you can examine the skin and match each piece back to its owner. I'll also need a description of the markings Lando burned onto his victims."

Thinking of the horrifying collection discovered in Hearst's suitcase, as well as the collection of stuffed and mounted animals he'd had in his home, Cate shuddered.

"I'd be glad to help," Mason said, his dark eyes bright with an emotion Cate interpreted as anger. "The bodies have already been interred, but I've got the autopsy photos and reports, so I believe we can pull together the evidence you need. Have the skin sent over and I'll get to work."

"Thank you," Cate said, surprised he'd agreed to her request so easily. "I was worried you might be too busy to help. I imagine you've been pulled into the investigation over at the burial ground in Bellamy Beach."

Mason exhaled wearily.

"I've been doing what I can," he said. "Luckily, the FBI has arranged to bring in a forensic archeologist to help. They're thinking other graves in the burial ground might need to be excavated and the bodies exhumed."

Disturbing images of crumbling headstones rising out of the dark, muddy ground flashed behind Cate's eyes. She swayed in her chair as the room started to spin.

"Cate? Are you okay?"

Jumping up from his chair, Mason circled around the desk to put a steadying hand on her arm, but the dizziness had passed as quickly as it had come, leaving Cate flushed with embarrassment.

"I'm sorry," she said. "It's just...I still get a little overwhelmed sometimes when I think of that awful place."

With a look of concern, Mason returned to his chair.

"It is a very disturbing situation," he said, keeping his dark eyes on her. "Hopefully we'll find out Hearst is responsible for the other remains. I'd hate to think someone else could have done...that."

Cate shivered again at the thought that whoever was responsible might be somewhere nearby.

"Are you sure you're going to be okay?"

Mason's voice was low and soft with concern.

"I'm fine, really. Although my memory's still a little fuzzy," she found herself telling him, although she wasn't sure why. "But I'm getting there."

"I'm glad to hear it," he said, with a faint smile that revealed dimples she hadn't noticed before. "And please call if you need anything else. Anything at all."

Following him back to the lobby, she studied his broad back and thick dark curls with new interest.

Why have I never noticed that he's a very nice man? And handsome, too? Or am I just imagining it? I could still be delusional from the Devil's Breath.

As he reached out to open the door for her, Cate took the opportunity to check his left hand, which was satisfyingly free of a ring.

That's good, right? It means he's still available. But he does work with dead bodies all day, so maybe his being available isn't a good thing after all?

She suddenly wasn't sure if his status as a dissector of corpses made him more interesting and eligible, or less so.

It certainly made him unique.

"Thanks again," she said as she waved goodbye. "I'll ask the CSI team to send you over the skin as we discussed."

"Good," he said with a smile. "I'll be in touch soon."

CHAPTER FORTY

Bailey walked into the FBI's Miami field office without even glancing up at the futuristic, all-glass building that had elicited a gasp of awe from her the first time she'd seen it. Traffic in from the coast had been snarled by a six-car pile-up near the turnpike, and she was running late for her meeting with SAC Ford Ramsey, where she was due to submit her final report on the Summerset Stalker investigation before heading back to D.C..

She would be attending Emma Walsh's memorial service that evening at sunset and would then be taking an early flight out of Miami International the next morning.

Wanting Ludwig to have a chance to say goodbye to Amadeus, she had gone by Sid Morley's place on the way into the city to drop the dog off for a final playdate.

Now, as she walked down the familiar halls, she had to admit to herself that, while she was relieved the Stalker had been caught and brought to justice, she was frustrated by the lack of additional information the task force had uncovered in the weeks since Hearst had fallen to his death.

Little was known about the serial killer's background.

While Hearst had implied to coworkers at the Offender

Review Commission that his parents were dead, so far the investigation had failed to turn up death certificates for either Elmore or Angie Hearst.

This had prompted a further search that revealed no recent financial or employment activity for the couple, who would likely be well past retirement age, if still alive.

Bailey had managed to find the military record for Elmore Hearst, who had served in Vietnam. The Department of Defense photo taken after his basic training showed a young man with the same thick, unruly hair and dark eyes as his son.

She'd noted that Elmore had been dishonorably discharged from the U.S. Army after serving ten months of a planned thirteen-month tour of duty, although she could find no details of his service or the circumstances that had led to him being kicked out.

The only information they'd managed to gather about Hearst's childhood, or his adult life for that matter, had been gleaned from the photos, letters, and journals they'd found stored in his home, along with his extensive taxidermy collection.

Stuffed birds of all kinds filled the living room, their wings aloft in mock flight. And in the bedroom, one whole wall had been covered in frames containing mounted butterflies and moths.

Only a single square of empty space remained where the killer had hung the skin he'd collected, which he'd labeled in Latin *Ala Angeli*, which translated into Angel's Wing.

The sight had sent a chill down Bailey's spine, as had the

discovery of a box in the closet, which was full of yellowed, faded photos, one of which had captured Elmore and his son on the beach, shovels in hand.

Rising up in the background like an ominous portent from the future was the Belle Harbor Lighthouse.

Bailey had studied the photo, along with the others in the box, trying to imagine what had happened to the little boy in the photos. What had turned him into a monster who killed young women and cut off their flesh?

She couldn't be sure Hearst had been responsible for the grisly remains Dalton West had discovered in the crypt but the fact that he'd taken Cate there made Bailey doubt it had been some sort of nightmarish coincidence.

An uneasy ache settled into her stomach as she pictured the old graveyard and the open crypt.

According to Cate's foggy memory, Hearst had planned to hide both their dead bodies in the crypt before he went on the run.

If Dalton hadn't shown up to save us...

Pushing away the disturbing thought, she went in search of Ford Ramsey. Once she'd delivered her report to the special agent in charge, she'd be free to go.

Somehow the idea wasn't comforting.

She didn't like feeling as if she was leaving loose ends behind. But she had little choice.

Roger Calloway would be expecting her back in D.C. the following day. She would likely be on a new case by the end of the week.

When she stuck her head into Ford Ramsey's office, he

looked up with the usual frown and offered her a curt nod.

"I was wondering where you were. Take a seat."

Moving into the sparsely furnished room, Bailey perched on a chair across from the SAC, who pinned his narrowed, impassive eyes on her.

"I understand you've been cleared by the Office of Professional Responsibility related to the death of Chadwick Hearst," he said. "Has your weapon been returned?"

Bailey nodded and patted the holster under her jacket.

She made no reference to the small Ruger which was strapped around her ankle. The Ruger was her personal weapon and, suspecting the bullet she'd fired at Hearst would never be recovered, she'd seen no need to mention the gun in her report of the evening's events.

"That's good," Ramsey said. "The forensic archeologist we're bringing in to help us excavate and investigate the Belle Harbor Burial Ground will be onsite next week and I'd like you to be there and ready to go when she arrives."

"But, I'm expected back in the D.C. field office tomorrow," Bailey protested. "Roger Calloway is–"

"I've already spoken to SAC Calloway and he agrees with me that this case takes priority," Ramsey said. "Unless you have a valid objection, you've been reassigned to the Miami field office for the duration of the investigation."

Sitting in stunned silence, Bailey stared at the Special Agent in Charge for a long beat.

"Well, do you have an objection?" Ramsey finally asked. "Because if you don't, I'd like you to lead the task force."

"The task force?"

Ramsey raised an eyebrow.

"You don't think the Bureau is going to work the case on our own, without the help of the local PD and the medical examiner's office, do you?"

"No, but I've never officially led a task force and..."

She hesitated as the creases on the SAC's face deepened.

"And you start now," he said curtly. "You unofficially led the team that took down the Summerset Stalker. Now you'll officially lead the task force that figures out who and what is responsible for the remains found in the burial ground."

Leaning back in his chair, he sighed.

"I know you're capable, Agent Flynn or I wouldn't have asked Calloway to allow you to stay. And frankly, I don't have anyone else to assign right now."

He offered her a rueful smile.

"Resources are limited and budgets are...tight. So, if you have no other objections, I suggest you make the necessary arrangements to extend your stay in the Miami area."

Bailey nodded numbly and started to get to her feet, but Ramsey motioned for her to sit back down.

"One more thing, Agent Flynn. The fact that Lando Gutierrez is in the wind complicates several investigations we're running," he said. "As you may have learned, he's a low-level operative within the Tumba Cartel."

"I've heard something like that," Bailey admitted. "Although I thought it might just be a rumor Lando had started to scare his couriers and competition."

The grim look on Ramsey's thin, over-tanned face told her that the drug dealer's involvement with the violent cartel was very real.

"We think the cartel arranged to pay his bail," Ramsey continued. "And are probably hiding him now, if they haven't already killed him to shut him up."

His tone suggested he didn't much care either way, as long as Lando wasn't around to cause more trouble.

"We have several undercover assets working within the Tumba Cartel," he said. "It's been suggested these assets may be able to help you find Lando if there's still anything left of him to be found. You should be contacted soon."

Nodding grimly, Bailey stood, checked her watch, and headed to the door. She had just enough time to make arrangements before she'd have to leave for Bellamy Beach.

* * *

The sun was low in the west when Bailey finally pulled the Expedition into the parking lot beside Bellamy Beach.

Based on the volume of cruisers and Interceptors in the lot, Bailey estimated the entire Belle Harbor Police Department had shown up to say goodbye to Emma.

As she walked toward the sand, a woman in a black silk dress with her hair swept back into a loose bun handed Bailey a program of service.

It took a second look for her to recognize Madeline Mercer, the CSI team lead as she smiled and moved on, not ready to make small talk.

Looking down at the program, she saw that a photo of Emma had been printed on the front. The picture had obviously been taken on her wedding day and showed a smiling, blushing bride surrounded by a swirl of white silk.

It was the first time Bailey had seen her friend's wedding dress, and she blinked back sudden tears at the thought of how wrong everything had gone and how sad it all was.

She moved across the sand toward a podium and several rows of chairs that had been arranged under a white tent.

Bailey admired the flower arrangements beside a small altar as she looked around for an empty seat.

"You can sit anywhere you want."

She looked over to see Zach standing beside her.

Her ex-fiancé appeared haggard and drawn, and she smelled alcohol on his breath as he moved toward her.

"My father and I will be sitting in the family row," he said, pointing to Gavin Walsh, who was already sitting in his designated chair at the front. "But we really should get together soon, Bailey. I've missed you."

Leaning forward, he attempted to pull her in for a hug, but she managed to slip out of his grasp and quickly cross to an empty row in the back.

As Bailey sank into a chair at the end of the row, a song began to play from speakers near the altar. She recognized the instrumental version of *Angel* by Sarah MacLachlan.

An elderly man with snow-white hair approached the altar as the last notes of the song faded away.

He wore a black shirt and white dog collar under his suit jacket, and he produced a sorrowful smile as he addressed the gathered mourners.

"Thank you all for joining us tonight," he said. "I'm

Reverend Cheever, formerly of the Belle Harbor Church of the Bible, and Zach has asked me to lead the service tonight as we watch the sun set over this beautiful beach, and over the life of a beautiful woman we will all dearly miss."

As the older man spoke in a sorrowful voice about a woman he had never met, and whom few of the people gathered at the beach had truly known, Bailey studied the large photo of Emma that rested on the altar.

Who could have ever guessed she would meet such a senseless end at such a young age? You just never know when death will come, or what life will bring next.

Distracted by the sobering thoughts, she didn't realize someone had taken a seat next to her until the service ended. Glancing over, she saw Dalton West sitting beside her, his fair hair slicked back from his clean-shaven face, his usual tactical jacket replaced with a black suit and tie.

Instinctively, she looked past him, wondering if he'd brought his sister. If so, she had no doubt Channel 3 News would be broadcasting footage of the modest memorial service on their eleven o'clock show.

"Don't worry, Sabrina's not here," Dalton said as he watched her eyes fill with relief. "I made her promise not to disturb the memorial service. Told her it would be bad for her reputation. But I wanted to pay my respects."

He met Bailey's eyes and held them.

"And I wanted to see how you and Cate are doing," he added softly. "We haven't spoken since the lighthouse."

The memory of Dalton dropping onto the metal deck behind Hearst flashed behind her eyes.

"I was hoping to see you at my debriefing at the police station," he admitted with a sheepish smile. "Detective Fraser wouldn't tell me much, but he said both you and Cate were doing okay. Is that right?"

Nodding weakly, Bailey was suddenly ashamed that she had never thanked him properly for what he'd done.

"I'm sorry I didn't call you," she said. "To thank you, I mean. It's just, I've been busy and..."

She hesitated and dropped her eyes. Her words sounded unconvincing even to her own ears.

I haven't been too busy. I've been too scared. I still am.

"I don't want your thanks," Dalton said with a sigh. "And you don't owe me anything. I was worried about you and just...wanted to see you."

Glancing up at his handsome, earnest face, Bailey couldn't hold back a faint smile.

"Well, you'll be seeing a lot more of me around these parts in the near future," she said. "Because I've been assigned to the Miami field office until the investigation out at the burial grounds is complete."

Dalton raised an eyebrow.

"That's actually a pretty depressing reason to stick around," he said. "But it makes sense for you to want to finish what you started. And I bet Cate's happy."

Bailey hadn't had time to think of her sister's reaction.

"I haven't told her yet," she admitted, her smile fading. "And if she isn't happy that I'm staying, I might end up back at my parent's house, which will drive me crazy."

She imagined her mother's reaction to the news and her

smile slipped away altogether. She'd simply have to make sure Cate didn't kick her out.

Either that or I'll be looking for a short-term rental.

Getting to her feet, Bailey began to walk back to the lot, pleased when Dalton fell into step beside her, blocking the lighthouse from view.

As they came to a stop beside the Expedition, Bailey remembered something Morley had mentioned when she'd dropped off Ludwig for his playdate.

"Morley told me that you plan on going after Lando Gutierrez," she said. "He said you were trying to get him to help you track Lando down."

Dalton shrugged.

"I was a bounty hunter for a few years before I turned to search and rescue," he said. "And this one seems kind of personal. It'd be nice to serve justice to a man who's hurt so many women."

Bailey cocked her head.

"I hear there's a pretty big reward."

"That's certainly a bonus," he admitted. "The reward money could be used to fund quite a few pro bono searches in the future. Maybe even save a few lives if we're lucky."

There was a mixture of hope and resolve in his voice.

He really believes he can make a difference.

Suddenly, she didn't want him to leave. And she didn't want to be alone. Not tonight.

"You know, I still haven't thanked you properly for saving my life," she said. "How about I buy you dinner? Although I do have to pick up Ludwig and-"

"How about we have dinner at my apartment and Ludwig can join us?" Dalton suggested. "I'm a pretty good cook."

His blue eyes were hopeful as he waited for her answer.

"Sounds perfect," she said. "So long as your apartment doesn't have a view of the lighthouse."

The End

ACKNOWLEDGEMENTS

IT'S ALWAYS EXCITING AND DAUNTING to start a brand-new series. I am grateful for the chance to introduce Bailey Flynn and her world to my readers and hope I have done her proud.

I couldn't have finished this book without the loving support of my family. I am beyond blessed to have my wonderful husband, Giles, and five amazing children, Michael, Joey, Linda, Owen, and Juliet, by my side.

The support of my extended family, including Melissa Romero, Leopoldo Romero, David Woodhall, and Tessa Woodhall, means the world to me.

This book is dedicated to the memory of my dearly missed sister and mother. They live on in my heart, and never leave me.

ABOUT THE AUTHOR

Melinda Woodhall is the author of heart-pounding, emotional thrillers with a twist, including the *Mercy Harbor Thriller Series*, the *Veronica Lee Thriller Series*, the *Detective Nessa Ainsley Novella Series*, and the *Bridget Bishop FBI Mystery Thriller Series*.

When she's not writing, Melinda can be found reading, gardening, and playing in the back garden with her tortoise. Melinda is a native Floridian and the proud mother of five children. She lives with her family in Orlando.

Visit Melinda's website at www.melindawoodhall.com

Other Books by Melinda Woodhall

Her Last Summer

Her Final Fall

Her Winter of Darkness

Her Silent Spring

Her Day to Die

Her Darkest Night

Her Fatal Hour

Her Bitter End

The River Girls

Girl Eight

Catch the Girl

Girls Who Lie

Steal Her Breath

Take Her Life

Make Her Pay

Break Her Heart

Lessons in Evil

Taken By Evil

Where Evil Hides

Road to Evil

Valley of Evil

Save Her from Evil

Betrayed by Evil

His Soul to Keep

His Heart of Darkness

Made in United States
North Haven, CT
22 July 2024

55311107R00189